THE YEAR OF EATING DANGEROUSLY

Mallory Caine, Zombie-At-Law Thriller #2

JAMES SCOTT BELL

Print version:

ISBN 10: 0-910355-44-4

ISBN 13: 978-0-910355-44-5

Cover art by Josh Kenfield

Published by
Compendium Press
Woodland Hills, CA

I have seen violence and strife in the city...Wickedness is in the midst thereof. Deceit and guile depart not from her streets.

 —Psalm 55

Is death life? That's the question, most likely. Yes, it is, of course, what else could it possibly be?

 —William Saroyan, *Obituaries*

PART ONE

THE WINTER OF MY CONDIMENTS

CHAPTER ONE

I LOOKED DOWN on the motorcycle gang and thought, *Lunch*.

There were eight of them. It was Tuesday, and we were in the hills of Sunland, in L.A.'s San Fernando Valley. It's a scrubby area of post-war homes and hot dirt and large patches of undeveloped land. The way old Los Angeles looked when the first Franciscans came by bearing beads and Catholic doctrine. Dry and barren.

Like my damaged soul, which may or may not be within my possession.

But I digress.

"Tie her up, bro," one of the gang said. "We'll take turns breakin' her in."

Her being a young, frightened Latina who was gagged and struggling between two thugs.

I'd gotten wind of the gang's meeting from a client of mine, Cal Dutton. I was cleaning up some unfinished appellate business for him and spoke to him at the county jail, where he was doing a stretch before being unloosed on the streets again.

During the course of our conversation he let something slip about being on the wrong side of a motorcycle gang, and that was making things dangerous for him in jail. He asked if I could do anything for him. He told me the leader of the gang was still on the outside, a guy by the name of Tony "Big Spin" Cleveland.

"What do you want me to do exactly?" I asked.

"Negotiate, that's what you do, right?"

"On behalf of clients who can pay me, yes."

"Aw, Ms. Caine." Cal Dutton was a white skinhead with a baby face. His prison tats didn't quite make up for the Elijah-Wood-Frodo-deer-in-the-headlights mug.

"Don't give me that. You still owe me."

"I'm sittin' in here!"

"I got you a deal to keep you out of state prison. You'd be in a cozy little crib in Solano right now, wouldn't you?"

He said nothing.

"Give me the details," I said. And he told me where they were going to meet in a few days. They had this regular spot, and maybe I could figure out a way to make the peace.

Not likely, I thought at the time, though there might be a way to kill those proverbial two birds. You know, clear up a problem for my client, and make provision for my own undead diet at the same time.

So, in my disguise as a streetwalker named Amanda, I had come to the meeting.

A girl's got to eat.

I don't want to have to do it, but this is the hand I've been dealt. Maybe by God, maybe by the devil, or maybe by blind fate, who likes to bat us around like a cat whacks yam.

There's nothing I can do to stop myself. I have to stay alive, even as the undead, in order to have a chance to save my soul from hell.

At least that's what I've been told.

And I've managed to find some consolation in going after the brains of those who have used up their Get Out of Jail Free cards in life.

That torments me, too. Because I've spent my professional life defending people accused of crimes, insisting they get a fair trial. A decision about life and death is one that should be made by an impartial jury, not an individual. The days of lynching and vigilantism are over.

Almost.

Setting aside the clutch in my gut, the inexplicable crosscurrents of desire and self-loathing, I made sure my wig was in place and started down the hill toward what I hoped would be a brain buffet.

IT WAS OVER A YEAR AGO THAT I WAS MURDERED, THEN BROUGHT back to life. A drive-by shooting, the cops said. They never caught whoever did it, but someone brought me back to life, voodoo-like. A *bokor*, a controller. And I was supposed to be the one controlled.

But I bucked it. I fought back. And got free somehow. But I have to find out who did this to me so I can have a chance of not spending eternity in hell.

I don't know if hell is real or not. They keep arguing about it. But here's the deal. When it comes to hell, I don't want to take the chance, thank you very much.

Meantime, I have to operate in this world just like everybody else.

Well, not exactly everybody. Because I have to eat flesh to live. I have to bite into brain for strength. I've given up being selective. I used to prefer more educated brains. Higher quality. But it's getting harder and harder to find those in L.A.

This is not a glamorous thing. It is an ugly curse that is as real as night terrors in children, as horrific as any image conjured up by a graphic artist on drugs.

And it all makes me very cranky. It makes me want to go whole hog, as they say.

Which brings me back to lunch.

I STARTED DOWN THE HILL TOWARD MY BIKER REPAST.

Big Spin was the first to notice me. He looked up and his bearded face did a double take like some old-time comedian. I almost laughed at the absurdity of it. Was I dealing with an outlaw or Oliver Hardy?

"Hi fellas," I said, as if I were a tour guide meeting my group of seniors for a bus tour of Hollywood.

Big Spin just blinked at me a couple of times. He held up his hand to his crew, a gesture telling them to stay in their positions. Except one. To the skinniest of the bunch he nodded up the hill, from where I'd come. Skinny started scampering up through the brush.

"No need to go nuts here," I said. I was standing at eye level with seven bikers, the eighth being up the hill behind me now. "But we've got a situation."

"Situation?" Big Spin snorted. He looked me up and down. "What's the situation, babe?"

"I am," I said. "That's my undercover moniker. The Situation."

"No way you're a cop."

"Did you hear me say that? I said *undercover*."

"You don't look like undercover, either. Know what you look like? A street piece."

"Is that any way to talk?" I said. "You don't exactly treat the ladies with much respect now, do you? So what I want you to do is release the girl and then line up for me right over there." I indicated a spot in front of their hogs, which were parked in an almost perfect row. I gave a quick scan to the other bikers. For some reason the Seven Dwarfs popped in my head. I started assigning names, like Sneezy and Dopey, to their faces. You think the craziest things when facing outlaws alone.

The Dwarfs were obviously waiting for Big Spin to tell them what to do. And just as obviously they wanted to do something really mean. To me.

Big Spin looked over my head. I turned and saw Skinny, dwarf number eight, scuttling down the hillside.

"Nothing," he shouted.

"I don't know what you think you're doing, little lady," Big Spin said to me, approaching. His fat gut was hemmed in by a black T-shirt with a Harley logo and food stains, framed by a denim vest that was a size too small. Why do these guys all wear the same costume? They are rebels, yes! Nonconformists! And they dress like all the other nonconformists they ride with.

"Just what I said." I smiled. "There's no need for unpleasantness here. Let the girl go."

"What makes you think she wants to?" He smiled back at me. Yellow teeth peeked through his fat lips like snipers poking out of a cave of flesh.

"The fact that she's trying to scream through her gag kinda gives me that feeling," I said.

"Before we do unto you what we're gonna do unto her, I gotta—"

"*Unto?* You don't look like a preacher—"

"I gotta know who you are. You got some kind of attitude. I kind of like it. So who are you?"

"You remember that drunken night in Tucson? Well, that wasn't me."

He was now about two gut lengths from me. "Maybe you *are* a cop."

"I eat cops for lunch." Which wasn't far from the truth. "I'm an advisor. I'm advising you to let the woman go. You see, I'm a witness now. But if you let her go, I will make sure you are not brought up on kidnapping charges."

This seemed to puzzle the big man. One of the other bikers, the one I'd labeled Dopey, said, "Let's do her, too."

Now I was starting to get mad. I normally would have taken on any one of them if they were accused of a crime. That's the Constitution I believe in. Even the scum of the earth are entitled to a fair trial—and to retain their liberty unless the government can prove its case beyond a reasonable doubt. That's the only way you can have freedom for everyone.

But since none of these jokers was my client, I had no qualms about eating the inside of their heads. Which was getting to be an increasingly complex proposition. The girl was the complication. I couldn't just unload on them with the 9mm I was packing.

Yes, zombies sometimes pack heat. We don't slobber or walk around with all that *Walking Dead* makeup on. You think we want people to know who we are?

Big Spin waved his hand at Dopey. Spin was one of these guys who doesn't like to be given suggestions, which is why I suggested, "Dude, just let the girl go and you and I will discuss why I shouldn't turn your whole tribe in to the local cops. How's that sound? Because if you don't, I'm going to have to cause some noise."

"Out here?"

"Gunshots will be heard," I said, which is when I chose to remove the Beretta from my purse. I pointed it directly at Big Spin.

His eyes got wide and angry.

"It would be hard for me to miss you," I said. "Now tell your boys to let her go."

There is a vibe to collective anger. When you're dealing with jackasses, there's also a smell. It wafted out of them and hit me in the nose. Sort of like sweat with a little bit of gas.

Big Spin waited to size up the situation, as it were. "If you shoot me, we got a bunch of other guys gonna shoot you. You just made a bad move. Now we got no choice but to take you out."

"Take me out? Like to a French restaurant?"

I heard the crack of a gun and something pass through me.

A bullet, I presumed. From the impact, I guessed it was also a 9mm. Now I had a hole in one of my nice blouses. I was wearing my hot purple number, usually reserved for nighttime on Santa Monica Boulevard.

I felt the hole in my clothes and body, which would soon close up while leaving a little white scar. "Look what you did," I said. "You're going to have to pay for this." Now it wasn't collective anger. It was pure shock and awe. Big Spin's lips moved like he was trying to say something along the lines of, *You just got shot! What are you doing standing up?*

But before he could form any more thoughts in that fevered brain of his, I shot him through the heart.

He fell backward and hit the ground like an overturned cement truck.

Behind me came ten more shots in rapid succession, and my clothes and torso got really messed up. I turned around and saw Skinny, with a look of horror on his face, finishing up what was in the magazine. I half expected him to do one of those movie moves and throw the empty gun at me.

I didn't give him time. I shot him, too. One shot.

Now there was a general disturbance. Dust kicked up as bikers bumped into each other trying to get away from the chick with the gun, the chick who would not die.

The Latina girl, having long since been forgotten, stood with eyes wide open. Trying, no doubt, to comprehend what was going on. She was maybe fifteen.

I am not the executioner type, no matter what you may think. As I shot each biker, part of me was shouting *Stop, stop!* I was a killer, a murderer, a vigilante.

This is not what I wanted to be. I wanted to be Captain Janeway on *Star Trek: Voyager.* Then Claire Kincaid on *Law & Order.* But this walking death I've been given has taken all that away.

When all my rounds were spent, I slid the magazine out and snagged another one from my purse.

The last living biker came at me with a knife, a big honking knife, the kind that makes an outlaw feel really baaaad.

I hate getting cut. That leaves a definite scar on my not so resilient skin. I have a hard enough time keeping it on this side of crusty, using special creams every morning.

He plunged the knife into my chest. I looked down.

"That really sucks," I said.

This biker, who I will now call Bashful, went *Ah!* and let go of the knife, then started to back away from me like I was an electrified fence.

I removed the knife and tossed it on the ground. I put a fresh magazine in the Beretta and shot him.

When the dust finally settled, all of them were dead or on their way to it.

But the girl was gone.

I couldn't go after her. I had a more pressing matter. I went up to my car, a yellow Volkswagen convertible Bug named Geraldine —it's yellow and bright and summery. I'm a summer, don't you think?—and I got a plastic cooler, my Sawzall, and a large ice cream scoop.

Twenty minutes later I had eight commingled brains in the cooler with some dry ice. I was a little blood spattered, but had a change of clothes in the car. A fresh brain will last pretty much all day without getting too chewy. But if you freeze it, it can last almost indefinitely. You can then thaw out chunks later or, on a hot day, suck on it as is. Like those frozen bananas you get at the beach sometimes.

My plan was to get these into my own freezer at home.

Where was the girl? Poor thing. Not only frightened out of her mind at what they were going to do to her, but also witnessing the gunfight at the O.K. Corral. I hoped she didn't see a woman sawing off heads and scooping out brains. That way lies madness.

As I was hauling my cooler up the hill I got the feeling I wasn't alone. I looked behind me and saw someone standing there in the midst of the carnage. It was a man in a white robe. He looked like some desert priest or wannabe guru. He had longish brown hair framing a gentle face. Blue eyes.

So what do you do when you are holding a box of brains and a dude is looking right at you? You say, "The trash men will be here in a while to take care of the mess."

Which is what I said.

"I know who you are," the man said.

"Send me a postcard," I said. I didn't want to kill him, too. But that was probably what I would have to do.

I put the cooler down and sat on it. The man in white was below me. He floated above the ground then and came closer.

A demon, I thought.

"I am here with a message for you," he said. "The one I serve wishes you to know something."

"Who is the one you serve, I guess is the obvious question."

"It is not something you need to know. What you need to know is that you are beginning to meddle. If you continue, the soul that you seek to restore will be lost forever. You must not get in the way of the kingdom. You will be allowed to live so long as you remain inactive."

"What is your name?" I said. I have learned that demons must answer when you ask them directly what their name is.

"It is not something you need to know."

That told me this was *not* a demon, but maybe a fallen angel. There are two types of beings on the dark side. Demons are the souls of the wicked dead, inhabiting bodies. But there are also fallen angels, according to the man who gave me all the information, a priest named Father Clemente.

I had to give it to the priest on this one. He's been right before.

"Then I'll take a wild guess," I said. "You work for Lucifer or one of his minions, am I right?"

The dark angel said nothing.

"You're part of this plan to set up some sort of war headquarters in L.A.—am I right about that, too?"

Silence.

"You got a lot more to worry about than one little streetwalker," I said.

"Your name is Mallory Caine," he said.

"You must be mixing me up with that famous lawyer," I said.

"You are being warned. You have one chance."

"Tell you what, angel face, I'll give her the message if I see her. Now will there be anything else?"

The dark angel let loose one of those malevolent smiles one sees in horror movies. Such a cliche, but I guessed he hadn't been trained well.

But then again, he had.

Because a wind whipped up. A big one. My Amanda wig went askew. Dirt and pebbles scraped my skin. I had to put my arm over my eyes.

I felt myself lifted off the ground, spun around.

Wizard of Oz time. I half expected Miss Gulch to ride by.

Instead, what whipped by was my cooler, the one I had so carefully filled with biker cranial matter.

I watched as the wind carried it through the dust storm and away from view. There was a deep chasm only about a hundred yards away. If it ended up down there, it was bye-bye meal plan.

That was, apparently, this angel's idea all along.

The wind stopped as quickly as it had started, and I *thanked* to the ground.

"Nice try," I said.

"You have two choices," the angel said. "You can stay out of things, or you can join us. But you cannot stand against us, for then you will surely die."

"Time for you to go back to hell," I said. "Or an abyss of your choosing."

At which point this joker vanished.

I went to look for my cooler but it had disappeared into the brush of the chasm.

Just great! All that work and nothing to show for it!

Nothing but a scrum of headless biker bodies.

Well, don't cry over spilled outlaw. I did what I didn't like to do —eat raw flesh then and there.

The lore of zombies is filled with two types: the mindless sort doing the bidding of a master, a *bokor,* the one who brings the dead to life. And the viral kind, the kind that suddenly develops jaws of death and eats human beings, especially brains.

There is a little truth to both, but I may be an exception. I have to eat flesh to stay alive; yet someone has tried to control me.

I have heard voices and resisted them. I have somehow, by force of will, managed to keep my own counsel, so to speak.

Although there is one voice to which I finally responded, one that apparently is friendly to me.

He goes by the name of Max.

But I didn't want him around now. I was about to descend into graphic-novel territory. I was going to gnaw the flesh of the dead.

BUT THE GIRL—WHAT IF SHE WENT FOR THE COPS? WHAT IF SHE made it all the way to the highway and was waving her arms and screaming?

Stupid! I was so consumed by my hunger that I let her go. And for all I knew there'd be a couple of squads of the city's finest.

I needed to get out of there. It was a distant place but not inaccessible.

I scampered back up the hill, hating the very thought of me. A bloody cannibal, that's what I was, even though it was not of my choosing.

When I got to the top of the ridge and prepared to jump in Geraldine, I happened to look left.

She was there.

Lying on her back like she was dead.

I went over to her, looked down. Her eyes were open and her mouth was moving. Like a catfish on the sand. Open, shut, open, shut.

She was in shock, is what she was.

She'd seen the whole thing from up here. Saw me cutting off heads and harvesting brains. How many did it take before she was out?

This was a fine thing. Now I had a catatonic young woman on my hands.

I should have just left her there.

Should have.

But I didn't.

Lousy zombie.

I piled her in the back of Geraldine and put the top up. Then drove out of Sunland. I knew a hospital in Panorama City. I went in the above-ground parking garage and found a spot near the elevators. I wrote a note about shock and attempted rape and stuck it in the pocket of the girl's blouse. She was out by this time, breathing normally. I saw a wheelchair sitting near the elevators and went for it.

I got the girl in the wheelchair. I punched the elevator down button. When it opened I wheeled her in and hit Lobby, then hopped out.

I got in Geraldine and drove out of there, still angry because I'd lost my biker brains. And feeling like an absolute loser.

CHAPTER TWO

NOT THAT I want you to get the idea all I do is eat flesh. Or think about it most of the time.

I actually do practice law. I defend people accused of crimes. I have a quaint notion that the government should be held to meeting its burden of proof before they throw you in the slammer. Or give you the needle.

See, if you don't do that, pretty soon they begin to run roughshod over people they just don't like.

And you never give a government that much power. Ever.

Even if you have to become a criminal defense lawyer and have doofuses constantly run you down about "defending people you know are guilty."

You know what, pal? When they arrest you for nothing, don't come crying to me.

On Monday I went into my office as usual. My space is above a tobacco shop and novelty store I call the Smoke 'n Joke, run by a very large woman named Lolita Maria Sofia Consuelo Hidalgo, or LoGo as she hates to be referred to. She has this crazy idea that I should be on time with my rent.

What world does she live in?

I was going to start setting up a trial notebook for an upcoming case when Nick popped in, unannounced.

Nick is Nikolas Papdoukis and he's a Kallikantzaros. In Greek lore, the Kallikantzaroi are goblins who snatch children. A boy born during the Saturnalia is fated to turn into this creature during the Christmas season. But a quirk of timing—the exact ides of Saturnalia, to the second—apparently made Nick a Kallikantzaros permanently.

He looks like a knotty little gnome. He's not going to make the cover of *GQ*, but he has overcome his kid snatching ways. Nick came to L.A. to start a new life and now helps me with investigations. He calls himself a barometer because he can feel things of a spiritual nature going on in the city. It comes in handy.

"Thanks for knocking," I said.

"There are things happening!" Nick said. He says that a lot.

"Have a seat," I said.

Nick jumped onto a client chair. His legs dangled and his feet did not reach the floor. "A motorcycle gang it was. Did you hear?"

The grisly scene out in Sunland was all over the morning news.

"I heard something about it," I said.

"I am a barometer. I feel a connection. What do you know about this?"

"The leader is someone who is connected to a client of mine in County. Maybe that's it."

Nick looked skeptical, but let it pass. "There is something happening! Something big." He touched a finger to his temple, closed his eyes. "Yes, and we are in the middle of this."

"How so?"

"It will be here, downtown, that the big thing will happen."

"Can you be any more specific?"

He shook his head. Then he opened his eyes and looked at me. "You are in danger."

"I'm always in danger, Nick. Criminal lawyer, remember?"

"No. There is a darkness closing in."

"Let's not be so dramatic."

But that was like asking a fish not to use his gills. Nick was nothing if not a drama-kantzaros.

"You listen to me," he said. "There is something wrong. Those bikers. There was something dark there. Girls, I think."

I sat up. "What does that mean?"

"I do not know! It only comes to me."

"A barometer that doesn't baromet?"

He looked hurt.

"That's okay, Nick," I said. "As long as we stick to what we're doing, no harm."

Only problem was, I didn't believe it.

CHAPTER THREE

MY BIGGEST CLIENT at the moment was a man who happened to be my own father.

Harry Clovis was shackled to a table in the attorney room at the men's central jail. Outside it was a hot Tuesday morning. Inside it was cool as a crypt. Which is what this place always reminds me of.

Dressed in the orange coveralls of the K-10 inmate, highest security, Harry Clovis was being charged with the murder of a former police officer. He did, in fact, cut off this officer's head with a sword. I know, because I was there.

The officer was a zombie, however. That little fact was somehow overlooked in the police report. But it was going to come out in court. It had to. It was our only way out of this.

There was one other pair in the attorney room. A local defense lawyer I knew, Gustavo Eli Gilboy, sat across from another shackled inmate, this one looking like a hype—he had the hollow-faced pallor of the heroin addict.

Gus himself had that lean-and-hungry look, but he dressed like a dandy from a '30s musical comedy. He was the Edward Everett Horton of defense lawyers. The faint smell of gardenia wafted from his ostentatious three-piece, dark gray suit. The pink tie was one of his trademarks, as was the old-school pencil mustache, black as night, and the moussed-back hair that fairly glistened under the jailhouse lights.

He smiled at me as I sat down. The word *icky* came to mind.

Gus and I had a history. We once were co-counsel on a murder case. He was hired privately while I had to work on the government's dime. Gus hardly knew how to try a case. I did all the heavy lifting. I had to undo damage he did on cross-examination. I had to scramble to keep him from calling bad witnesses. I had to do everything in my power to keep his gardenia-scented mistakes from losing the case for both of us.

The jury came back with an acquittal for both clients based on the self-defense theory I had so carefully laid out.

"We sure showed 'em, didn't we?" Gus had said after the verdict. "We make a pretty good team."

"Yeah," I said, "if I'm the Dodgers, you're the peanut guy in the stands."

He didn't like that. But I didn't like him. Mr. Plead Out was his nickname, and he was far too eager to collect his fees and make a deal so he wouldn't have to do what he was no good at—go to trial.

I'm a trial lawyer and I don't mind admitting it. I want to fight.

Which I was going to have to do with my dad.

The first fight was getting him to listen to me.

"I need to confess," he said. "I need to just confess to my sin and be done with it."

"Dad, listen, that's enough of that talk." We were following a familiar pattern here, and my insides were starting to roil again. My dad had run out on me when I was born, ended up trafficking in drugs with a biker gang. He was in Mexico for awhile, even in prison down there. He'd had some sort of religious epiphany then and now was prone to visions.

And big pronouncements, like this confession thing.

"You don't understand," he said. "You don't understand confession, for you are the undead."

Out of the corner of my eye I could see Gus look over at us.

"Keep your voice down," I said. "Or I'm going to walk right out of here."

"No, stay."

I took my voice down to a whisper. "Then quit calling me undead. I know that already, and I feel everything you feel."

"No," he said. "You do not feel the burden of sin. You kill."

Which is why Harry Clovis had once tried to kill me. He was a zombie hunter and had targeted yours truly, until he discovered, by chance, that I was the daughter he had abandoned.

"Dad, we can beat this thing," I said.

"I want to make my peace with God."

"I thought it was God who told you to come to L.A. and kill zombies. How can that be sinful if God told you to do it?"

He closed his eyes. "I am so confused."

"Then quit talking about confessing, will you? You cut off the head of a zombie. That's self-defense. We'll prove it."

He opened his orbs again and said, "I have had a vision, Mallory. A vision of darkness such as I have never seen before."

"Oh no."

"In the vision there was given to me a reed like unto a rod."

"What the heck does that even mean?"

"Listen, Mallory!"

"Voice down," I said.

"An angel said to me, 'Rise, and measure the temple of God, and the altar, and them that worship therein. And the Lord will give power unto his two witnesses, and they shall prophesy a thousand two hundred and threescore days, clothed in sackcloth.'"

"All right, Dad. We'll go shopping for sackcloth when you walk out of the courtroom a free man."

He shook his head violently. "And when they shall have finished their testimony, the beast that ascendeth out of the bottomless pit shall make war against them, and shall overcome them, and kill them. And their dead bodies shall lie in the street of the great city."

"City?"

"Yes."

"What city?"

His eyes narrowed. "I am in its jail."

"Los Angeles?"

"The city of sin!"

"Dad, the voice."

"The time grows short. You must find the two witnesses. They are here!"

Now everybody was looking at us. Gus, his hype client, and the deputy sheriff standing watch. The deputy gave me a warning look. If I couldn't control my dad's voice, well, interview over.

"Look at me," I said. "I'm only going to say this once. You are not going to confess to anything. And no more talk about the visions, either. I want you to keep quiet. I don't want you talking to anybody, except to me. Is that understood?"

"How is she?" he said.

"Who?"

"Your mother."

"Come on."

"Will you see her for me?"

I leaned back in my chair. "I don't know if that's such a good idea."

"Please."

"She's been very delicate lately."

"I'm an old man now. I've changed. I am not who I was. She needs to know that."

"She's not the same, either. You running out like that really did a number on her."

He drooped his head.

"Dad, let's get you out of here. First things first."

"I must atone."

"What about me?"

"You?" he said.

"You tried to kill me once. You sorry about that?"

"I'm so, so confused. You are undead. You shouldn't exist. But you're my own flesh and blood."

"Think of it this way," I said. "I'm a zombie lawyer. The perfect front. And this is what I do. The law. You need to help me help you. Once you're out, you can figure what to do with your life."

"My life is over, I'm afraid."

I reached over the rail and slapped him. The smack resounded in the interview room.

"Hey," the deputy said. "You can't hit a prisoner!"

"He's my father," I said. "I can smack him if I want to." To which no one said anything.

I WAS STANDING OUTSIDE THE INTERVIEW ROOM, GETTING MY briefcase closed, when Gus Gilboy and his gardenia smell snuck up behind me.

"My, what a performance in there," he said.

"Get lost, Gus."

"Hitting your client? That's not good for business."

"Good-bye."

"Not so fast," he said. "I couldn't help overhearing—"

"Look, what you think you heard or did not hear doesn't make any difference to me. You leaving me alone makes a difference to me."

"I get the distinct impression you don't like me, Ms. Caine."

"You're on a list right below boils," I said.

"What did I ever do to you?"

"It's what you do to your clients," I said. "You sell them out."

"I make them good deals."

"You make deals, not good ones. You're a volume business. Like a guy selling computer parts in a boiler room. You take your fees and you plead them out."

"Don't try to pose as a saint, Ms. Caine. I know all about you."

For a second I thought he did. The undead part.

But he said, "You make a big pose to represent the poor and

tempest-tossed and all that other phony stuff. All you want is the fame and the glory."

"Please, Gus, do you have anything of substance to say? No, wait, you're Gus Gilboy—what was I thinking?"

"You don't want me as an enemy, Ms. Caine."

"And you don't want me as a friend. So what does that leave us with?"

He smiled like a pot head listening to Ramsey Lewis. "See you around, Ms. Caine."

He left me in his cologne wake, and I almost gagged. I decided to wait for a minute or two before following him out. Let the smell dissipate.

Sometimes those pauses can change the course of your life.

CHAPTER FOUR

BEFORE I LEFT the jail I ordered up another client. A former client, actually.

Cal Dutton was the one who'd given me the tip on the bikers. I had a few questions I wanted to ask him.

But when they brought him into the attorney room and he saw me there, he started to shake.

"Sit down," I told him.

The deputy got him in a chair and put his hands in the table shackles.

"I don't got nothin' to say to you."

"You just did," I said.

He clammed.

"How you doing, Cal?"

Cal's eyelids twitched. They moved like rippling water. He was trying hard to look stone cold, but he was hot and bothered.

"Talk to me," I said. "I want to know what they were into, your boys."

"Ain't my boys."

"Not anymore, they're not."

"Did you?"

"Did I what?"

"Somethin' to do with it?" His face told me he knew all about the killings. Of course, that sort of thing couldn't be kept out of the jailhouse communication system, which is often faster and more efficient than the U.S. Postal Service.

"Lawyers don't do that sort of thing as a rule now, do they?" I said.

"I can't tell you nothin'."

"You know what you're going to do, Mr. Dutton? You're going to get out of here and get yourself in trouble again. And when you do, you're not going to want a public defender. You're going to want me. You're going to come to me and ask me to rep you, because you know I'll get you the best shot. And then what'll I say? 'Sorry, man, you didn't give me squat, so I don't choose to give you squat. Have a nice day.'"

"Ms. Caine, come on now."

"Am I right?"

He shrugged.

"What I want is a lead. I want to know what your boys were going to do with that girl."

"How you know about that?"

"I have sources, too, Cal."

He leaned forward. "Ms. Caine, if it ever got out that I said something—"

"No one's going to find out, not on my watch. You have my word on that."

He shook his head. "Ain't good enough. Not when you're in here. Maybe when I get out."

"Cal—"

"Hey!" he shouted to the deputy. "I'm done here."

"You're not done, Cal."

The deputy came over and started to unlock the shackles. "Wait a second," I said.

"I'm done!" Cal shouted. "Get me out of here now."

"His call," the deputy said.

"You know you can't get away from a good lawyer," I said,

looking right into Cal's eyes. He closed his so he wouldn't have to look at me.

The deputy led him away like a bovine to slaughter.

What was Cal Dutton so afraid of? It was more than not wanting to give up a name in violation of street thug *omerta*. Cal Dutton was scared out of his criminal mind. And I had to find out why.

CHAPTER FIVE

WHICH IS why I went back to the hospital in Panorama City. Maybe the girl could give me something. But first I'd have to find out who she was.

No easy task.

At the desk I was met by a skeptical-eyed and ample-waisted security guard.

"I was told a teenaged girl was checked in here anonymously," I said. "Would have been Sunday night."

"Who are you?" the guard said.

"I'm a lawyer." I showed him my bar card. "I got a tip from the woman who brought her in. Thought the doctors might like to know more about that."

He looked at a computer terminal and tapped the keyboard a few times, like he was going to issue me a plane ticket. Then he turned back to me. "Can you wait here a moment?"

"With breathless anticipation."

He waddled off.

I sat on a couch and looked at a two-year-old *Newsweek* magazine. The cover story was a social prediction. It hadn't come true. I tossed it aside and watched a plant growing instead. A few minutes later a deputy sheriff came striding into the lobby. He was tall and earnest and pink cheeked. Maybe thirty-five. His name pin said *Snodgrass.*

"You're the lawyer?" he said.

I stood and faced him. "It's not like a disease," I said.

"May I ask what your interest is in this matter?"

"May I ask what this matter is?"

"You are the one who made the inquiry. You tell me."

"There's something wrong here, because the sheriff doesn't show up unless there is."

"Lawyers don't usually show up, either."

"I'll give you that one," I said. "Here's what I know. A teenager, Latina, was brought here by someone after she had been attacked. Or so it looked like. That someone is someone I know."

"We'd like to talk to him or her. Can you give me a name?"

"You know I can't do that. Client confidentiality and all."

"Are you saying this person is a client?"

"A very intimate one. So I'm not going to be giving you any information on that."

"What makes you think I'm going to be giving *you* any information?"

"If you do, you might be able to get something in return. Like finding the guys that attacked her."

The deputy frowned. "How do you know it was guys, plural?"

He was sharp. And I had been sloppy. "I'm just telling you what I heard. If you want to know more, give me information on the girl. My client would like to know if she has been taken care of."

"May I have your name, please?" he said.

"Not just yet," I said.

He blinked hard. "I'm going to ask if you will come with me."

"Where?"

"Where we can talk."

"We can talk right here. And I'd like to see her."

"She isn't here," he said.

"Where is she then?"

"I can't tell you that," he said.

This was starting to feel strange. In my position you can't be too careful with cops or anyone else in uniform, from security guards on up.

"Maybe you'll hear from me again, Deputy Snodgrass." I said.

"I'm not finished talking to you," he said.

"Yes, you are."

I walked out.

CHAPTER SIX

I TORE down the freeway in Geraldine, about as much as you can in tight traffic. I did my best but still I got passed by Beemers and Lexi, SUVs and sporty little numbers. But I didn't care—the top was down, the wind was whistling through my hair, and I felt alive. By that I mean alive again, like when I was totally human and totally flawed and totally trying to do what I thought I'd been called to do, which is practice law and fall in love and get married and have kids, and take my son and daughter to their soccer games and softball practices, and to ballet and music lessons, to stress out whenever they got sick or had a recital, to build them up and inspire them, but not too much, not hovering over them like a helicopter parent, but nurturing them and letting them bloom. I wanted all that and I had it all mapped out until I was dead.

I couldn't go to the old places. I couldn't eat the food I used to love. I couldn't go out to a club and dance for fear that I'd want to eat the guy who asked me. Maybe take a chunk out of his arm if I had too much champagne. I couldn't walk into a store without wanting to eat the help, except on Rodeo Drive where the women were too skinny to eat and had no brains to speak of.

Oh, but to drive, drive around my city, the place where I came

into my own, where I had tried cases and saved some of the inno-
cents from being run over by the cops and prosecutors. I'd done a
little of that, a little bit of good I'd say, and that was the one thing
I had left—to do good through law—and that's what I was going to
do, dammit.

Behind me a honk, a big truck in the fast lane was on my tail.
What was he doing? Violating all the laws, both criminal and
unwritten, that you don't put a truck in the fast lane and you don't
honk while hugging the tail of the car in front of you.

I put my pedal to the floor, but the truck stayed right with me.
What was this? Even in crazy L.A. this was not something that
made any sense. Maybe if I'd ticked him off somehow and there
was road rage, but I hadn't. Little old zombie me, I was just
minding my own business.

But there he was. It's funny how you can read intent from a
grille. I just knew this guy had his sights set on Geraldine's fine
rear end.

He wasn't going to go away.

Reminded me of that old Spielberg movie they showed sometimes, *Duel.* The one about the killer truck trying to get this guy. I
can't remember the guy who was in it, but he was this skinny, innocent guy and the monster truck decided to kill him. You never see
the driver of the truck, either, which made it all the more
frightening.

So who was driving this truck? I wanted to separate him from
his brain.

WONK! He blasted me with his horn.

Okay, pal, crazy man, you want to play that game, go ahead. I
pulled over into the next lane.

The truck followed me, as if we were one vehicle separated
only by a small length of chain.

And it was weird, the way it was happening. Me in my bug and
this guy in a big rig; there shouldn't be any way he could keep up.
There should have been other cars in the way, but it was almost

like the cars were cooperating with him. Or he was somehow in control of the traffic. I don't know if that was true or not—I can't prove it. But I can't prove love is real, either. You just know.

Now I was getting mad. Where was the CHP when you needed it?

WONK!

I made one more lane change. He was right behind me still.

No prob. I could get off at the next ramp and pull onto the streets. He couldn't maneuver there. I'd lose him in the little lanes.

But it was like he knew my thoughts because he whipped into the slow lane, sped up, and jammed me from the side.

I looked up at the cab and caught only a glimpse of the face.

What I saw was this: a baseball cap turned backwards. Normal enough for a trucker, but it was underneath the cap that was the difference.

He had a horn sticking out of his forehead, like a rhino horn, curling up. And just below the horn, one eye. One, dead center.

A cyclops.

Below the eye was a hook nose and under the nose a curved smile.

I wondered if anybody else could see this. I didn't know much about the one-eyes then. I'd seen all manner of creature, from vampires to werewolves, not to mention my kind, showing up in L.A. But never a cyclops.

I found myself wishing for a BB gun. You know, the kind your grandmother always said would put out your eye?

All I needed was one good shot.

But not while I was driving.

I tried to get away, tried to maneuver like a NASCAR driver on the stretch of freeway. We were at the curve of the 101. I tried to get cars in between me and the truck. But every move I made was anticipated.

The cyclops blew his horn. The sound filled my head like an explosion of bowling balls.

My arms reacted by turning the wheel hard left. I almost clipped a Honda.

I righted myself but came back too far right, slipping into the slow lane once again.

The truck had somehow maneuvered to the left of me, leaving me between the mad cyclops and the freeway wall to the right. The city fathers, in their idiotic spending ways, had erected sound walls all up and down the freeway corridors of the city, cutting off views and giving taggers a whole lot of canvas to play with.

Now it was an inescapable crusher as the truck began to wedge me in. Veering right and staying slightly ahead of me, he made it seem like I was driving into a funnel.

I slammed on my brakes but the one-eyed trucker seemed to know my every move. Metal screeched against metal, and the acrid smell of hot brake fluid filled Geraldine.

My windshield shattered. I was being trashed.

There is one sure way to kill a zombie, and that is by stuffing the mouth with salt and stitching the lips together.

But being crushed in a car could do real damage to the body parts. I already had a couple of knife wounds from the past, and bullet holes from my luncheon stopover in Sunland. Clothes could cover those things up. But if I had an arm or a leg severed, I'd be alive but there'd be less of me to go around. It would make practicing trial law more of a challenge than it already was.

There was no way out.

The last bit of blue of the Los Angeles sky disappeared from my vision. Black clouds gathered, coming together in something like a sea of ink, overtaking my sight and then my mind.

ZOMBIES HAVE DREAMS.

At least this one did. In my dream I was looking down on Los Angeles from the outside deck at the top of City Hall. I could see the pagodas of Chinatown and the towering glass buildings of the financial center. The Times building and the new police headquarters. Disney Hall and the four-level interchange.

Beyond all of that stretched the blanket of the metropolitan basin, all the way to the sea. From my perch I saw the Pacific Ocean and the string of planes landing and taking off from LAX. It was what Randy Newman called another perfect day in his song about the city.

Then from out of the sea rose this giant red ... thing. A monster made up of one huge eyeball resting on scaly shoulders. Around the eyeball were horns, ten of them, and the body was like a scabrous lizard. It moved like Godzilla, the old Japanese flick variety.

Across the breast of this beast was a blinking neon sign that said, **Eat for Free.**

I watched, frozen, as the monster planted its two feet on the beach and turned its eyeball left and right, as if taking in the entirety of the city.

It then looked directly at me. Even though we were many miles apart, I knew it had my number.

It raised its two monster arms, which were like a T. Rex's, in a motion that reminded me of Moses in *The Ten Commandments.*

Then behind him the water turned to blood.

Deep, ruby red, the ocean from Malibu to Catalina Island transformed and started to boil. Steam rose up from the waters, creating a fog that blew in and started to cover the city. I lost sight of the monster as the smoky veil rolled toward me. When it got to City Hall there was no way you could see farther than a few feet. I heard cars crashing on the freeway below. And the screams of people shrouded in sudden darkness.

Then I heard a bubbling liquid sound, like soup on a hot stove, only a hundred times louder. I looked down through the cloud, down at the street, and a little bit of the fog cleared so I could see.

What I saw was red-hot lava. I knew, the way you know in dreams, that it was the ocean of blood brought up by the monster, covering and destroying everything in its wake.

I had to get down there to do something about it.

I ran to the elevator and found it was missing. The doors were open to the long shaft and cable.

I jumped on the cable and started sliding down, fast, because of the grease. I wrapped my legs around the cable to try to slow myself down but it wasn't any use.

I zipped down like a bullet train and hit the bottom of the shaft in a way that felt familiar. I was dazed but alive and looked up.

The elevator had somehow reappeared and was shooting down to crush me. A laughing head peered over the roof of the cab. It was the cyclops.

I scampered up, moving like I was in the tar pits, and dove through open doors on the first floor just before the elevator would have hit me.

A security guard was sitting in a rocking chair, head down as if asleep. He looked vaguely familiar. I shouted at him, "We have to stop it!"

The guard lifted his head.

It was my own father, Harry Clovis.

"Dad, get up!"

He shook his head.

"The city!"

He blinked his eyes.

I shook him by the shoulders, trying to get him out of his torpor. He blinked again and said, "It is no use."

I heard the churning of waters outside the building. I ran from my father to the great doors opening up on Spring Street. Outside the ocean of blood was hot and flowing. Screaming pedestrians were getting sucked into it, disappearing.

I had to stop it, but how? I looked around and saw, at my feet, a single silver spoon. The kind you might eat cereal with.

I picked it up.

I was going to try to stem this tide with a spoon?

I looked up and saw the monster. He was standing right across the street in front of the criminal courts building.

And from the giant eyeball I heard a voice say, "Eat for free."

SPEAK TO ME...

I opened my eyes. Smelled gasoline. Heard cars and saw fuzzy figures. The light brown uniform of a CHP officer.

"A little late," I muttered.

"Don't move," the Chip said. "We'll have you out of there. Help is on the way."

"Where am I?"

"You had an accident."

I felt for my arms and legs. Everything seemed to be there. The only thing that needed clearing was my zombie brain, which was scrambled.

"Did you get the number of the truck?" I said.

"Don't try to joke about this—"

"No, I mean it. The truck that rammed me into the wall."

"You just take it easy, ma'am."

"Let me out of here." I was wedged in Geraldine and, in fact, was more concerned about her. I loved her, and she was going to be all broken up, bearing the scars of the city and its mad drivers.

"We have to wait—"

"Did you not hear me?" I said. I pushed against something, the dash I guess it was, and started to slip out.

"Don't do that!" Chip said.

"Out of my way," I said. Like a baby performing its own cesarean, I emerged from the metallic womb and spilled onto the asphalt.

"Ma'am, please—"

I got to my feet. "I'm okay, Officer."

He looked at me in astonishment. "But you. You were..."

"It's all right," I said. "I need to get out of here. I've got work to do."

"I can't let you. I mean, I've got to get a statement. You've got to see a doctor. How could you—"

"I want you to make sure my car gets hauled to an auto body shop. I'm going to call for a ride."

I gave him my card and walked away from the scene of my own accident.

CHAPTER SEVEN

WHAT A DAY.

When I got back to my loft, in one of those renovated buildings you see around downtown these days—mine is on Main Street, a former high finance building, a great facade built in the '20s—I just wanted to kick back and pretend I was just another urban professional, home from the wars.

I wanted to have a meal, a glass of wine, and watch a movie on TCM.

And I wanted someone to watch it with. I wanted Aaron Argula.

Aaron was the deputy district attorney. We had first met in law school—before I became a zombie. That's when we had a chance to be happy. But he ran off with somebody else and I got murdered and brought back from the dead.

Those things tend to put a strain on a relationship.

But now Aaron was back in town and making overtures toward me. I wanted him. But we had a couple of things going against us.

First of all, I was a criminal defense attorney and he was my natural enemy, a DA. Second of all, whenever I was around him, I wanted to eat his brain.

We had seemingly insoluble problems.

I didn't want to think about that tonight. After all I've been through, I just wanted to make believe my life was not that distinguishable from the millions of others in the city and county of Los Angeles.

Boy, what a dope I was.

I OPENED MY FREEZER AND TOOK OUT MY LAST BIT OF BRAIN, AN accountant's, which I had in some Saran wrap. I unwrapped it and placed it in a microwave bowl. I took a Tupperware container of flaxseeds out of my refrigerator and sprinkled them on the frozen brain. I've discovered that flaxseeds help keep my skin tone, which is an ongoing project with me.

I pretended I was Rachael Ray. I looked out at the cameras and exalted in what I was cooking. Even though my taste buds are pretty much dead, I wanted to pretend I was whipping up something wonderful. Maybe I could put the recipe up on the Internet.

What was it Blanche DuBois says in *Streetcar*? A woman's charm is fifty percent illusion?

Maybe life is like that. Maybe we need fifty percent of it to be an illusion so we can get through it without wanting to set things on fire.

So I microwaved the brain and flaxseed mixture on medium for two minutes. It came out moist and steamy. Brain is a little stringy, so you need a set of sharp knives. Which I had.

I then poured myself a glass of Carlo Rossi rose. You see, it's no use spending massive amounts of money on expensive wine when you can't really appreciate it. Carlo Rossi does the trick for me. That trick is making me think I'm living like a real person.

I took the bowl and the wine and the knife and fork out to my living room. I sat on the couch and put the meal on the coffee table. Then I grabbed the remote and flicked on the TV

I went to TCM. They were between movies. They were showing an old newsreel. Joan Crawford was making some sort of plea that the audience buy war bonds. She had the Joan Crawford early '40s look. No other actress went through more permutations in the face than Crawford. You can almost record some of the middle part of the twentieth century by the shape of her lips.

Lips I wanted to eat. That's one thing that takes a little bit of that pleasure away from watching old movies. When I see Clark Gable, I want to eat his ears. When I see Wallace Beery, I want to eat his nose.

The only actor I don't want to eat is Cary Grant. I want him to stay just the way he is.

I looked at the schedule and saw to my horror that the next movie up was *I Walked with a Zombie*.

Gack. The last thing I wanted to see. Movies never got zombies right. You either have a slobbering, halfwitted mangle the masses right out of apocalyptic comic books, or you have the wide-eyed, mindless puppet on a string.

I can move pretty fast if I need to, thank you very much.

The movie also played a role in my last murder case, which I wrote about in the memoir entitled *Pay Me in Flesh*.

So I flipped the channel and found something even more horrible: a talk show.

I turned the TV off.

I was just about to slice my first taste of brain when someone knocked on my door.

What?

Who could be coming to see me? One of my neighbors? It wasn't exactly the opportune time.

Another knock.

I went to the door and looked out my peephole.

Aaron was smiling at me, as if he knew I was looking at him.

"Let me in," he said.

My zombie heart jackhammered the inside of my rib cage. Aaron has a hot Italian look, with a thatch of black hair and eyes as blue as the Mediterranean. Even through the hole his hotness burned like sunlight through a magnifying glass.

"Come on, Mallory!"

"Aaron, what are you doing here?"

"I was in the neighborhood, selling cookies, and I thought I'd drop by."

"No, really."

"Um, I wanted to borrow a couple of eggs?"

"This isn't really a convenient time."

"I'm not leaving until you let me in. You love me, remember?"

"I can't let you in. I don't love you anymore"—*liar*—"and I'm not decent."

"I'm not decent, either. That's why we get along so well."

"I'm not going to let you in."

"Mallory—"

"Good night, Aaron."

"One kiss."

"No."

"I'll stay here and serenade you. I'll sing until the neighbors complain."

"You are such a jerk."

"Open the door and give me a kiss, and then I'll go away."

I had to be careful. I was ravenous now. My whole body craved flesh. Last time I kissed Aaron in a situation like this I ended up biting his lip and drawing blood.

And in my weakened state I opened the door just a crack.

Aaron pushed right past me.

"Hey!" I said.

He didn't stop. He was almost to the living room before I thought to shut the door.

"What are we having for dinner?" Aaron said, looking into my bowl of brain. "Looks nasty."

"Get out!"

He faced me. "What's the deal, honey?"

"I don't like people busting into my place. You ever heard of the Fourth Amendment?"

"Ah yes!" he said. "The poorest man may, in his cottage, bid defiance to the king!"

"And you're no king, Aaron. You're just a guy who is really and truly hacking me off."

He stepped closer. "Part of my charm."

He made a grab for me and I stepped back. And subtly put myself between him and the bowl on the table.

"What do you see in me, Aaron? I'm petulant and stubborn, just like you. Would *you* want to be with you?"

"I could save on the monogrammed bathroom towels, now couldn't I?"

"I'm serious," I said.

"Why? We're young and in love."

I issued a snort. "Don't you remember that time you tried to kiss me and I bit your lip?"

He put his finger on his mouth. "How could I forget?"

"Have you ever asked yourself why I did that?"

"All the time. And I come up empty."

"What if I did it again?"

"I'd be very upset. I might charge you with lip assault. I could do it—"

"What if I can't help doing things like that?" I said.

He frowned. "What do you mean, can't help?"

"What if I had a condition that made me do things like that?"

"A biting condition?"

"Have you read the medical literature? There was a whole cover story on lips in the *New England Journal of Medicine*."

"Now when you break out the jokes I know you're hiding something. What's going on? Tell me, Mallory, straight up."

Tell him what? That I was a zombie and that I missed him and would do anything to be able to be with him, but I can't because I'm undead?

Then what's a self-respecting deputy DA supposed to do with that? And I'd eventually have to tell him the whole truth, about the cop I ate, though it was clearly self-defense before it was self-feeding. The cop was dirty and tried to kill me first. The world, not to mention the city, is better off without him. That much I do know.

But they ended up arresting an innocent, a streetwalker turned vampire named Traci Ann Johnson. I'd proven her innocence to Aaron, but that still left the cop murder open.

In a way, Aaron would always be looking for me.

"Can we at least try it?" Aaron said.

"Try what?"

"A kiss. One kiss. No biting. What do you say?"

"No."

"Then I have no choice but to stay. What *is* this?" He started for the sofa, once again looking at my bowl.

So I grabbed him quick and laid a kiss on him.

My brain kicked into a zombie-human hybrid of mass explosions.

His lips, soft and supple and warm. A thrill charged down my spine at the same time another charge headed up, crying out, *Eat him! Eat him!*

It would be easy enough to do. I'd killed men quick—a simple thrust through the nose with Emily, the metal hook I use as a brain deadener and extractor.

Aaron would never know what hit him. He wouldn't suffer. Which was important to me.

The kiss lingered. He gently sent the tip of his tongue gliding over my lower lip, seeking entrance to the cave.

My jaw muscles quivered.

Then I pushed him away. "There! You satisfied?"

"You want me," he said.

"In more ways than you can imagine."

"That's all I need to hear." He started to unbutton his shirt.

"No," I said.

"Yes," he said.

"*No* means *No*. You're a county prosecutor. You want to rape me?"

"Listen to your own body, Mallory."

"I will end your career if you undo another button."

He stopped.

I felt tears forming in my eyes. I don't like to cry. It messes up my skin. "Please get out, Aaron. Please."

"I need you," he said.

"Now," I said.

He paused, then buttoned up his shirt. He looked so lost then. I almost wanted to forget everything I'd just said and run to him.

I didn't.

He left without another word.

CHAPTER EIGHT

I WENT UP to the roof of my building. From up here I can see the city 360 degrees. City Hall, Bunker Hill, Pershing Square, the Biltmore. All lighted up like life was normal.

Not for me, God, remember? I hate what you've done to me, and what is happening under your watch. Why don't you do something about it? Why don't you save my damned soul for me and get me out of this body of death? "You don't look so hot."

I whipped around and saw him. The Owl. It was Slapsie Maxie Green, my guardian fowl. His accent is '50s Jewish comedian, which is really annoying coming out of a bunch of feathers.

"Why do you sneak up on me like that?" I said.

"You know, I once bet on a horse that was so slow the jockey kept a diary of the trip."

"What does that have to do with anything?"

"It's a good joke!"

I shook my head. "You're the joke."

"Now that hurts."

"Why? You're a mouthpiece for somebody or some god, and you won't give me what I need to know. How do I even know you're who you say you are? How do I know you're not a demon?"

"Demon, she says! I'm wounded."

"Cry me a river."

"Milton Berle, now he was a demon. Stole my best material."

"I don't want to hear—"

"The Thief of Bad Gags, they called him—"

"Shut up!"

If an owl could show a hurt look in its eyes, Max did. Big deal. I wasn't in the mood.

"I want to know who shot me and I want to know now," I said. It had happened when I was working for the public defender's office and went to see a client in South L.A. When I was done with the interview, I got in my car and the next thing I know I've been shot. A drive-by. I died on the street. Then came back to life. I don't know how, but I was a changed woman, oh yes.

"Believe me," Max said, "I would tell you if I knew. But guess what? I don't have that information."

"Why don't you?"

"There's a reason for everything, and I got things I can say to you and things I can't. I talk to the other guys, and they say this is not normal."

"Other guys? Like you?"

"Oh yeah, the watchers. We got a regular group. Meet once a week for poker."

I tried to stay focused. "Can you at least tell me what I need to do to find out? The cops are a dead end. I had a deal with a cop named Richards, but he reneged. He's in with the mayor's people, I'm sure. So I need help. Why can't you help me?"

"Who says I can't help?"

"You did. You said—"

"I said I couldn't *tell* you, not that I couldn't *help* you."

"That's a technicality!"

"You're the lawyer! You're the one with technicalities already."

"I so want to stuff a pillow with you."

"Believe me, you don't want that. Owl feathers are tough."

"But if you were a pillow I could hit you when I was frustrated, like now."

"Listen to me. There's an old joke—"

"Please don't tell me a joke—"

"A guy walks into a bar with a piece of asphalt under his arm. He says to the bartender, 'Give me a drink—and one for the road.'"

I didn't laugh.

"That's funny," Max said.

I said nothing.

"But it's also got a point," he said. "I can give you one for the road."

"One what?"

"Clue. It's all I got. But I was with you on the night you were shot."

"A lot of good that did me."

"After. After you were shot. After you were reanimated."

"Who reupped me?"

"I don't know! And I couldn't tell you if I did."

"I'm getting tired of this."

"Listen, after you were out of there, out of the morgue, somebody came to claim your body. But you were gone."

"Who was it?"

"I didn't see his face."

"His?"

"He was male, I think."

"You think?"

"The point is, they must have a record of it down at the morgue, wouldn't you say?"

"This'd be a helluva lot easier if you could talk," I said.

"Talking has never been my problem, *Tchotchke*. It's having something to say that's the tricky part. Gotta fly now."

"Wait—"

"Use your noodle," Max said, ascending.

"Just tell me if things are going to get worse or better," I said. "Can you tell me that much?"

He flapped his wings, hovering. "The world is in some shape. Pessimists never had it so good."

"That's your answer?"

"Keep fighting," he said, and flew away.

Keep fighting? That's the advice I get from on high?

When I was six my mom got me a Cabbage Patch Kid. It was a stretch for her because we didn't have much money and Mom was paying rent and buying weed and trying to sell her beadwork. Plus she had to fight a couple of other moms at the store to get the thing.

So I tried real hard to like the doll—for Mom's sake.

But I was not a Cabbage Patch sort of kid. Somehow I knew that.

One day I went out to the courtyard of the place we were staying and saw a boy of five, Milton, playing with a *Masters of the Universe* He-Man action figure.

That I had to have. That was my destiny.

I entered into my very first negotiation.

"Cheap doll," I said.

"It's not a doll," Milton said.

"You wish it was a doll," I said.

"Do not."

"Do too."

"Do not, do not."

"Do too, do too, one more time than you."

Milton started to cry.

"Milton, don't cry. I'll give you my doll if you want."

"You will?"

"Yes."

"Okay."

"But what have you got for me?" I asked.

His eyes narrowed. "You can't have my He-Man."

"Who wants that piece of junk?"

"It's not junk!"

"It's not a Cabbage Patch, either. Just for that, I'm keeping Francesca Janice. She's going to be worth a hundred dollars someday."

"A hundred!"

"Uh-huh."

"How do you know?" Milton said.

"I have special powers of knowing," I said.

"Uh-uh."

"Uh-huh."

"Prove it," Milton said.

"I can take off my thumb."

"You can?"

It was a trick I'd seen an old man do, pretending to take off his thumb when he was really hiding it in his palm. It worked on me when I was five. I figured it out when I was six.

So I did it to Milton and his eyes lit up. He then traded me his He-Man for Francesca Janice.

And for two glorious days I bonded with the Master of the Universe.

Then all hell broke loose. Milton's mother came over to our place screaming and yelling about what I'd done, and my mom told her to "mellow out."

I was forced to give back the He-Man. I got back my Cabbage Patch Kid with Milton's saliva all over it.

I learned that day you have little time to enjoy anything in life before hell breaks loose again somewhere.

FOR TWO MONTHS THINGS QUIETED DOWN IN THE CITY. No demons or cyclopes came within my line of fire, but it was like those Civil War battles that took place after months of quiet. Out there in the forest, forces were gathering, but you couldn't see them.

Meanwhile, you knew there would be a battle soon enough, with casualties and bodies piling up. Somebody would be coming for He-Man.

So I tried to keep on. I tried to find out more about who killed me and why but got nowhere. Whoever had set me up had done a superb job.

Which left me to do what I do. Kill. Eat. Not get caught. Kill, eat some more.

And practice law.

So that's what I did. Preparing my father's defense and handling a few misdemeanors here and there. Barely making enough to pay the rent.

Then in the middle of April, the world got deadly again.

All because a little boy walked into my office.

PART TWO

IN SPRING, A YOUNG ZOMBIE'S FANCY LIGHTLY
TURNS TO THOUGHTS OF FLESH

CHAPTER NINE

IT WAS mid morning and I was in my office on Broadway, working up a suppression motion on behalf of my dad. I was attempting to keep his sword from being admissible.

You never want the alleged murder weapon showing up in trial if you can help it. That's terribly inconvenient for the defense. But I had the good old Fourth Amendment on my side. All I would need is a judge with the courage to do the right thing.

Not easy to find.

Judges are elected. And if the electorate these days thinks you're soft on crime, they don't care if you uphold the Constitution. They just want you stripped of the judicial robes.

Which made my task all the more challenging. I was putting all my persuasive powers into that motion—I was going to have the judge weeping for justice before I was through.

Or so I told myself.

Little lies like this keep criminal defense lawyers going.

Around ten there was a knock on the door. A soft little knock like someone sheepish about intruding. If they had money, though, I welcomed it. There is rent to pay on this place, modest as it is. The building is between 3d and 4th and had seen its best days when Abbott and Costello were all the rage.

I went to the door and opened it. I had to look down to see who it was.

It was a boy of about ten. He had light brown skin, smooth as innocence, and thick hair the color of licorice. His eyes were wide and brown and nervous.

"Hello there," I said.

He trembled and his breathing quickened. I knelt down. "Are you all right?"

"You are law?" he said with a slight Mexican lilt.

"I'm a lawyer, yes. Do you know what that is?"

He nodded.

"What's your name?"

"Jaime."

"Did you need something, Jaime?"

He nodded.

"What is it you need?" I asked.

"Help."

It was quite clear to me he was scared of something. "Come in," I said. I closed the door behind him, then led him to my one good client chair.

"My name is Mallory," I said, sitting on the edge of my desk. "Now, why don't you tell me what the trouble is?"

"It is my mother," he said.

"Is she in trouble?"

He shook his head.

"Shall we call your mother?"

"No!"

The suddenness and vehemence of his reaction threw me. "Jaime, you don't have to be afraid as long as you're here. People can tell me whatever they want and I listen, and then I try to help them."

"I have no money," he said.

"Well, that makes two of us," I said. "I think we'll get along just fine. I don't want your money. I just want to help you if I can. What is it about your mother you need to tell me?"

"She is trying ..."

"Don't be afraid."

"She is trying to kill me."

Slow down, Mallory girl, I told myself. You could be stepping right into a minefield. Family disputes are one of the least predictable areas in the entire field of law. Kids lie about parents, parents lie about kids, wives and husbands lie about each other. You have to walk a fine line of legalities if you get anywhere close to family law, especially when children are involved.

I said, "How did you find me?"

"I see your name. On the sign. I hear your name sometime."

I had a rep among the people down here, primarily a Latino population, with a mix of Asian and African American. You do some good work, and it gets around. You do work people can afford, and it gets around even more.

So it wasn't much of a surprise if my name had floated to a boy named Jaime.

"What makes you say your mother wants to kill you?" I said. His face was unmarked. I hoped there wasn't anything beneath the clothes.

"She want to eat me!" Jaime said.

Now that is a matter I know something about.

"Tell me why you think that, Jaime. I mean, what did she do?"

"Bit me," he said. He held up his arm and I saw the dried blood on his long-sleeved shirt.

"Let me have a look at that," I said. I unbuttoned the sleeve and rolled it up. An ugly bite mark was right in the middle of his forearm. In a perverse jolt of my nature, I looked at the boy's wound with a mixture of desire and repulsion.

Which is why I have some very bad days.

"We need to get you to a doctor," I said.

"No! I am afraid."

"Afraid of what?"

"She will find me."

I did some quick legal calculating. Child protection is a priority in the law. Over the decades, through cases hard and heartbreaking, the laws had evolved to hold up the best interest of the child in all these matters.

It was a sign of the times. Parenting skills were not exactly what they had been in generations past.

So the law protected children and that was a good thing. What my role would be was yet to be seen.

"We can do this in secret. I'll go with you," I said.

"What will happen to me?"

"First, you'll get your arm taken care of. Then we'll try to figure out what's going on at home."

"No home!" he cried. "I do not want to go home again, not ever!"

"Do you have other family? Somewhere you can go?"

He shook his head. "We come from Texas."

"Just you and your mother?"

"But she is not my mother! Don't make me go back there."

"All right now. Here's what we have to do. We have to let some people know what's happening at your house."

"Who?"

"It's called child protective services," I said. "The doctor will have to report—"

"No! I don't want to go there!"

"This is what they do," I said.

Tears started to roll down the boy's smooth cheeks.

I fought the urge to wrap my arms around him. I had to keep professional. But I wanted to. And inside came that old familiar feeling, a dark and hopeless feeling—wanting to have children of my own, but my undead body denying me that.

I almost wept then.

But Jaime, I had decided, was my new client. *Pro bono publico,* as we lawyers like to say. Roughly translated, it means, no money but the same amount of work.

I told myself not to do it, not yet, not to dive in with both feet. I'd been burned before.

But he was little and he was crying and I knew I couldn't say no.

JAIME GAVE ME HIS ADDRESS, WHICH WAS A RUN-DOWN apartment building on the east side of Los Angeles, in Boyle Heights.

Using our very sophisticated interoffice communication system, I opened the door of my office and shouted, "Hey Nick!"

A moment later, Nick came out to see what I wanted.

"Nick, this is Jaime," I said.

Nick looked at the boy. The boy looked at Nick and pushed back into his chair. Nick is not, at first glance, a friendly looking sort. You have to warm up to him.

"I need you to keep an eye on him while I go visit his mother."

"No!" Jaime said.

"It's all right," I said. "Nick is a friend of mine."

Jaime didn't look convinced.

Nick smiled. When he does, little crinkles form at the comer of his eyes. Kind of endearing in a way.

"Hello there, young man," Nick said. "Do you believe in magic?"

Jaime said nothing but watched Nick carefully.

"Would you like to see something magical?" Nick said.

Jaime didn't protest.

"Let me show you," Nick said. He reached into his pocket. He rummaged around there for a moment. Then said to me, "Mallory, can you lend me a quarter?"

I laughed. Nick is perpetually money challenged. I fished a quarter out of my purse and put it in his weathered old hand.

"Now watch!" Nick said as he tossed the coin from hand to hand. He made a final toss and closed his left fist. He held the fist out to Jaime. "Blow on my fist," Nick said.

Jaime looked at me.

"It's all right," I said.

Jaime issued a birthday cake blow toward Nick's fist.

Nick opened his hand.

No coin.

Jaime's eyes rounded with wonder.

"Where did it go?" Nick said.

Jaime shrugged, totally into the moment.

"Ah! Wait!" Nick put his right hand up to his nose and snorted. The quarter fell into his open left hand.

Jaime broke out in laughter.

Nick said, "Well, what do you know!" He wiped the quarter on his shirt and then handed it to Jaime. "For you, young man."

Jaime took it with obvious delight.

"I'll be back in an hour," I said to the duo.

CHAPTER TEN

I DROVE without incident to Boyle Heights. My Geraldine had been nursed back to health by a great body shop whose boss I decided not to eat. This is a deal I have. You give me good service, you keep your brain.

That's only fair.

Boyle Heights is an area of L.A. that has long been one of the poorer sections. In the '20s and '30s, as the white population established restrictive covenants in their new burgs, the Heights was about the only place poor folks of color could get property.

And so the legacy continues. It's almost all Latino now, with a smattering of black and very old white.

The so-called security gate at the front was unlocked. I entered into a courtyard of dried grass and a two-story apartment building in an L-shape. The grass was strewn with children's toys and a couple of crushed beer cans. I made my way to apartment number seven.

I knocked.

A moment later the door opened a crack and a voice said, "Como?"

"Mrs. Gonzalez?" I asked.

"Si'?"

"My name is Mallory Caine. I'm a lawyer. May I speak with you please?"

"Lawyer?"

"May I come in?"

"I don't think—"

"It concerns your son," I said.

Silence.

"He came to see me. He's afraid of something."

The woman opened the door. She was small, a bit round, but friendly in features. She wore brown pants and a plain white blouse. The only thing remarkable about her was her fingernails, longish and painted blue.

"Where is my son?" she asked. There was concern in her voice, but I couldn't tell what the motivation was. Did she want him back to do him harm? She didn't look like a child abuser. But that's not something you can tell from the outside.

"Please." I pushed in past her and waited for her to close the door.

The apartment was small but neat. It smelled like cooked meat. I don't like that smell anymore. On one wall was a wooden cross and that was about it for the decorations. There wasn't much sunlight coming in through any of the windows. I think the apartment backed up against an alley.

"Now you tell me," the woman said. "Where is Jaime?"

"He's safe. He's at my office."

"I want him here." Her voice was insistent but not crazy. Not like somebody who would bite her own child.

"All right," I said. "If you could just answer a couple of questions for me?"

She shook her head. "First Jaime."

"I'm sorry," I said. "First my questions."

"You have not the right!"

"But I do, Mrs. Gonzalez. I am an officer of the court, and I have a minor who has come to me with some concerns. If you will allow me to ask you a few questions, I'm sure this will all be cleared up."

"Concerns?"

I wasn't going to tell her that her son thought she wanted to eat him. She did not seem like a zombie to me. The cooked meat was one clue.

I remembered a scene from a movie I'd seen as a kid. It was *Invasion of the Body Snatchers,* and it started with a boy running away from his mother. The hero stops and tries to help the boy, but he's insistent. He keeps saying it's not his real mother. And it turns out he's right because she's a pod person who has snatched the mother's body.

I have to admit, with all the things happening in L.A. lately, I was open to anything.

"Do you live alone here?" I asked.

"Yes."

"Does Jaime have a father?"

"No."

"I understand you came from Texas."

"Yes, but—"

"What brought you out here?"

"Work," she said.

"What sort of work do you do?"

"I am a legal citizen, if that is what you ask."

"No, I'm asking what sort of work it is that brought you out here."

"I work at Central Market."

The Grand Central Market has been a Los Angeles mainstay since 1917. It is, in fact, just a pickle's throw from my office.

"There are markets in Texas, too," I said. "Was there something special about L.A.?"

She didn't answer. I've looked at enough witnesses in my time to tell when there's something the witness is trying to hide. She was very good at the hiding but not good enough to slip it by me.

Now a clumsy lawyer, in court, rushes right in and tries to force out the secret. Like on all those cheesy lawyer shows and movies.

Doesn't work that way in real life.

You have to dig for the information with a gentle trowel. You have to burrow around the witness until you find a leak. Then you coax out the hidden info.

Unless you can catch a liar in the act, and that's when you really give them the hammer. I didn't know enough yet to make that judgment. She could have just been deeply suspicious of me, which is not a hard thing to be around a lawyer.

"Perhaps you'd like to give me the story on your own," I said. "Shall we sit down?"

"I want to see him," she said. "I want to see him now." Her eyes were wet. She went to an old recliner, sat down, put her head in her hands. "He is in need of help, and I have not the money."

"What help?"

"They say he is sick. He has something in his head. He try to hurt himself sometime."

I said nothing about seeing his arm. I just wanted her to talk.

"They don't know what it is, but he will see things. It sound like he is making up stories. But he really is believing he is seeing these things. Sometimes they are devils. Sometimes they are birds."

"What kind of birds?"

"Sometimes black, sometimes owls."

Owls again. Besides the ones I've mentioned, I've also had a run-in with Lilith, an ancient demon goddess who flapped around as a screech owl in ancient times—and even now. We had not concluded our business. I knew I would see her again.

"Go on," I said.

"I take him to a doctor in Houston. I use all of the money I have for him to see. He cannot tell me what is wrong with Jaime. But he says if I go to Los Angeles. Someone there may help. But I have run out of money and my little boy is suffering. Sometime he look at me and it is like he does not know me. Do you know how that breaks my heart?"

I could only imagine.

"Mrs. Gonzalez, do you have any paperwork on this? Do you have some report from the doctor in Houston? It would help us to figure out what is best for Jaime."

"I know what is best for him. Is best for him to have God help him. But he will not go into a church. He is too scared of something."

I was beginning to feel like a real intruder here. Butting in on this woman's pain and interfering in a family relationship that was already troubled. Maybe what I thought she'd been hiding was just this, her child's medical condition. Who wants to have that known?

"Nevertheless," I said, "if you have something of a medical nature, that would help."

"I do not have nothing. I went to the hospital and they tell me that this was not an emergency. They said I should see, you know, doctor of the head. Maybe you help? You are a lawyer, cannot you make them help my boy?"

"Let me work on it with you," I said.

"We cannot pay for this."

"You won't have to this time. I know where we can go. But there is still the problem of Jaime being afraid."

"You must bring him home."

She was right. Sooner or later, probably sooner, the law would tell me I had no right to keep Jaime from his mother. Especially if he had a medical condition. If this was true, his vision of his mother eating him was indeed probably something in his mind.

But I kept seeing the bite mark on his arm. What about that? Could it really have been self-inflicted?

I wasn't ready yet to just give him up.

"Mrs. Gonzalez," I said, "I will bring Jaime to you. And then we'll get him to a doctor. We'll get him the help he needs."

"Yes," she said. "I want that. Please. Hurry."

CHAPTER ELEVEN

WHEN I GOT BACK to the office, Jaime was playing with Nick. Some sort of chase-around-the-room game. Which was funny because Nick was about the same height as the boy.

It was nice to hear the boy laughing. To see a look of joy on his face. I wanted him to have that for the rest of his life.

I put my hand out and stopped Nick by palming his head.

"Easy there, Sparky," I said. "What is this, a playground?"

Jaime came squealing around a chair and grabbed Nick's leg. "Got you!" he shouted.

"You have got the Kallikantzaros!" Nick said. "You will get your wish!"

"I need to talk to Jaime," I said.

Must have been my voice. Jaime let go of Nick and his face went back to the look he had the first time I saw him.

"Jaime, I have been to see your mother."

"Do not make me go!" Jaime said.

"Now wait," I said. "She talked to me about your medical condition. Do you know what a medical condition is?"

He nodded.

"You've been to see doctors?"

He nodded.

"There are times when we think we see things and we really don't," I said. "Even grown-ups have this happen sometimes."

"No, she is not my mother!"

"What if I came along with you? And you and your mother and I went to see a doctor together?"

Jaime said nothing.

"I'll stay with you all the way," I said. "And you can still talk to me. Would you let me do that with you?" Nick told Jaime to sit for a moment, then walked me to the window. He spoke low so Jaime couldn't hear.

"I am a barometer," he said. "This is not good for Jaime. There is something bad there."

"Any idea what?"

He shook his craggy head. "But I have no doubt the boy is in grave danger."

"You know I can't hold him," I said.

"But I am telling you—"

"I can't tell the court that a mini barometer told me to keep him from his mother."

"Then think up something."

"Like what?"

"Anything."

"The law is not magic, Nick. I can't just start producing rabbits."

"You are a lawyer. You know how to manipulate anything!"

"You give us too much credit."

"Save him."

"I'll do everything I can, Nick." I looked over and saw Jaime, his eyes wet. And I felt something that reminded me of love. Not that I can truly love anymore. I can only get a whisper of it, like the scent of a flower as you walk by a garden you cannot enter.

This time I didn't fight my feelings. I went to him and picked him up and put my arms around him. I held him as if he were my own. And then the familiar feeling arose, the one that makes me think of eating even those I love. I quickly let him go.

"Take him outside," I said to Nick. "I'll be right with you."

When the door to my office had closed, I stifled a scream. Once more I felt what I did not want to feel. To God, or the sky, or whomever—I clenched my teeth. I looked up with my jaw shut, daring any divinity to try to make a fool of me.

It would happen soon enough.

SOMETHING WAS WRONG AT JAIME'S APARTMENT BUILDING. When a black-and-white is parked in front, it's never good, especially in Boyle Heights. I pulled Geraldine in behind the police car. The top was down. I told Jaime to stay in his seat.

The moment I got out, Mrs. Gonzalez ran from the front of the building toward us.

Behind Mrs. Gonzalez was a uniformed LAPD officer.

"Jaime!" Mrs. Gonzalez held her arms out toward the passenger side. Jaime stayed in the car. I stepped between him and the onrushing mother.

"He's still a little shaky," I said. "Let's take it slow."

"Out of my way," she said.

I had to put my hands on her shoulders to stop her. "Please," I said.

"Put your hands down and step out of the way," the officer said. He was young and sincere and there is nothing more intractable on the street than a young, sincere LAPD patrol officer.

"I represent the boy," I said. "I'm a lawyer."

"You have to back away."

I didn't move.

"Now," he said.

"Let's be reasonable about this," I said and stepped to the side to talk to him directly. "I am representing to you that I am the boy's representative as of today and—" From inside the car Jaime squealed. "No!"

I turned around and saw Mrs. Gonzalez trying to lift her son out of the car. He was flopping around, resisting.

"Do something," I said to the cop. "We need to get him to a doctor. And I'm going with him."

"You're not going anywhere," the patrolman said. "Except to the station if you don't back off."

"Arrest me? That's what you're saying?"

"If I have to, yes."

Now Jaime was in full-throttle scream. He'd managed to wriggle away from his mother and jump to the backseat.

The officer calmly stepped to the car and lifted Jaime up by the back of his pants. Holding him like a hooked bass, he began walking his wailing catch toward the apartment building.

"You can't do that," I said, knowing he could, and that there was nothing I could say to stop him. Sometimes bluster works, but not on young, enthusiastic cops.

"Stay away or you'll be arrested," he said over his shoulder.

"I am sorry," Mrs. Gonzalez said to me. "He is my son." It's true, he was. I knew I was out of line. I'd violated one of the rules of the good lawyer—don't get personally involved.

CHAPTER TWELVE

I AM NOT proud that I am an expert in removing the human brain.

It's just that I'm good at it.

With Emily I can go in through a nasal cavity and grab some of that soft, though fibrous, material and bring it out like a long string of sausage. You have to be careful, though, because if you're indelicate the hook tears right through the stuff. It's like taking out very cold Jell-o that has some fruit mixed in with it.

I suppose this is over-sharing, but this is a zombie memoir, so deal with it.

The other way, if you've got the right tools and some privacy, is to saw off the head and go up through the neck or take off the dome of the cranium and scoop out chunks directly. That's more of an inconvenience, though.

I had been trying, in my pathetic way of justification, to seek the flesh only of those who deserved to have it torn from them.

But who was the one making that determination? Me. Without benefit of judge or jury, burdens of proof or evidence.

In other words, I was going against every instinct I had as a criminal lawyer. The Constitution does not have a provision that allows the consumption of brains by zombies. It does not protect the right of the undead to feast upon the flesh of lowlifes.

But this world had become strange and maddening for me, and until I could figure how to get out of it, how to right myself, how to find out who was behind all this and give him or her a straight ticket to hell, I was trapped and had to eat.

So, as Amanda I got myself down to Santa Monica Boulevard, where I ply my trade as a hooker.

Not really trade, as the johns never get what they think they're paying for.

My comer is near the Hollywood Forever Cemetery, where many stars of the past are buried. Ever heard of Douglas Fairbanks? Maybe the biggest silent film star of all, entombed in this gorgeous memorial with a large pool in front of it. Something royalty might have gotten. And I guess in those days the screen stars were treated that way.

Valentino got a crypt in a wall there. Tyrone Power a nice location near the big pond.

Sometimes I go there just to reflect.

But not tonight.

Some of the other girls were there, this section of town not having been cleaned out for awhile. We are just like the street dog vendors. Sometimes the cops chase us away and we move to another location. Sometimes they just let things alone because there's more going on around town than they have time to take care of.

These days it was more like the latter. It had started, I think, when Traci Ann Johnson, vampire, used to work this corner with me. Then all sorts of creatures started showing up. Bloodsuckers and werewolves and demons and screech owls and eyeballs that appeared in guacamole.

I have a history with eyeballs. Someone or something has been watching me since I was a kid.

Why was I born? Just so I could have people watch me? Just so I could be a piece in a game?

I didn't want any part of it, but I was stuck. Can't live, can't die, can't get out of here with a soul intact.

A car drove up, a Benz. Pretty.

I leaned in the passenger side window.

It was a freshly scrubbed young man trying desperately to look cool.

"Hi ya, handsome," I said.

"You want to go for a little ride?" he said. I took him for some west side kid with too much family money. Money used for tats and a hard look.

"Well, that just depends," I said. "Good-looking guy like you, where'd you go to school?"

"Huh?"

"You in or out of school?"

"What's that got to do with anything? We doing something here or not?"

"What are you, eighteen?"

He hurled the B word at me and for that alone I should have eaten him. But instead of getting angry, I got sad. Immensely, deeply.

"How'd you get to this place?" I said.

"Get in and I'll show you."

"Get over yourself, junior. Go make something of yourself, other than some white bread wannabe gangsta woman-hating lowlife."

What was I *saying*?

Junior started cursing.

"Shut it!" I said. "You got limited chances in this life. Don't blow it. And I'm a cop and if I ever see you or your car around here again I'm going to haul you in and call Mommy and have a family talk."

"Cop?" He blanched. "Show me your badge."

"You want to try me, short stack? Get out of the car."

"Hey, wait—"

"Go earn a girlfriend. Be a real man. You make me sick."

He burned rubber getting out of there.

And I was still hungry. Still angry at myself. Stuck between two worlds.

What I needed was a fresh criminal.

I walked down Santa Monica Boulevard. The cemetery was dark save for security lights and the illumination of the sign.

What about the people in the ground? Their ghosts? Their souls?

I found myself thinking about those things, the realm of after-death.

Where was Rudy Valentino these days? Was he doing the tango in heaven or hell, or was there some other dance floor?

People don't think about death much. It used to be life was a preparation for the big sleep. What was it the poet said? "Sleep is lovely, death is better still, not to have been born is, of course, the miracle."

Clearly I was out of miracles. I had been born.

When I was, my father told me, there were blackbirds all around trying to get at me. My mom was in the backseat of a Ford Maverick in the desert outside Las Vegas. An owl chased the birds away. An owl form, actually. Inside it was the spirit of a man now dead, who has been assigned the role of protector.

Turned out to be Max, my guardian.

He says he's been watching me all my life—and fighting battles unseen. But he cannot give me more details. Some he knows, others he doesn't, but there's some sort of big cosmic chess game going on, and I'm a piece on the board.

I reject that. If God is behind it, he can play the game without me.

Life sucks.

Death sucks.

Undeath sucks.

The only thing that doesn't suck is practicing law.

I kept on walking. A couple of cars pulled up and I rejected them. A guy out prowling for a little action doesn't deserve to die for it.

This was how I was thinking at the time.

And then I heard a voice say, "Amanda."

It was, of all the unlikely people, Detective Mark Strobert of the Los Angeles Police Department. He was driving one of those standard-issue Crown Vics LAPD detectives ride around in, looking for hookers to hassle.

Once he'd picked me up as Amanda to try to get some information out of me on Traci Ann Johnson. He didn't know I was Mallory Caine, lawyer. He thought I was just Traci Ann's coworker on the street. He took me to a Mexican place to eat. That's where the bowl of guacamole revealed an eyeball in the thick of it, looking at us.

Let's just say Strobert lost his appetite.

Strobert had been hit with some other out-of-the-ordinary things, like the werewolf in court who stabbed my vampire client through the chest with a wooden spike.

His world was rocked.

So what was he doing here?

I spoke in a thick Jersey accent, as Amanda. "Detective, what brings you down to the boulevard?"

"Can we talk?"

"Here?"

"Not here. Hop in."

"Now hold on there, sweets. You're not going to take me out of commission, are you?"

"Are you doing anything illegal?" he said with a knowing smile.

"Little old me?"

"I'll pay you for your time."

It wasn't money I wanted. My stomach was growling. I was about to tell him to kiss off when he said, "Please." What was I thinking letting that get to me?

I guess the answer is, I wasn't thinking at all. I was feeling something, and if you could have cut it out of me with a scalpel, it might have resembled sympathy.

. . .

"You're a mess, honey," I said.

We were having coffee at a little all-night diner on Western. Strobert looked like a defeated man. His green eyes, which I'd once mistrusted, didn't seem as lustrous or confident as they once were. He'd lost his swagger. And when you're an LAPD detective, that's half your image.

"You're quick with the compliments," he said.

"Show me the money." I had to keep up appearances.

"You don't trust cops?"

"I really have to answer that?"

He gave a half smile as he took out his wallet, then a twenty, which he put on the table. I snatched it up.

"My time is your time," I said.

"Tell me about zombies," he said.

Poker face, I told myself. "You mean those gross things that eat brains?"

He nodded.

"Fiction," I said. "Why?"

"You haven't seen any stuff like that go on down on the boulevard?"

"I'm too busy," I said. "I've been picked up by more than a few jerks, if that's what you mean."

"That's not what I mean."

"What *do* you mean?"

"I just want information, is all. Wherever I can get it."

"Why me? I'm a streetwalker. You could talk to a thousand other people."

"Maybe I wanted to see you again."

"Whoa." I put my hands up. "Not interested."

"You know what I think?" he asked.

"No."

"You want to know what I think?"

"No."

"I'm going to tell you anyway. I think you're in the wrong line of work."

"What are you doing here?" I said.

"Can't a guy take an interest?"

"No."

"Listen!" He slapped the tabletop, got embarrassed, and put his hands in his lap. "I know there's something going on in this town that I can't figure, and I'm somebody who has to figure. I have to know."

I liked him then. I knew I could like him a lot if I let myself.

I didn't let myself.

"You know," he said, "I believe what it says on the side of our black and whites. Protect and serve."

My mind wanted me to say, *Protect and Serve Warm.* But the words stayed right where they should have.

"You know what makes a good detective?" he asked.

I shook my head.

"The ability to see, ask the right questions, and persist. Like a bulldog. Only the questions that you answer are supposed to add up. They're supposed to have some basis in logic or experience. But how do you make anything out of an eyeball rolling around in fresh guacamole? How do you do that? How do you protect a town where there's things you can't explain or hunt down?"

"Detective, why are you telling me all this?"

"For some reason I trust you," he said. "Sometimes you can trust people on the street more than the ..."

"Than the what?"

"Nothing."

"The people you work with?"

"It's nothing."

"Or the people in power?"

"Look, just leave it at that. *Can* I trust you?"

"Sure."

"It's kind of hard to figure people these days," he said. "People used to be decent back in the old days. In my grandfather's day. He was a World War II vet, and he came back home here to Los

Angeles and helped build up the greatest civilization on earth. That whole generation, you know?"

"Sort of."

"What about your parents?"

"Maybe we don't need to go into that," I said.

He heaved a heavy sigh. "I just need to know."

My heart was going out to him but I pulled that beating thing back into my undead chest.

"Why don't you stop what you're doing?" he said. "Why don't you go back to school or something and get a real job?"

"I don't need career advice. Thanks for the coffee. And maybe you better not roust me again."

"What if I want to see you?" he said. "I mean, just see you?"

"Me? A hooker?"

"Stranger things have happened."

"I would say you need to look at some stress leave." I got up, gave him a final look, then walked out into the night.

In another lifetime, a boy-meets-girl-and-they-don't-want-to-eat-each-other lifetime, I would have stuck around. I would have wanted him to kiss me. I would have put my hand in his and talked.

Now that was out of the question. And as I walked up the street I felt like I was drowning in the middle of the ocean. No hope of any rescue. Sharks underneath.

CHAPTER THIRTEEN

I MUST HAVE WALKED for at least an hour before a car pulled up. It was a guy with one of those mounted saints on the dash. He was maybe fifty, thin, unruly brown hair. No wedding band.

Nervous.

He asked about giving me a ride somewhere and I said sure and got in. Before taking off, he asked if I was a cop and I said no. Then he asked how much half an hour would be and I told him to drive to a specific location I had in mind. A place where we wouldn't be seen.

As he drove, I said, "Who's the saint?"

"Hm? Oh, St. Francis."

"You a good Catholic?"

"Why are you asking me that? I didn't pay you to talk."

"You haven't paid me at all. Park there."

I pointed him to the quiet spot between two corner walls. This is where things could happen in relative quiet. My place. Like a fisherman with a favorite fishing hole.

"So now what?" he said after he killed the motor.

"Answer me," I said. "Have you been to confession?"

"You're making me mad."

"I'll make it up to you."

"So what? I go to confession. I'll have to go after this, too."

"No, you won't."

He just stared at me.

I reached into my bag for Emily.

"What are you doing?" he said.

"This won't hurt a bit," I said.

KILLING GETS IN YOUR BLOOD. IF YOU DO IT ONCE, IT'S EASIER to do it again. If you do it and your conscience doesn't bring you to your knees, you are truly the walking dead.

I was part of L.A. history now, though no one knew it yet. We seem to grow them here in Los Angeles.

There was a woman who came here from Louisiana named Louise Peete. Had all this Southern charm. This was around 1920. She learned about a wealthy businessman named Jacob Denton who was planning to travel and wanted to rent out his mansion. So she used her well-educated sweetness to get Mr. Denton into bed. Then she moved into his mansion and started figuring how to get his money.

After a month Denton disappeared.

Denton's family hired an attorney and a detective, and they found Denton's body buried in a shallow grave in the basement of the mansion. He'd been shot once in the head. Louise Peete was sent to prison for life.

But eighteen years later, after stints in San Quentin and Tehachapi, Louise was paroled. She had always maintained her innocence and many people believed her, including an elderly couple named Margaret and Arthur Logan. They invited Louise to live with them at their home in Pacific Palisades. Margaret paid Louise seventy-five bucks a month, plus room and board, to watch her aging husband while Margaret helped the war effort at an aircraft plant.

Louise started forming a plan to gain control of the couple's money, but Margaret became suspicious. So Louise shot her in the back of the head and buried her in the backyard. She got rid of Arthur by taking him to a psychiatric hospital and making up all sorts of stories about his insanity and violent temper. The poor man was committed and died six months later.

Louise was actually in the process of breaking open the family safe when the head of LAPD's homicide division came calling.

It was 1944 and once more Louise Peete was tried for murder. The jury took only three hours to return a conviction. She was given the death sentence.

The prosecutor told jurors, "Mrs. Peete was a Dr. Jekyll and Mrs. Hyde. She must've sat in her prison cell all those years, figuring out what went wrong the first time in plotting a new crime."

For some reason I can understand Louise Peete. On April 11, 1947, she was put in a gas chamber at San Quentin.

I am under a death sentence, too.

CHAPTER FOURTEEN

I HADN'T SEEN my mom in a while, so the next afternoon I drove out to Glendale. My mom's bead store is just off Colorado Boulevard. As I approached the front door, I saw a big sign in her familiar scrawl: **Sale! Today Only!**

I went in and saw my mother, Calista Caine, ex-hippie and braless bead store owner, in a state of suspended animation. Only she wasn't up in the air. She had her eyes closed and hands lifted up to the ceiling of her store. The place smelled, as it usually did, of old incense and fresh ganja. Mom, at her age, still got baked on a regular basis.

"Mom, what on earth are you doing?" I said.

"Shhh," she said and continued communing with something above her.

Whatever. She occupied her own zone of reality and had ever since I could remember. We led a vagabond existence when I was a kid. Mom was always looking for some ecstatic deliverance from this world. There was a time when I thought she was a member of the cult-of-the-month club. But she always seemed to find a job. She always made enough for us to live on.

"I haven't got time to wait," I said. "Can you put your call on hold?"

Mom didn't respond. She seemed to go deeper into a trance.

Okay, if she was off sailing around outer space, I'd take the time to see what she was doing to her body these days. I went behind the glass display to the little office in back. It was set off from the rest of the store with a red paisley curtain. In the office was a hookah and a computer and a small flat-screen TV. And sure enough, on some tinfoil, was about an ounce of hippie lettuce with a few scattered seeds.

Mom insisted she got toasted because she had a medical condition. I call it *Dippus perpetuus*. Roughly translated, ongoing dippiness. But she's my mother and I keep trying to protect her health.

And then I saw something else: a syringe.

I charged back out to her. "What do you think you're doing?" I said, making no effort to use my inside voice.

"Quiet..."

"Wake up." I pulled her arms down and took her chin in my hand and made her look at me. Her eyes were dilated. "We're going to the hospital," I said.

"You interrupted!" she said. "I was talking to God."

"Oh really. Did he tell you to shoot smack?"

"Don't talk to me."

"Come on." I tried to take her arm and guide her toward the door. She went with me a couple of steps and then yanked her arm away and turned nasty.

"Get out!" she yelled.

"Mom—"

"Get out or I'll call the police."

"You'll call the cops on me?"

"I want you out of here."

"Mom, you're out of control—"

"Out!"

I realized then that no amount of reasoning was going to get her out of there. So I went back into the inner office and started gathering up the paraphernalia.

Mom whipped back the curtain. "Stop!"

She looked bigger than she'd been just a moment before. Like she was engorged with rage. It freaked me, because Mom was not one given to extreme anger. She was of the mellow variety of drug users. This was coming from some other place.

I kept cleaning up. The syringe went in the tinfoil that held the weed. I folded it up.

Mom came at me and grabbed my left arm. "Give that back to me!"

I pulled free. "Not going to do it," I said. I held her off with my left like some NFL running back with a great stiff-arm.

Mom started screaming at me, pawing at me again.

In the midst of all of that I bumped her and she went down. Flat on her keister.

She put her hands over her face and started crying.

I ignored her. Let her weep. Weep out the demons inside her that were making her—

Demons.

Suddenly I had an idea who—or what—could have been behind this. And the moment that thought hit me, the entire room went dark.

The darkness that overtook us was a form. Vaguely familiar. When it started to take human shape, I knew exactly who it was, coming to visit.

"Lilith," I said.

The form became the shape of a woman, naked save for two snakes that twisted around her body. Lilith was beautiful in that dangerous way of enticing wickedness.

"And so we meet again," Lilith said. One of her snakes hissed at me.

"Oh shut up," I said, and the snake head went silent.

"You are not wanted here," Lilith said.

"What have you been doing to my mother?"

"You have no rights here," Lilith said. Her voice was sultry, in that deep Bette Davis way that the reedy little waifs who pass for actresses today don't have. But this wasn't acting. I knew about Lilith from the last time we'd met.

At least this was what Father Clemente had told me. Lilith had been the first wife of Adam, but after a little tryst with Lucifer in the garden, and I do mean tryst, she was cast out to become a demon—her wicked and rebellious spirit to wander the earth. Often manifesting herself as a screech owl, she has been a temptress in league with her lover, Satan.

Nice gal.

I wasn't afraid of her this time. If she couldn't do away with me before, it was because something was holding back her power in that regard. It gave me all the confidence of a defense lawyer with a surprise witness.

"Don't tell me about my rights, Lil," I said. "If anybody doesn't have rights around here, it's you."

"You speak like the shameless lawyeress you are. I laugh at your words."

"Take your snakes and go find some rats to eat."

The snakes both hissed at me this time. Imagine that, snakes that can hear and respond. Sort of like talk show hosts.

"Your vain words have no power," Lilith said. "The power is not with you, but with her."

She turned to my mother. Mom was looking a little dazed. The effect of drugs and being knocked down. But one thing she wasn't was scared. She didn't look freaked at all by snake woman.

"What's that supposed to mean?" I said.

"I am here by your mother's choice," Lilith said. "Her choice is what controls."

"Is that right, Mom?" I said. "You want to do what this demon says?"

Mom didn't answer, just looked at me with doe-in-the-headlights eyes.

"Mom, tell this serpentine witch to leave you alone."

Mom said nothing.

"At least, tell her you want me to stay and help you get clean."

No response.

"Mom!"

"Please go," Mom said.

Lilith broke into a broad grin. And then, hands held out in front of her, she made a witchy face and I got lifted up off the ground.

She'd done this to me before.

Upside down now, I got whirled to the front of the store. An old man had just come in. He went, "Hey!"

The door whipped open, and out I went, dumped on the sidewalk.

The door slammed shut.

I looked up and saw the old man, still inside, pressing his frightened face to the glass. I got up and opened the door for him.

He stumbled out, his old eyes blinking like pistons. "What... was ... that?"

"I guess the sale is over," I said.

CHAPTER FIFTEEN

MY PHONE BLEEPED. It was Nick.

"Come quick!"

"Where?"

"Jaime's apartment. You must come now!"

"What's wrong? Where is he?"

"Come now!"

I burned Geraldine's rubber back to Boyle Heights and met Nick outside the apartment complex.

He was not alone.

A couple of children, maybe eight years old or so, were standing on either side of him, staring.

"I cannot shake them," he said.

I really couldn't blame the kids, for Nick resembles the least attractive of Snow White's dwarfs.

"What about Jaime?" I said.

"He is gone."

"What do you mean, gone?"

"And the mother, too. I went to check, and the neighbor, he said she took him."

"Take me to this guy."

Nick led me to the last apartment on the left, on the lower

level. The apartment next door to Jaime's. Nick knocked on the door and a Hispanic man of about fifty answered. He was swarthy, paunchy, and wore a wife-beater with a mustard stain on the front.

"You again?" the man said. "What is it you want?"

Nick jerked his thumb my way.

"My name is Mallory Caine," I said. "I'm a lawyer. I have come to help Jaime. What can you tell me about where they went?"

"I say nothin'."

"You told my investigator that Jaime's mother took him away?"

"This little man, investigator?"

"You have a problem?" Nick said.

I put my hand on Nick's shoulder to calm him down. "What happened?"

"All I say was she went away with her boy," the neighbor said.

"Does anything about that seem strange to you?"

"I don't think I say more."

I paused, then went to Jaime's apartment and tried the door. It opened.

"Hey," the man said. "You can't go in."

"I haven't got time to explain," I said. I went in. I wanted to see if there was any indication of packing or sign that she was taking Jaime away for good. Nick followed me and then came the man himself. He continued to protest that I shouldn't be in the apartment. I ignored him and kept looking around. I went in the back to where there was a single room. It was spare but looked like a boy's room. A boy who liked sports. Basketball. There were posters on the wall of basketball players, Lakers and Clippers and UCLA.

The man came back and said, "If you don't leave, I am going to call the police."

I faced him. "There are things happening that you don't know anything about."

"I don't trust lawyers."

"You're in a long line. Jaime may be in bad trouble."

"I don't know who you are or why I should listen. You and that little man may be bad people."

I heard Nick yell, "*Ahhhh!*"

The neighbor and I ran back into the living room. Nick was standing on the back of the sofa reaching up to where the wooden cross was hanging. He took it off its tack and brought it down.

"You put that back," the neighbor said.

"What are you doing, Nick?" I said.

He turned and jumped onto the sofa cushions. It acted like a small trampoline as he bounded to the floor. He looked like a Bizarro World Mary Lou Retton.

He held the cross out to me and turned it over in his hand. On the other side was the figure of Jesus.

"She had Jesus' face to the wall," Nick said.

"So?"

"It is sometimes used by those who follow the dark way." The man now looked like he was thinking deeply. "What is it?" I said.

He shook his head, sat on an old pink chair. "Graveyards," he said.

"What's that?"

"She liked to visit graveyards."

Nick and I looked at each other. To the man I said, "Tell me everything you know."

"Is the boy really in trouble?"

Nick said, "In terrible danger."

"She used to say she talked to the dead," the man said. "And something like the ghosts needed feeding."

Nick grabbed my sleeve and practically dragged me out to the street.

CHAPTER SIXTEEN

NICK USED his iPhone to find graveyards on a street map. Technically a graveyard is connected to a church of some kind. You don't see many graveyards in Los Angeles. Most every place with dead people is a cemetery, unless you count the Los Angeles City Council chamber.

I drove Geraldine as Nick shouted directions. It was twilight now, which only added to the horror movie vibe. There was a full moon rising. It was going to be a good night for werewolves, for bodies to rise from a grave or zombies to feed.

We found two small graveyards connected to churches that looked well over a hundred years old. But the yards were small and nothing was in them but markers and leaves and neglect.

Nick ordered me to turn down Whittier Boulevard. He kept his eyes on his iPhone, looking up on occasion to see where we were.

"There!" he said.

It was a church coming up on the right. A small sign I could barely read in the gloom, even with their pitiful sign light. St. Somebody-or-other, I couldn't quite make it out. As we drove past the driveway, I could see it had some kind of expansive graveyard

—the markers were glowing in the moonlight—with a chain-link fence around it. There was an anemic flower garden just inside the fence. But no other sign of activity.

Nick ordered me to drive slowly around the block. His head was fixed like a hunting dog's. The barometer seemed to be sensing something.

I turned right as Nick kept his eyes on the graveyard. Across the street was a 7-Eleven and a KFC. You could bury your dead, then ply yourself with fried chicken, and finish off with a Slurpee. L.A. was nothing if not sufficient for all needs.

"Hey Nick, what did you mean back there when you said it wasn't good?"

"It is just a theory," he said, keeping his eyes on the yard.

"Share it with me."

"I do not wish to alarm you."

"Alarm me."

He stiffened.

"What's going on?" I said. I was at the next corner, ready to turn.

"Look!"

I did.

And saw nothing.

"Go, go!" Nick said.

"Go where?"

"The entrance! We have to get in!"

"I don't see anything—"

"Hurry!"

I gunned Geraldine down the street.

"Here!" Nick said.

I braked Geraldine to the curb. Her tires screamed at me. We were next to a gated entrance. It was open.

Nick was already out of the car, his short legs churning. I jumped out and followed. It was like chasing after a runaway dachshund.

"Slow down," I said.

Nick didn't slow. He ran right across the soft, mushy grass of the buried dead. It was squishier than normal grass and the heels of my shoes kept sticking. I felt like I was running in snowshoes.

There was a silver sheen to the place and no outside lights. The trees were like sentries with multiple skinny arms. I lost sight of my investigator.

"Nick!"

No answer.

I kept on. There was a small mausoleum off to the right. I could barely see one wall and the rectangular plates that marked the tombs. It's almost redundant to say there was no sign of life, but I was looking for one sprightly Greek imp. Without anther plan I headed for the mausoleum.

I almost tripped over Nick. He put up his hand and put a finger to his lips. Then he used that same finger to point out into the darkness.

I saw nothing. At least nothing that moved. More of those ghostly trees. No sound except the ambient noise of cars on the street and the faint chop of a police helicopter, scanning some distant neighborhood for untoward things.

It should have been right overhead.

I leaned down and whispered, "Is it Jaime?"

Nick shook his head but didn't speak.

And then I saw it. An indistinct form maybe fifty yards away, slowly coming towards us.

Nick took my hand and squeezed it. I squeezed back. I wasn't afraid of whatever it was, unless it was someone with a bag of salt and a sewing kit.

As the figure got closer, I determined it was a woman. But looks can be deceiving. I'm talking transcreature, like shape-shifters.

Or it could be some actual citizen visiting a grave, in which case all this cloak and dagger from Nick the Barometer was a pointless waste of time. We still had to find—

The woman, or what I supposed was a woman, stopped. She

was close enough that I could see her shape, her hair, and then I knew.

"Mom?"

"Hello, honey," she said.

"What are you doing here?" I said.

Nick said, "This is what I would like to know!"

"It's all right, children. I know exactly why you're here. You're looking for that little boy," she said.

"Yes!" I said.

"He's safe."

"Where?"

"I will take you to him."

I said, "First tell me why you know about Jaime."

"Sweetheart, there are so many things you do not know." She sounded high, like one of those hippies holding flowers in front of a guru from India with a scraggly white beard, circa 1968.

"All right," I said. "I want to see the boy."

"Of course."

"Does Lilith have anything to do with this?" I said.

"Come," she said.

"We both come," I said. "Nick, you and I will—"

I stopped when I realized he wasn't there.

"Nick?"

He didn't answer. I couldn't see a sign of the little guy anywhere. When did he slip away? Or was he taken?

"One more question, Mom," I said. "When I was a little girl, what was my favorite toy? The one I wanted to have with me most of all?"

"Honey, why are you asking me such things?"

"Humor me, Mother."

"All right," she said. "You were very attached to a Cabbage Patch doll. I had to fight to get it. But then, wait a moment, you gave it away for another, a figure with muscles."

"Close enough," I said. "Are you all right yourself?"

"Yes, dear. Now—" She stopped abruptly when something moved behind her.

Then I heard Nick scream, "Liar!"

With that one word what had been my mother was something else. Roundish and hairy, open mouth with huge, pointed teeth. Bulging eyes and hands with long nails curling off each fingertip. She held them out like daggers.

It charged at me. I jumped to the side but the razor-sharp talons ripped through my arm.

Now I was mad. I was getting sick of having my flesh torn up. It doesn't kill me, but I do care how I look, you know? It's hard enough keeping my skin moisturized and all my joints in place. So getting knifed and shot with bullets and slashed by this *thing* was too much.

The monster growled. The effect was like the Abominable Snowman at the Disneyland Matterhorn ride mixed with an angry pit bull. It came at me again. I ducked as it whipped its spikes at me and, as the momentum sent it past me, put my leg out. It tripped and went down, rolling a couple of times.

It lumbered to its feet.

I looked for Nick but, again, he was nowhere to be seen.

Another lunge by the frothing furball. I sidestepped and gave it a kick to the middle. The thing doubled over and I gave it a swift foot to the face.

It backed up and shook its head like a boxer who'd just been clocked. But other than that it was going to keep coming at me, I was certain.

Out of the corner of my eye I saw something moving. I looked, which was a mistake. It was Nick, and he was stumbling toward the street, carrying something in his arms. I couldn't make out what it was.

But in trying to see I'd turned my back to the creature. And now it was on me, knocking me on my face. I smelled dirt and grass and felt the weight of the thing on me.

I heard Nick yell, "No!"

I managed to lift my face. The monster on top of me roared. I couldn't move. This thing was going to slash me to pieces and I'd be a walking skeleton with flesh hanging off me. I'd be just like those zombies you see in the movies. I'd be unable to help anyone because my cover would be blown. All this flashed through my mind.

And that's when the first flame hit.

I don't know about you, but fire is not my best friend. I used to love fires on a cold night. Old school, made with real wood and burned in a real fireplace. The crackle and the warmth.

My mom didn't do a lot of things right, but one of the things she tried to give me was a nice Christmas. And in those years we lived in a rented house in Gardena, and she made a real fire in the morning. Then she'd make me hot chocolate and Christmas toast, which was plain white bread, buttered, with some red sprinkles on it, the kind you usually put on cupcakes.

So fire had a special place in my heart. But once I became undead, I didn't like it anymore. It's something that threatens, that takes off skin, and I can ill afford that.

Now I was about to see it as my salvation. Because this flame came shooting over my head and hit the thing sitting on me.

It screeched and fell off my back.

I rolled the other way, not knowing if this combustion was going to continue.

The fire subsided and there was a moment's pause. I got to my feet to assess and tried to get my bearings.

The taloned monstrosity was ten feet to my left. It roared again.

And once more the fire came.

And in the light of the flame I saw what the source of it was.

Jaime Gonzalez.

The stream of flame issued from his *mouth*, conflagrating the demon's head like the embrace of a small sun. The monster screamed and covered its face with spiked hands.

I could not believe what I just saw.

Even more, Jaime looked like *he* couldn't believe what he'd just done.

And the thing, smelling like burnt toast, backed away. It wasn't growling now. In fact, it looked confused.

As I was. Jaime Gonzalez was a little flamethrower. This bent my mind all over the place. What was I dealing with here? Why hadn't the little guy brought this up to me before?

I'd have to figure that out later. We still had a monster problem that wasn't yet solved.

Then I heard a man's voice say, "What in the Sam Hill?"

I turned and saw a figure appear from behind the mausoleum. He seemed to be an older man and a little stooped over.

"Go back!" I said.

"You can't be here," he said. "This's private property. There's dead people here."

"Don't come any closer."

"Now what is—" He stopped when he saw the creature. It was looking back at him with what I can only describe as deadly curiosity.

"Sandy, is that you?" the man said.

I jumped in front of the man and pushed him, trying to get him out of there.

Instead he started to go down and I rode him to the ground. Him face down, me on top.

I felt the thing stomp on my back.

Then felt the heat of more fire.

A screech, and the pressure lifted.

"Get off me!" the old man said from underneath.

I got off and took a ready position, in case the creature tried to strike again.

It looked ready to do just that—but then shot up into the sky and disappeared.

"What in the name of..." the man said.

I went and helped him up. "I'm sorry, sir, but it was for your own good."

"What in the Sam Hill did I just see? Where is Sandy Koufax?"

Then I heard Jaime weeping in the shadows. I left the old man and went to the boy. Nick was by his side. Jaime had ropes around his body.

CHAPTER SEVENTEEN

I STROKED JAIME'S FACE. "It's all right now."

He sniffed. Nick and I started taking off his restraints. As we did, the old man came to us. In the calm and moonlight I could better make him out. He seemed to be in his seventies, African American, thin but not gaunt. Based on his confusion, I did not suspect him to be a shape-shifter, but I was ready to pounce if he tried anything.

"Now you tell me what went on here," he said. "There was fire!"

I stood and faced him.

"Who are you, sir?" I asked.

"I keep the grounds. I watch the place," he said. "And I just saw a man who looked like Sandy Koufax. As a young man!"

"It wasn't," I said.

"Well, then who was it?"

"It wasn't a *who*."

"I saw that. . . thing ... I better call the police."

"You don't need to do that," I said.

"I think I do."

"I'm a lawyer," I said.

"You say that like it's a good thing. Well, no sir, that ain't no good thing in my book. The less lawyers we got, the better, far as I'm concerned."

Great.

"This is quite serious," I said.

"I'm serious, too. You think lawyers is the only ones can be serious?"

"This child's life is at stake."

He looked at Jaime.

"I represent the boy, and something just tried to kill him."

"Holy mother of…"

"Exactly."

"Then shouldn't we ought to call the police?"

"Not yet. Not now."

"I don't know—"

"Nick, tell this man what's going on."

"We're protecting the boy," Nick said.

"And what I'd like from you is your name and willingness to testify about what you saw here tonight."

"But I still ain't sure what I saw!"

"None of us are," I said. "But maybe together we can find out the truth."

The man thought about it, looked at Jaime once more. "I guess you could find out easy enough who I am anyway."

"True," I said.

"Well then, does the name Leon 'Cool Train' Jones ring a bell?"

"I'm sorry, no."

"You heard of the Los Angeles Dodgers?"

"Of course."

"You remember the World Serious of 1965?"

"You mean World Series?"

"That ain't good enough. I call it the Serious. 1965."

"I'm afraid I wasn't bom yet."

"Yeah, you and a whole lot of other people. You heard of Sandy Koufax and Don Drysdale and Maury Wills?"

"Sure."

"Well, I was on that team, young lady. And we won the World Serious. I stole three bases in one game."

"Mr. Jones, if you'll allow me to take the boy now. I want to come back tomorrow and get a statement from you. I'll need it if we're going to help the boy."

"Does he play baseball?"

"I don't know."

"Because a boy ain't got a boyhood if he don't play baseball, and he looks like he ain't got much of a boyhood going on."

"I'll contact you, Mr. Jones."

"You can call me 'Cool Train.' On account of I was so fast."

"I see—"

"They used to say I could turn off the light and be in bed before the room got dark."

"Yes—"

"So you call me anytime, and I'll help you. Fast. 'Cause that's how I do things."

"We will be in touch, Mr. Jones."

"Cool Train."

CHAPTER EIGHTEEN

NICK SAT with Jaime in the back of the Geraldine. I gave them a few minutes to calm down as I drove away from the church, then said, "Jaime, do you think you can talk?"

"I think," he said in a little boy voice that broke my heart.

"Okay then, how did you get to the graveyard?"

"The one who is not my mother," he said. "She tie me up and put a thing on my mouth."

"I think he means a gag," Nick said.

"She tied you up and brought you there?"

"Uh-huh."

"Did she carry you?"

"Uh-huh."

"Do you know why?"

"Uh-uh."

"Where did she carry you?"

"To a place, where there are graves and those things."

"What things?"

"The things that say the names."

"Like a gravestone?"

"I think."

"All right," I said. "What did she do next?"

"She put me on one and then started to say something."

"Do you remember what it was?"

"Uh-uh. I did not know the words."

"Was it in another language?"

"I think."

"Jaime, what about the fire? Fire came out of your mouth. How did you do that?"

"I don't know! It was the first time."

"First time that you ever did it?"

"Uh-huh."

I glanced at Nick via the rearview mirror. He looked confused and concerned. His barometer was apparently stuck at this turn of events.

Just how does a ten-year-old boy shoot fire out of his mouth and not know anything about it? And what did that make him? Was he nonhuman himself? Or was he a boy with a dragon-like skill? And if he was the latter, how did he acquire that particular capacity?

"Don't take me back to there," Jaime said.

"I won't," I said.

"Please don't take me back."

"No. Never again."

"We better think about where to hide him," Nick said.

"We can't go to my place," I said. "What about yours, Nick? I don't think I've ever seen it."

"It is small, like me."

"Can we all fit?"

"Not that small!"

NICK'S PLACE WAS INDEED A TINY APARTMENT NEAR EXPOSITION Park and the Coliseum. He wasn't much of a housekeeper. The spare furnishings had clothes draped over them. The smell of honey and some kind of roast meat hung in the air.

But he did have a bed. He said he'd take the couch. I helped him change the sheets on the bed and we put Jaime there. He was asleep in seconds.

Poor kid. We now knew he was the focus of some sort of demonic activity, but for what reason we didn't know. And he had a supernatural ability with fire that was a great big kicker to the whole thing.

And yet he was in one sense just a scared little boy.

I decided to wait awhile until I left. I grabbed a book from Nick's shelf—I think the title was *The Untold Story of the Kallikantzari Jockeys*—and sat in a chair by Jaime. Listening to his rhythmic breathing was comforting to me. But it was also like that sense of dread you get before the mythic other shoe drops. I want to find the shoemaker someday and give him a piece of my mind.

CHAPTER NINETEEN

I LEFT Nick's and did some walking up Vermont Street, past the Coliseum, and turned right on Exposition so I had the USC campus on my left. I took another left on Figueroa and thought I'd just take a nice long walk home.

If I played my cards right, as they say, I could head down one of the darker streets and maybe pick up a snack.

This is what it's come to, I thought. People as after-hours repast. Like on a cruise with a twenty-four-hour pizza bar, for those who haven't stuffed their faces enough.

And then I heard Max's voice. "Don't."

I looked around. And there he was, sitting in one of the anemic street trees we have in L.A. His big round face and yellow eyes staring at me.

"Well, well," I said. "Out for a field mouse?"

"I know what you're up to, *Tchotchke*," Max said. He flapped out of the tree and settled himself on a retaining wall separating me from a parking lot. I was aware of the traffic on Figueroa but unconcerned what they'd think of a woman talking to a fowl. Much stranger sights have happened downtown.

"So what?" I said. "I don't care if you know what I'm up to. I just don't want you in my head."

"Oh, Miss Hoity-Toity!" Max said. "She's too big for her panty-hose now."

"I don't wear pantyhose. I strangle owls with 'em."

"Oy, the disposition of an untipped waitress she has."

"You're not onstage anymore, Max."

"At least you got an even disposition—always crabby."

"I'm going home now," I said.

"After you eat?" he said.

"That's none of your affair anymore."

"I got a job to do," he said.

"That's all I am to you? A job?"

"No," Max the Owl said. "You're a major production, you are. Stubborn."

"I don't like anybody telling me what to think."

"When you want my opinion you should give it to me?"

"Exactly."

Max flapped his wings to his side, exasperated. "I don't like to see this, Mallory."

"Take it up with your boss, whoever he is."

"Michael is his name," Max said.

"Oh really? Where does this Michael live?"

"He's the archangel, you silly person. The general."

"I've had enough of the general, the war, the chaos! You people have messed things up around here and you better set it all straight."

"You are part of this!" Max said. "You were set apart!"

"Hey, I don't want to be some Harry Potter. I don't want to be set apart, or the one, or the anointed, okay? You can't get me out of being undead, so what use are you to me?"

A man staggered up to us. He was bundled up in an old, smelly jacket and had about five days' growth of beard. And a bottle in a brown paper bag. He was out of Central Casting for the wino role.

But we are a town of stereotypes.

Max the Owl looked at the man, who had stopped and was looking back and forth between me and the owl.

"Wuzuhhhm," the wino said.

I walked on. I didn't care to have any more conversation with owls or drunks, thank you.

And then I heard Max scream.

I spun around. No wino now but a tiger, and it was on its hind legs. With an owl in its mouth.

THERE ARE THINGS YOU SEE ON A REGULAR BASIS IN LOS Angeles, and things you don't see.

For example, it is quite common to come across odd pets in people's homes. Your iguanas, Komodo dragons, snakes, all manner of dog and cat, of course. Turtles and chickens.

But it is not so common to see tigers on Figueroa Street, especially shape-shifting ones.

So what do you do when an annoying bird is about to be chewed by a tiger you have nothing against? These are questions you aren't really prepared for. Max was a spirit of some kind. Maybe he could just vanish out of his owl suit and find another host.

Or maybe this was going to be his demise. I didn't know the rules.

I also didn't know how to handle a tiger.

Max screamed again.

I took a couple of steps and kicked the tiger in the gut.

I've studied street fighting, but it was for humans, not giant cats.

Still, the kick was sufficient to get the tiger to spit out Max and issue a defiant roar.

With nothing to lose I said, "What is your name!" The tiger rose up even higher on its hind legs.

"I am Baal! You have nothing to do with me."

"What are you doing—"

There was a screech of tires. I looked. A cop car had stopped next to us.

"They have guns," I said to the tiger.

"Meddler!" Baal said.

"It's what I do. Get used to it."

One of the cops was out of the car, his gun drawn. "Don't move!"

I looked at him. "You talking to me or the tiger?" I said.

"Don't move, ma'am, or you might spook him." His gun was trained on the tiger. His partner, a taller, skinnier, younger cop, had the car's shotgun. He came around the vehicle like John Wayne.

Meanwhile, Baal was just watching with what seemed like detached bemusement.

"It's a demon," I said.

Then a wailing voice on the other side of the retaining wall. "Oyyyy ..."

Max. He was still the owl. And hurting.

"Shoot it," I said.

The tiger looked mockingly at the uniforms.

"It's a demon and a tiger!" I said. "And it wants to bite things!"

The tiger roared.

"What do we do?" the first cop said.

"I don't know!" the tall cop said, retreating behind his black and white. "What about animal rights?"

"It's a demon!" I said. "Are you guys nuts?"

"Ma'am, quiet!" the short cop said.

"You think you can't shoot a demon tiger on the street?"

The tiger spoke. "You are all so weak. Lay down your arms and worship the one who is to come."

The two cops looked like they had just been hit with white powder. All blood drained from their faces.

At which point Baal the Tiger leapt over the cops, who both screamed. Baal continued to rise, up into the night sky, until it was out of sight.

I heard groaning from the other side of the wall. "Max?"

"Oy."

It sounded like it was coming from behind an old Ford Taurus in the parking lot. I jumped the wall and found his feathered form lying on its back.

"Max, are you all right?"

"Am I all right, she asks me! Look at me. I got tiger spit all over."

"Are you in pain?"

"What, this? This is nothing. I'll tell you what pain is. When you tell a joke and get the crickets, that's pain."

The tall cop came to the retaining wall. "Ma'am?"

I gently picked Max up and placed him on the hood of the Taurus, then faced the cop.

"Everything's all right," I said.

He still looked dumbfounded. "Can you tell me what that was?"

"A demon named Baal," I said.

"But—"

"Officer, don't even try to understand."

"I need to write a report," he said.

"Tell him," Max said. "Tell him everything."

The cop looked at Max. "Did that owl just talk?"

"I can see this is going to take awhile," I said. "But unfortunately, I'm late for dinner."

"Mallory ..." Max said.

"Good night to one and all," I said and headed into the darker corners of downtown.

CHAPTER TWENTY

THE NEXT DAY I went to the Grand Central Market. The place still does an active business after almost a hundred years.

This was where Jaime's real mother, if she ever was his real mother, had worked. So I asked around and got directed to a man named Wong at one of the produce counters. I'd taken a picture of Jaime with my phone and showed it to him.

"Oh yes. Boy. Good boy." He was a jovial, fast-talking man who continued to move heads of lettuce and tomatoes around like chess pieces.

"I'm looking for Jaime's mother," I said.

"She quit," Mr. Wong said.

"When was this?"

"Oh, two week maybe. She was good."

"How long did she work for you, Mr. Wong?"

"Oh, maybe one year."

"And when was the last time you saw her?"

He stopped to consider. "Last day here. When she walk out."

"She quit and left?"

He shook his head. "I call her. She not come in. She says she quit."

"When was that?"

"Next day."

A Latina with a shopping bag jostled me from behind. Wong saw her as a potential customer and started showing her his tomatoes.

"Was she acting strangely at all?" I asked him.

He waited until the woman walked on. "Who are you?" he said.

"My name is Mallory Caine. I'm a lawyer."

"What kind law?"

"Mostly criminal."

"Lots of criminal here," he said. "Maybe you take care of for me?"

"I'm not a prosecutor, Mr. Wong."

"You defend?"

I nodded.

"You tricky, eh?" he said and laughed, as if he'd made the most original lawyer joke in American history.

"I'm trying to help the boy. We don't know where his mother is. What I want to know is if you saw any strange behavior in her in the last few weeks?"

He thought about it, then shook his head. "I think maybe she was in love."

"Love?"

"You know, with man."

"She was seeing a man?"

He shrugged. "I see her with him one time. That's all."

"Can you describe this man?"

"Oh yes! Very tall."

"That's it?"

"Oh, very tall! Like Shaq."

"Shaq?"

"Lakers!"

"So he was tall like a basketball player?"

Wong nodded.

"He was black?"

"White."

"Anything else about him you can remember?"

He looked up, thoughtful. "Hat. Round hat."

"Round?"

Wong appeared frustrated trying to think up a better description. Then his face brightened. "Larry and Hardy!"

I pondered that a second. "You mean, Laurel and Hardy?"

He smiled widely and nodded.

"This tall man wore a hat like Laurel and Hardy?"

"Yes!"

So I was looking for a seven-foot white man in a derby hat. But who wore a derby anymore? It was out of fashion—

No, it was *in* fashion in certain quarters. And when it came to those trends, I knew exactly who to ask. I made a mental note to talk to Ginny Finn.

I gave Mr. Wong my card. "If you can think of anything else, I would appreciate your giving me a call. My office is almost next door."

He put the card in the pocket of his white smock. "You take some tomatoes now, yes?"

I DROVE OVER TO MED ZEPPELIN, A MEDICINAL GRASS SHOP IN West Hollywood. The front of the place has a giant mural of Salvador Dali such that walking in from the street gives you the impression of entering Dali's mouth.

Inside are tables and a coffee bar, bookshelves, and framed prints of 1950s drive-in movie favorites, like *Attack of the 50 Foot Woman* and *The Blob*. I picked up the unmistakable odor of aromatic cannabis. It was an unofficial "weed week" in L.A. and every way inclined citizens could blaze tree was being exploited.

The social action at Med Zeppelin was in the back, on the patio, where the majority of customers flamed Jane in relative obscurity. There were tables here, too, for those with red-rimmed eyes and iPads for writing screenplays or poems or business plans.

They had a small stage for performances and at the moment

there was a guy on it, clad in jeans and an actual beret, wearing a bright orange soul patch, reading. I listened for a moment and decided he was another of these liberal arts college grads who wanted to play Bukowski for awhile.

Seven or eight others sat enraptured at funky tables. I think I was the only one for whom rapture was not an option. At least not chemically.

Ginny Finn was sitting just offstage, wearing her mix of retro *Jetsons* and Lolita garb. She's an organizer of meet-ups for the L.A. costume culture. Her goal in life is to be a "live-freak dork," as she puts it, and find underground movements before the mainstream does. She got out in front of steampunk by a full year, which is when I first met her. She came to me when I was with the PD's office, on a drug charge. Simple possession. But I got it tossed out on a search point. The officer in question had taken his pat-down a bit too far.

One thing Ginny Finn knew was where the weirdness was and how to connect with it.

"Hey, Cainie!" she said when she saw me. She was one for setting up her own vocabulary and nicknames. Her hair this day was deep purple, and her green bodice covered a healthy bosom. An ivory broach with a likeness of Elroy, the kid from *The Jetsons,* rested on the left side of her cleavage.

"What's up, Ginny?"

She stood and gave me a peck on the cheek. "Awesome Hello Kitty anniversary party is what's up. You want in?"

The would-be beat poet onstage frowned at me as he recited, "Kissing you is like eating the grass off the back of a diseased cat."

Brilliance!

"What do I have to do?" I asked.

"We need a Kuromi," Ginny said.

"A who with a what now?"

"Kuromi, Goth femeny of My Melody."

"Once again, you speak a language with which I am not familiar."

Fake Bukowski raised his voice. "Your skin is the rotten fish I vomited once in high school."

Genius!

"I'll give you language lessons," Ginny said.

"Maybe another time. What I need now is information."

"Bring it, mama."

"Can we get out the earshot of the poet laureate?" I said.

Ginny took my arm and walked me back inside. Thankfully I didn't hear another word from the ersatz hipster.

Just inside the door by the rack holding the latest edition of *L.A. Weekly,* I said, "I need to know if you have any bead on a very tall guy in a derby. I know it's not much but—"

"Stretch!"

"Excuse me?"

"Could be a guy who showed at the cherry blossom viewing at Lake Balboa. He was the tallest. I called him Stretch."

"Do you know who he was?"

"We don't do names, you know."

"I know it's a long shot, but—"

"Long shot! That's it. He was a basketball player. I think somebody said he played for the Clippers."

A professional basketball player who liked steampunk? Could he possibly be the same guy at the market? Highly unlikely, but sometimes that's all you have to go on.

Ginny said, "Listen, Cainie, if you want me to put the word out..."

"No. I'd rather this not get any play on the street."

"Real trouble?"

"It could be. You ever seen anybody breathe fire?"

"I dated a guy once, used to do the act at Farmers Market."

"Not a novelty act. Somebody who can really and truly breathe it out from inside."

"Like a dragon?"

"Exactly."

"No, but I want him! We have a Zombie Apocalypse lunch

coming up at the Getty. You know, that's absolutely the best place to be for the real Zombie Apocalypse."

"Silly girl. No such thing as zombies."

"We can pretend, can't we?"

"Some of us, maybe," I said.

CHAPTER TWENTY-ONE

I WENT BACK to my office and used my iPad to download a team photo of the Los Angeles Clippers.

The Clippers were reputed to be the worst sports franchise in history, owned by a man named Donald Sterling. It's a place for great college basketball players to be drafted into, spend a couple of years getting seasoning, then heading as fast as possible to the free agent market. In a town that seems to be all Lakers, all the time, the Clippers were the steamed beets of local sports—the last thing you'd order on a menu—and only if there wasn't anything else on it.

The team had a roster of twelve, eight of them black and four white.

The white guys were divided up into two power forwards, a center, and a shooting guard.

I copied their pictures and blew them up and made a lineup card of the four white faces and printed it out.

I walked over to the Central Market and showed the lineup to Mr. Wong. He gave it a look and immediately pointed to the center, one the team identified as Rudolf "The Roof" Gamboni.

· · ·

I TOOK A WALK TO STAPLES CENTER, WHERE THE CLIPPERS PLAY when the Lakers aren't in town. It takes up a city block on Figueroa just south of Olympic. They've got statues outside of Magic Johnson and Jerry West and some other legends, including longtime Lakers announcer Chick Hearn.

It's one of those places in Los Angeles that pays tribute to the past while, at the same time, charges average citizens a small ransom to take part in its activities.

Except where the Clippers are concerned. They almost give those tickets away.

A lone security guard sat out front of the main entrance. He was overweight and putting the strain on a canvas chair. He gave the guard stare from behind his shades. Maybe that should be the next statue they put here: the legendary fat security guards of L.A.'s history. I flashed the rotund watchman my bar card and said I was a lawyer here on official business, and I needed to talk to Rudolf Gamboni. The Clips were playing a game that night and were scheduled for a shoot-around right about now.

The guard looked uninterested. He seemed to be lost in a dream of hot dogs and SWAT teams.

"Closed practice," he said.

"Did you miss the part about me being a lawyer?" I said.

He shrugged.

"This is a matter that could be embarrassing to the Clippers," I said and then realized that wasn't much of a threat.

"I can't let anybody in," he said.

"You mean you don't have the authority to let anybody in, right?"

He said nothing.

"But I'm betting that if you went in and reported what I just told you, someone who is in authority might think it a very good idea to handle this matter now, rather than letting it get all messy in a public way."

I couldn't see behind his shades but it seemed he was blinking like Venetian blinds.

He pulled himself up and said, "I'm not supposed to disturb practice."

"What's the Clippers record right now?" I said.

"Ten and sixty-five," he said.

"They *need* to be disturbed. You could be doing them a great favor."

"Wait here."

He disappeared inside and came back five minutes later. "Coach Redmond will talk to you," he said.

I went in and walked past darkened concession stands and through the first aisle I came to. The team was out on the floor in practice garb, casually shooting around on both ends of the court. I made my way down to courtside, where a concerned-looking man in a Clippers sweatshirt said, "You from the District Attorney's office?"

"No, from my own office," I said.

"Good," the man said. "Because the only crime we're guilty of is impersonating a basketball team." He put out his hand. "I'm Tucker Redmond, coach."

"Mallory Cain. I wonder if I might have a word with Mr. Gamboni," I said.

"Well, even though the *Times* and *Sports Illustrated* beg to differ, I take a half interest in the affairs of this squad. You mind telling me what this is about?"

"Not at all. Mr. Gamboni may be a man who knows something about a missing woman. I want to ask him a couple of questions."

Redmond's face blanched. "Please don't tell me this is a rape allegation. I can't take a rape allegation."

"I assure you, sir, it's not anything like that."

He issued a sigh of relief. "Thank the good Lord."

"You sound as though you half expected it."

"Ms. Caine, what I expect, sad to say, is for a shoe to drop, size seventeen. That's what Roof wears."

"You're worried?"

"Of course, I'm worried! Rudy Gamboni has suddenly developed into one of the best three-point shooters in the league! Better than Dirk Nowitzki! And he isn't getting hurt like he used to, sprained ankles and all that. It's almost like a gift from heaven and I don't want anything to rock that boat."

"I promise I'll keep it nice and easy and out of the news."

"Don't say 'news'! Please."

"I will be discreet, Coach."

"Can you keep it under ten minutes?"

"Promise."

"All right then. Maybe the Roof can use a break. He's a machine out there." He turned to the floor and shouted for Gamboni.

The tallest one on the floor finished his shot, a beautiful three-pointer from beyond the arc, and started toward us.

Redmond excused himself as soon as Gamboni got to me. We sat in the courtside seats, Gamboni's long legs stretched out in front of him like phone poles in sneakers.

"You do a story on me, yes?" he said with a goofy smile and a sheen of face sweat. He wore a red-and-white jersey over his stick-like frame. His hair was curly and black and matted down. A nose like a broken ankle hooked over his upper lip.

"No story," I said. "I'm a lawyer."

"I have three lawyers," he said. "And an agent."

"Are you satisfied with your representation?"

He leaned toward me and whispered, "Can you get me out of contract? This place, it is hell."

"I'm not here seeking you as a client, Mr. Gamboni."

"You call me Roof, eh?" His toothy smile devolved into a leering grin. "I am quite the man with the ladies."

"I'm sure you are—"

"I have hot Italian blood."

"Buddy, you don't want to say that to me."

"Eh? And why not?"

"It could cost you an arm and a leg."

He frowned. "I have many millions! The chicks they like to party with me."

"Do they like the way you dress?"

"Eh?"

"With that silly derby hat?"

"That is my fashion!" he said. "I make a statement!"

Good. It was confirmed out of his own mouth that this was the guy I was looking for.

"Mr. Gamboni, I want to talk to you about a particular woman, the one you met at the Central Market a few weeks ago, name of Gonzalez."

He stiffened. "What is your game, lady?"

"This isn't a game, Rudy."

"Roof."

"If you don't mind, I'd rather not sound like a dog when I talk to you. I just want to know where Mrs. Gonzalez is."

He shook his head. "Do not know anybody by that name."

"You were seen at Central Market with her."

"I am never there. It is too crowded."

"If you are never there, how do you know it's too crowded?"

"You think you're smarter than Gamboni?"

"Isn't it obvious?"

"I say no more."

"You want me to get nasty on you, Rudy? You want me to make this hard? You want the papers and bloggers to pick this up? You want other teams looking at you as a free agent to think you're just too much trouble?"

"You can't do that," he said.

"Make trouble? You watch me. It's a specialty of mine."

"You cannot touch Gamboni."

"Quit referring to yourself in the third person."

"How many persons?"

"Forget it. Just tell me what you know and I promise I'll keep things quiet."

"Nothing. I know nothing."

"You need to know this is a big deal," I said. "As far as I'm concerned, Mrs. Gonzalez is missing, and you may be responsible for it."

Gamboni pulled his legs in and stood up. Way up.

"I take my chances," Gamboni said. "I have the powerful friends."

I stood up and faced his chest. "You're going to feel some heat."

"Ah, we lose to the Heat all the time. Gamboni can take it."

"We'll see about that," I said, wondering how many meals he'd make.

He loped back onto the floor. Someone passed him a ball. He took a fall-away shot from fifteen feet and swished it.

CHAPTER TWENTY-TWO

WHEN I GOT BACK to my office, the cops were waiting for me.

Two uniforms and one suit, a woman with a badge. They met me just outside the Smoke 'n Joke but were not in a laughing mood. The woman was a hard-looking one or trying to be. She had short blond hair and an equine face. Her clothes could have used a buck-up. She looked like she was dressing for the librarian-in-sensible-shoes contest.

"Jaime Gonzalez," the suited woman said. "Where is he?"

"And I should know who this is?" I said.

"You are Mallory Caine, are you not?"

"At least until further notice."

"Do you deny knowing Jaime Gonzalez?"

"Now your questions have gotten a little pointed, Detective. I didn't get your name."

"Broderick."

"Detective Broderick, I am not going to answer any more of your questions. Unless you have an arrest warrant in your pocket, I am going up to my office. Have a nice day."

I tried to get by but she stepped in front of me. "We don't have to do it this way. You just give up the boy."

"Give up? I have no idea what you're talking about."

"I think you do."

"Shall we continue dancing then?" I said. "How 'bout those Lakers?"

"You don't want to get on my bad side," Broderick said. "I have a special concern for children."

"But what you don't have is probable cause. You have come here to accuse me of something. I suspect what you have is a statement by someone who says they've lost their child and for some reason has put the finger on me. I have a lot of enemies, Detective Broderick. You can't practice law in this town with any success and not have that happen."

"We can clear this up if you'll just answer some questions."

"I have work to do," I said. "And I don't talk to cops unless I have to. And I don't have to."

"That can change very quickly."

"Then change it," I said.

They did. They slapped cuffs on me and took me away.

"WHY DO YOU WANT TO MAKE SUCH TROUBLE FOR US, HUH?" Broderick said down at central station.

"Trouble is my business when it involves sloppy cops," I said.

"You're not going to get it any easier if you pay us compliments like that."

"You either charge me or let me go."

"We got some time here, while we get the paperwork together."

"You're not going to hold me and you know it."

"What does it look like we're doing now?"

I sighed. "Broderick, that's your name?"

She nodded.

"I hate to be hard on my buddies on the force—"

"You have buddies on the force?"

"People know I'm a straight shooter. So what's the deal here?

You have no idea what's going on with this boy and his so-called mother."

"You want to tell me?"

"You ever heard of a shape-shifter?" I said.

"That's the rap on you," Broderick said. "You're into weird things, like vampires and werewolves."

"I'm not into anything," I said. "It's what shows up. Did you get a report last night about a tiger on Figueroa Boulevard?"

Broderick said nothing.

"A couple of uniforms, sounding very freaked out?"

"Look, Ms. Caine, we have one job, to find Jaime Gonzalez. Are you going to help us out or not?"

"You brought me down here to ask me that?"

"Yes."

"No," I said. "You brought me down to try to intimidate me, because you're taking your orders from the chief, who is taking them from the mayor. How'm I doing?"

"That kind of talk is not going to help you."

"And the sheriff, I include him, too. All law enforcement in this city is funneling into one source, and it's at City Hall. I'm the one who should be asking *you* questions."

"Ms. Caine—"

"I'm leaving now. Don't try this little dance again."

"Or what?"

"There's still a judge or two on the federal bench who can make trouble for you. Don't make me go there."

Broderick only smiled. I hate it when cops only smile. But this one had more than a little dark vibe to it. Maybe I was picking up a little of Nick's barometer-ness. I did not like what I was picking up.

As soon as I got out of there, I decided it wouldn't be safe to keep Jaime at Nick's. Jaime would need some good power on his side.

CHAPTER TWENTY-THREE

A LITTLE CHURCH ON SELMA, in Hollywood, had been the scene of some really bizarre demonic activity. When I was working the Traci Ann Johnson case, the demons attacked me here and even once hung the rector, Father Clemente, upside down.

That really ticked him off. He got out the holy water and the prayers and beat back the demons that way.

I knew this was the place Jaime would be safest. Jaime was not so sure as we pulled up in front.

"It looks scary," he said to me.

"No need to be scared," I said. "Father Clemente is a friend of mine, and he'll take care of you."

"No! Do not leave me."

"Jaime, listen to me. You're ten years old. You're a boy, but you're a big boy. It's time to be brave. It's time for you to know there are some very bad things in the world. I wish it weren't true. I wish all boys and girls could grow up without any of that. But you can't, and you have to be strong. Can you be strong for me?"

He blinked at me a couple of times. "Okay."

"That's the ticket. Let's go inside."

Father Clemente listened as I explained the situation. Despite his austere looks—sort of white haired and wild—he could be warm and even funny. I hoped Jaime would like him.

"I can offer him sanctuary," Father Clemente said. "He will be safe from all demons here. But the police will come to see you, won't they?"

"They have already," I said. "I'll take this to a judge. Just as long as Jaime is safe."

"As long as he is within these walls, no harm will befall him."

He turned to Jaime, who was sitting on a pew looking not at all sure of what was going on.

"Jaime," he said, "what is your favorite food?"

"Pizza," he said.

"Well guess what? That's one of my favorites, too!"

"Really?"

"We get it from Micelli's, just around the corner. Fresh and hot. Would you like some?"

Pizza secured, we sat at a table in the kitchenette of the church. Jaime happily munched and sipped the world's greatest drink, Coca-Cola.

Father Clemente was smiling as he watched the boy eat. Then he turned to me. I, of course, was not eating pizza. That pleasure had fled, unfortunately.

Low, so Jaime couldn't hear me, I said to the priest, "There's something going on here, in Los Angeles."

"There is always something going on in Los Angeles," he said. "I told you about that."

Yes, he had. I remembered his words:

Back before evil existed, before mankind walked the earth. Back when there was God and the angels and one beautiful angel in particular.

His name in Hebrew means the "shining one."

It has cognates in Akkadian, Ugaritic, and Arabic. The Septuagint,

Targum, and the Vulgate translate it as "Morning Star." In Latin, he is "Light Bearer," or more commonly, Lucifer.

Don't you see? He has been plotting his comeback. Launched from earth once again.

And Los Angeles, I greatly fear, is his war headquarters.

Now, sitting with Father Clemente, I could see in his eyes there was more in that head of his.

Jaime had his fill. Father Clemente took us to the library, where old, leather-bound volumes lined the shelves. He sat Jaime down in a big chair and opened a cabinet. He came out with several colorful books. With unmistakable covers.

Dr. Seuss.

He placed them on Jaime's lap and asked if he'd like to read them. Jaime nodded, somewhat tentatively. Then slowly opened the first book.

Father Clemente patted the boy's head. Then he went to the shelf and pulled down a vintage book. He brought it to his desk on the other side of the room and motioned for me to pull up a chair beside him.

He opened to the title page, which read *The Curses of La Ciudad de Nuestra Sehora, La Reina de Los Angeles.* It was dated MCMX.

Father Clemente turned a few of the large, yellowed pages, some of which looked like they might crack under the strain.

"Here it is," he said. "The curse of the Gabrieleno."

"What is that?" I asked.

"Los Angeles was once a broad, arid land occupied by a people called the Gabrieleno. They were an indigenous, peaceful race, a fishing folk. They believed that porpoises guard the world, swimming around in the seas to keep the earth safe from cosmic harm. But with the coming of the missions, these people were subsumed under the largesse of the Catholic Church, for good or ill is not for me to say. I am, after all, a priest. But you will see that the battle was joined."

"Battle?"

"It is said that a chieftain of the Gabrieleno placed a curse on the land then, standing right in the middle of where MacArthur Park is now. In his native language he shouted that if God has come by way of these priests, then there should come another, equally strong force to retake the land. And that there should be no peace until then, and that the church should not be victorious. This chieftain was reportedly hanged from a tree in the park. No one knows who did the hanging. It may have been one of our own."

"A priest?"

"A lapsed priest whose name has been erased from church records. But the point is that there has never been peace in the city since then. Los Angeles was an American garrison during the Mexican War. It became a violent cow town in the 1850s, when northern California lived off southern California beef. And then, in the mid-1870s, with the coming of the Southern Pacific Railroad, immigrants poured in to what would become an agricultural empire. But with that also came cowboys and gamblers and bandits and desperadoes. Border town mayhem ensued. They used to say back then, around 1850 or so, that there was one murder for each day of the year in Los Angeles."

"Surely things got better, though. More order."

"On the surface perhaps. But morally, not so. A prominent clergyman from the East came out to Los Angeles a short time later. A reverend named Woods. He hoped to bring the gospel to the city. He kept a diary. The first two weeks he was here, he noted ten murders. He called the city not one of the angels, as the name indicates, but of the demons. Ordinary citizens walked the streets armed with pistols, Bowie knives, and shotguns. A young cowboy named David Brown was sentenced to hang. Woods offered to see him before the sentence was carried out. Brown refused to see Woods, telling the sheriff he would rather have a bear in his cell than a minister. Shortly thereafter Brown was dragged from the jailhouse and lynched. The head of the lynching party? Stephen Clark Foster, the mayor of Los Angeles."

"Ah, the mayor's office," I said. "Why am I not surprised?"

"In the last entry in his diary, Wood notes that on the Sabbath there was revelry and drunkenness and noise. Horse racing and gambling and dogfighting. Children crying, men cursing. He wrote this is a nominally Christian town, but in reality it is heathen. And then he entered this in his diary." Father Clemente read from the book:

"If it had been God's will, I should have liked to have contended for the truth in this place, this retreat of Satan, but God by his Providence has otherwise decided. My right arm is broken. Whether it will ever be restored to strength, the future will develop.

It seems a plain indication of Providence that I leave this place, and the wicked will rejoice at it I have no doubt."

FATHER CLEMENTE LOOKED UP AT ME. "THEN CAME THE TURN of the century. And Los Angeles became the city of churches and the city of sin, both sides of it growing up together. You had the coming of the movies and everything that became Hollywood Babylon. You had Bible institutes and street preachers mixing with swamis and spiritualists and people who could read your head and tell you your fortune. You had neighborhoods with palm trees outside and brothels with crooked cops outside. It's no coincidence that the first girlie show on Broadway was followed in a few weeks by an outbreak of speaking in tongues at a little church on Azusa Street. Manifestations were breaking out all over that there was something going on between two forces, forces of darkness and forces of light. It was as if there was a turf war among the angels."

"All this going on as the city grew up," I said.

"Precisely. People would light candles in churches or reefers in parks. Con men were on the make and politicians on the take. There was even a pyramid shaped building in Alhambra, where fake seers would take your money and chart out the planets and the future for you."

Father Clemente turned a page in the book, where the chapter ended, and pointed to the last line. "The curse of the Gabrieleno will no doubt continue, until and unless the people of the city themselves rise up as one to resist the dark powers. The final chapter is yet to be written."

The old priest looked at me with some intent.

"Now we come to you," he said.

The good father knows all about my, um, condition.

"I am still . . . you know," I said. "I have not gotten closer to the one who reupped me."

"I have been praying for you to find that person and to be delivered."

"Well, keep it up, Father. I need all the help I can get."

CHAPTER TWENTY-FOUR

The Fourth Amendment rocks.

That's what I said.

The framers of the United States Constitution did not want police kicking in your door at night. They did not want secret squads sneaking into your home while you are away and stealing your letters and diaries and then using those things against you in court, to get you whipped or jailed or hanged.

The framers actually believed in the dignity of the individual against the state. They distrusted the state and those who wield its power.

It doesn't matter if you're rich or destitute, living in a mansion or a garage. The poorest man in his cottage may bid defiance to the king, is the way they put it.

You want to search the place, go get a warrant. Convince a judge by sworn testimony that you have probable cause to believe evidence of a crime exists in the place you want to search.

And if you don't, here's what's going to happen. We are not going to let you use the evidence you gathered. What? You say that's unfair? That you have the guilty party?

Tough. There's no other way to get you to obey the Fourth Amendment.

Deal with it.

But should a criminal go free because the officer blundered?

You got it.

Because if that doesn't happen, it will be easier to flout the rules just because a police officer doesn't like the cut of your jib. If you don't believe me, go back to Alabama in 1932 and live there as a black man for a few years.

That's not our country anymore, pal.

In California, motions to suppress evidence are governed by Penal Code Section 1538.5. The defense, in this case me, has to show that the cops did not have a search warrant. Then the burden shifts to the prosecutor to show there was an allowable exception. The Supreme Court has been stingy with these, but courts all over the land have been trying to broaden the exceptions.

I'm the broad who stands in the way of more broadening.

MY MOTION TO SUPPRESS EVIDENCE WAS HEARD ON A THURSDAY morning. Our judge for this party was Katherine Haynes-Stuckey. She was around fifty years old and wore her blond hair in the style of Nancy Grace, which is to say severe and threatening. She was not considered the brightest bulb on the judicial bench, so it would be my task to educate her on the law of search and seizure.

Aaron seemed in good spirits this morning. This was the second time in a row we faced each other in a murder trial. The other one was the vampire Traci Ann Johnson, which ended a little abruptly. A werewolf planted a stake in her heart as she was testifying, and suffice to say we had to take a break.

Another thing that had to please Aaron was the police presence in the courtroom. Several uniforms were here to watch the proceedings. That's because the victim was a former cop, a guy named Bracamonte. But I knew he'd been a zombie when my father sliced his head off in my presence.

The evidence at issue this morning was the alleged murder weapon, the long sword that my father had been wielding against zombies for some time. Without that, the prosecution would have no case.

"Your honor," I said, "when the police SWAT team broke into the home of the defendant, Harry Clovis, they did not have a warrant. Under the rules of procedure the burden of proof now shifts to the People, who must show by a preponderance of the evidence that an exception to the warrant requirement was in play. In other words, Mr. Argula has to put up or the evidence goes out."

Aaron smiled. "I am prepared to move forward," he said. "But I find that I must make another motion first."

Judge Haynes-Stuckey said, "What would that be, counselor?"

"A motion to exclude Ms. Caine from representing the defendant."

I just about busted out of my blue suit—which would not have been pretty. "That's an outrage, your honor!"

"It's the law," Aaron said. "She has a conflict of interest with her own client. She cannot be both an advocate and a witness."

This was a cheap trick. I tried not to let my anger show. I'd give him an earful later on, then maybe eat his ears after.

"Your honor," I said, "Mr. Argula's concern for my client is touching, but he should also know that my client's right to choose a counsel of his choice supersedes the conflict potential, if my client knowingly accepts the situation and chooses to move forward."

Judge Haynes-Stuckey gave a thoughtful nod, which was the most I could expect. "Then I will address the defendant," she said. "Mr. Clovis, will you please stand?"

"Eh?" my father said.

"Stand up," I said.

He got to his feet, facing the judge uncertainly.

"Mr. Clovis, you know that you are charged with murder, don't you?"

"God hath numbered thy kingdom, and finished it."

"Mr. Clovis—"

"Thou art weighed in the balances, and art found wanting!"

"Ms. Caine, will you please instruct your client?"

"Dad," I whispered, "not now. Just answer her questions."

"What questions?"

Aaron said, "Your honor, this is an obvious attempt to fake incompetence to stand trial."

"You shut up about my father," I said.

"Ms. Caine!" the judge said.

"And I object to the prosecutor's insinuation that we are faking anything."

"That's quite enough," Judge Haynes-Stuckey said. "Ms. Caine, is your father prepared to answer?"

"Please try again, your honor."

"All right. Mr. Clovis, pay attention. Do you understand that you are charged with murder?"

"Thy Kingdom is divided—"

I elbowed my father in the ribs. He went *Oomph,* then said, "Well, yes."

"And that you are entitled to be represented by counsel?"

"I have one," he said.

"But as you know, Ms. Caine is both a witness to the events and is your daughter as well. That presents certain dangers."

He shrugged. "I don't care."

"You have to care," the judge said. "It's my job to make sure you do care and that you do understand the consequences of your decision."

"It's in God's hands now," Harry Clovis said.

"That's not good enough," the judge said.

"Excuse me, your honor," I said.

"What is it?"

"Under the First Amendment, Mr. Clovis has the right to exercise his religion. If he believes that this trial, indeed his very life, is under the hand of God, denying him the counsel of his choice is tantamount to denying him religious freedom."

"Hey," Harry said, "that's pretty good."

I thought so myself. It certainly was giving the judge something more to think about.

Aaron looked gobsmacked. Or admiring.

I'll take admiring.

"Mr. Clovis," Judge Haynes-Stuckey said, "are you willing to be represented by Ms. Caine even though you know there is potential for a conflict of interest here?"

"I'll take her any day of the week," my father said. Which made the whole thing worth it to me right there.

CHAPTER TWENTY-FIVE

WE RAN the hearing on the motion to suppress. Aaron put on his chief witness, Detective Mark Strobert of the Los Angeles Police Department.

It seemed like I couldn't get away from this cop. Maybe it was fate.

"Detective Strobert," Aaron began, "you were the lead detective on the killing of a police officer, one Cruz 'Bud' Bracamonte, last year, is that correct?"

"Correct."

"How was Officer Bracamonte killed?"

"His head was cut off. The coroner concluded that the cut was consistent with a blade of some length, like a sword. It's in the report."

"You were called in at what time?"

"Eleven-seventeen. I made a note of it."

"What was the basis of the call?"

"It was an anonymous tip. Someone reported seeing the attack, got the license number of the truck. The tipster also reported that a bearded man with a sword had a woman with him, and it appeared to the tipster that the woman was under some duress."

"And you were able to place the license plate?"

"We were, because we had had the defendant under surveillance. We suspected him of violent activity and so went immediately to the location where the truck was registered."

"That was the address on Normandie?"

"That's correct."

"What did you do when you got there?"

"I had called in SWAT because I thought we might have a hostage situation."

"Your entry was effected how?"

"Battering ram. SWAT went in first."

"What did you find?"

"I found the defendant and Ms. Caine. We also found what appeared to be a large samurai type sword. This was consistent with the report from the tipster. I subsequently spoke with Ms. Caine."

Aaron turned to give me one of his triumphant trial lawyer looks.

"What did Ms. Caine tell you?"

"She said that the defendant was her father and that she was acting as his attorney."

"What did you do in response to that?"

"I had the defendant taken to Hollywood station for incarceration and treated Ms. Caine like a lawyer."

"And you seized the sword?"

"We did."

Aaron went to his counsel table. The sword was underneath. He brought it out in its terrorizing glory— unsheathed—and brought it to Strobert.

"Is this the sword, Detective?"

Strobert gave it a quick glance. "Yes, it is."

"I would like this marked as 'People's 1,'" Aaron said.

"'People's 1,'" the judge said.

Aaron placed the sword on the clerk's table and looked at me. "Your witness."

"Good morning, Detective Strobert," I said.

With a cool professionalism, Strobert said, "Morning."

"You were in command when the SWAT team broke down the door of Mr. Clovis's humble home, yes?"

"I wouldn't phrase it that way, Ms. Caine."

"You can answer the question, can't you?"

"The team was instructed to enter the dwelling," he said.

"Enter seems a rather benign word, doesn't it?"

"Those were the instructions."

"The door was locked, was it not?"

"Yes."

"And SWAT used a battering ram to break it down, correct?"

"For safety purposes."

"Ah, there's the rub," I said. "You claimed on direct examination that exigent circumstances dictated this incredible overreach."

"It was an emergency situation, and it wasn't an overreach."

"You told Mr. Argula that you believed there was a potential victim inside the house, is that correct?"

"Yes. And a sword was involved."

"The potential victim was me, yes?"

"Yes."

"When in actuality, as you now know, I am the daughter of the defendant."

"I didn't know that at the time."

"You didn't really know anything at the time, Detective, did you?"

"We had probable cause to believe you were in danger."

"Based upon an anonymous tip."

"Yes. We get those all the time."

"So you do not know the identity of this tipster?"

"That's a common occurrence," he said.

"But as an experienced officer, you are no doubt aware that an untested, anonymous tip is not sufficient to establish probable cause."

Strobert paused, then said, "I do what I do to protect the public."

"So your answer is that you don't know the law?"

"I do know the law."

"Are you aware, then, of *People* v. *Reeves*? A decision by the California Supreme Court?"

Aaron stood up. "Your honor, Detective Strobert is not here to argue the law. That's my job. If your honor would like us to do that now, we can excuse Detective Strobert."

The judge looked at me. "Have you any further questions of a foundational nature, Ms. Caine?"

"No," I said. "I think we have all we need to know from the good detective."

Strobert shot me a look. His green eyes were angry but not all that unfriendly. Usually cops hate my guts after I've put them through cross-examination. But, hey, just doing my job here, boys and girls.

Then, when Strobert walked past Aaron, I got this sudden flash of sad irony. I realized I still wanted Aaron, but that Strobert had something that drew me, too. And if I wasn't careful, I was going to be liking two men I ultimately would want to consume.

Now I could address the judge directly. "Your honor, in *People* v. *Reeves,* the California Supreme Court held that an anonymous tip could not establish probable cause for a search, absent sufficient corroboration. Nor can it provide an excuse for exigent circumstances. Otherwise, any vindictive neighbor could call in an anonymous report on the guy across the street, and we'd have police breaking down doors all over town. This was a clear violation of the Constitution, and as such any evidence seized, including the sword, must be suppressed. As a matter of law."

Judge Haynes-Stuckey looked, well, blank. "Mr. Argula, I hope you have some authority on the other side."

"This is absurd," Aaron said.

"Is that *People* v. *Absurd?*" I said.

Aaron ignored me. "Your honor, the community caretaking function of the police cannot be overstated."

Oh, brother.

"And our law enforcement officials, under great stress already, put their lives on the line every day."

Oh, brother again.

"In this case, a credible tip came in that a man with a sword was holding a potential victim hostage, and this after a horrible killing of a former police officer, with something that would have been like a sword. To go for a search warrant with this information would have been a dereliction of duty."

The judge said, "The tip mentioned a sword, and that seems to me to be corroboration, to establish the tip as trustworthy."

"Doesn't he have to at least cite a case?" I asked, letting incredulity drip off my tongue.

"No," the judge said. "The sword comes in. Anything else?"

"Just the execution, I gather," I muttered.

"What did you just say?"

"How just is retribution," I said.

Haynes-Stuckey looked annoyed and I let her stay that way.

CHAPTER TWENTY-SIX

"Trial work is an aphrodisiac," Aaron said. "Don't you agree?"

We were sipping martinis at Musso's, on Hollywood Boulevard. The classic interior was old movie town. You could still hear the ghosts of Cary Grant and Marlene Dietrich here.

Why I allowed myself to be with Aaron was beyond me. Maybe love is like that. But I still didn't want to admit this to myself.

"Where are you tonight?" Aaron said.

"Hm? Right here with you."

"Doesn't seem like it."

"How could I not be?" I said. "Here in this place where so many charming men have sipped martinis? Cheers."

I lifted my glass and we clinked. Our ancient waiter—it is required, I think, that the waiters here look as if they came to America via Ellis Island—asked if we would like to order. Aaron was hungry, but naturally I wasn't, except for the waiter himself. So Aaron ordered a Cobb salad, then looked at me again.

"And so we come down to it," Aaron said. "The DTR."

"Define the relationship?" I said. "Are you still in high school?"

"Now the way I see it—"

"Wait a second. Who said you get to define it?"

"I'm only giving you my offer. You will have to accept it before we have a binding deal."

"Oh brother."

"Or you can negotiate," Aaron said, tossing on that charming smile of his. "But I'm a hard man to deal with."

"Stubborn is more like it, but go ahead. And remember, I have leverage."

"What leverage?"

"You dumped me, remember?"

"You bring that up again? I thought we—"

"Quit saying *we*. It was *you!*' I felt my zombie cheeks flushing. We still have blood pumping.

"But can't we ... *we* ... move away from the past?" Aaron asked.

"No, Aaron."

"Why not?"

"Because I'm giving up sex," I said. "We can have a fine platonic relationship."

"That's not normal at all."

"The times we live in aren't normal."

"What do you mean?"

"Look around you, Aaron! You prosecuted a vampire. Is that normal?"

"Only in certain parts of Hollywood."

"That's not funny."

"I'm still not sure about any of that. Vampires. Werewolves."

"You saw it with your own eyes, didn't you? You saw a man turn into a wolf and run out of the courtroom."

"I thought I did," he said.

"You did! You saw me on the thing's back. You've seen demons, too."

"I don't believe in that stuff."

"And what's been happening in this town?"

"L.A. is great! Have you seen what the mayor's done?"

"The mayor is a corrupt little smiler."

"Which doesn't have anything to do with us. Mallory, I want you to marry me."

I opened my mouth but nothing came out. Had he said those words to me before, when I was truly alive, I would have grabbed them. They were words that would have showed me a future just like I wanted it. We'd start out in an apartment, then maybe buy a house in Pasadena. I love Pasadena. And we'd work and charge ahead, two lawyers making it in Los Angeles, until that time when I'd bring home the pregnancy test and it would be blue. I'd keep practicing up until a few weeks before due date, then the baby would come and be perfect. I wanted it! I wanted Norman Rockwell.

But that wasn't what I got. Instead, I was in a Matt Groening "Life in Hell" cartoon.

I threw my napkin on the table.

"Don't say that again," I said.

"Mallory—"

"We're not getting married. There's too much that's happened, too much that's going to happen."

"What do you mean, *going* to happen?"

I was about to answer but stopped. Because in the back of the restaurant a spectral presence hovered by the door. And I could not help thinking that it looked like Cary Grant in an impeccable white suit. Whatever it was had the Grant hairstyle, too. And he was homing in on me.

"What's wrong?" Aaron asked.

"Him? Nothing."

"Then what are you looking at?"

The ghost arrived at the table and there was no question about it. It was Cary Grant. And Aaron obviously couldn't see him.

"Good evening," Cary Grant's ghost said.

"Good evening?" I said.

"Huh?" said Aaron.

Cary Grant said, "I know someone who can help you." Oh, that voice. Unmistakable.

"Who?" I said.

"What?" said Aaron.

"He'll contact you," Cary Grant said. "And may I say what a lovely outfit you're wearing."

"Thank you."

"Thank who?" Aaron said.

Cary Grant smiled. "He will show up at your office. It's been a pleasure speaking with you."

"Must you go?" I said.

"Go?" said Aaron. "Who are you talking to?"

Cary Grant said, "Gary Cooper and I are meeting some people at the Troc. There's still a lot of us who meet where the Troc used to stand."

And with that he was gone, gliding to, and then through, the back door.

"What's happening here?" Aaron said.

"I'm sorry," I said.

"Tell me, please."

"Aaron, we need to act like professionals here."

"No. Not us. We are in love with each other."

"It's over, Aaron. Once and for all, accept it."

Aaron's face got as cold as the martinis. "You mean that?"

"I just said it, didn't I?" I was trying so hard not to cry. I dug my nails into my palms.

"Then this is it," he said. "From now on, I consider you an enemy."

"What is *that* supposed to mean?"

"I will fight you in court and out."

"You're acting like a high schooler who got turned down for prom."

He slipped out of the booth, reached in his pocket, and pulled out a couple of bills. He tossed them on the table.

"The drinks are on me," he said, then unknowingly followed Cary Grant out.

CHAPTER TWENTY-SEVEN

THE NEXT DAY I went to the church on Selma to check on Jaime. He was in the fenced-in yard, being watched by a nun. The nun was a young one, wearing a full habit.

When Jaime saw me he ran up and hugged my leg.

The nun smiled. "He's been asking about you all morning."

"I want to go with you," he said.

I pried him off and sat him on a bench. "You know I have to go to see a judge about you, right?"

He shook his head.

"It's the law," I said. "We have to do this so it's right and legal."

"Do I have to go back home?"

"I am going to tell the judge not to make you."

"Will he make me?"

"I'm going to argue very hard with him."

"Please don't make me go back."

I put my arm around him and he put his head on my chest. I looked at the nun. She was smiling bravely. Trying to buck me up, I guess. That was nice.

But then I saw something behind her. Perched on the chain-link fence surrounding the churchyard was a black bird with yellow eyes.

"Let's go inside," I said.

This was not much of an existence for a child, but until I could figure out how to best handle the situation, this is where he would stay. At some point I was going to have to face the proverbial music, in a court of law. But that was my meat, and I was going to be ready for it.

I started to get a crazy thought. That maybe Jaime and I could just leave this place. If this was indeed where all the demonic stuff was going to go down, why not just get out and go start a life together? Maybe in the Midwest somewhere. I'd hang a shingle and he'd be my son and ...

Of course that couldn't happen. What would I say to him? *Mommy is a zombie, honey. That's why the neighbors keep disappearing. And please don't unlock the freezer downstairs, you hear?*

No, there wasn't any way I was going to be settling down anywhere with Jaime. It was just my wild dream.

But zombies are allowed to have those sometimes.

CHAPTER TWENTY-EIGHT

WHEN I GOT BACK to my office, the sheriff was waiting for me.

First the cops, now the sheriff. I don't mean a deputy. I mean the head honcho himself. The big dude. The top of the heap.

Sheriff Geronimo Novakovich.

The product of a Native American mother and Russian emigre father, Sheriff Novakovich's rise had been rapid. After establishing himself on patrol, he learned how to play politics. And there is no rougher brand of politics in Los Angeles than in law enforcement, especially the sheriff's office. People elected to be sheriff generally keep that position forever, until death or retirement. It's no small thing to unseat a sheriff who does not wish to be unsat.

But Novakovich did it, and at a fairly young age. He was forty-one and had movie-star good looks. His skin was a soft brown. Not so dark that he looked Latino and not so light that he seemed a suntanned Norwegian. He was just right for appealing to the broadest possible Angeleno constituency.

He was also as ruthless as a New York wiseguy. And now here he was, at my office. Alone.

"Is there some sort of memo to law enforcement to show up at my place of work?" I asked.

"This is an informal visit," Novakovich said. "A friendly chat. Shall we go on up?"

We were still inside the Smoke 'n Joke, with LoGo giving me the landlord stare.

"I have work to do, Sheriff. Maybe you should make an appointment."

He smiled. "I've heard that about you. You have a mouth on you."

"It's right here, just above my chin."

"I specialize in taking people like you down a peg."

"How nice," I said. "Now maybe you can tell me how I got to be gristle in your brisket."

"I'd prefer we take this to your office," he said.

"What's wrong with right here?" I said. "Hey, LoGo, can we talk here?"

"Give me my rent!" she said.

"On second thought, let's go up," I said.

So up we went. I asked the sheriff to have a seat and asked what there was I could do for him. And to please make it fast.

"It's about one of your clients, goes by the name of Amanda, I believe."

I kept my face impassive. We were playing poker. He knew I knew more than I was going to tell him, and he wanted me to know he knew that I knew. Something like that. It's SOP with law enforcement and defense lawyers.

"Of course, I can't reveal anything of a confidential nature, Sheriff."

"I understand that. I went to law school, you know."

"I did not know that."

"Oh yes. But I couldn't pass that doggone bar exam. Well, that wasn't meant to be. Fate had something else for me to do. But I did learn that if you have a client who you know is about to commit a crime, you better doggone well reveal it."

"I feel threatened by your use of the word *doggone.'*"

"This isn't a joke, Ms. Caine."

"What do you call it when the sheriff himself comes to a lowly law office and starts throwing out threats? I don't like bullies."

"Now Ms. Caine," he said, putting his hand over his heart, "what have I ever done to you?"

"It's not me, it's the people of this county. You've let the medical conditions at the jail slide so low the feds are all over you. But you keep putting up excuses. Then when one of your subordinates talked to a federal commission, you ordered your second in command to deny his promotion request, even though he was more than qualified. In other words, you operate like a small-town sheriff, not a big-city one. You're vindictive and petty and hold grudges. Shall I go on?"

"Please do. I'm fascinated with myself."

"You fill your office with people who've been loyal to you on campaigns, and put that ahead of merit. You pad your expense account and take trips on the county dime that a Washington pol would blush at. You've had an affair with a local reporter and you play hardball with your wife in the divorce courts. That about covers it."

Novakovich kept his cool expression on, but I could tell there was heat underneath.

"Do you know what I do with people like you, Ms. Caine?"

"I hope you're about to threaten me so I can sue you."

"Me? Nah. I was about to tell you how much I admire your straight talk. I can be a very good friend."

"My friend list is about full up, Sheriff."

"You're going to need me someday, Ms. Caine. You're going to wish that you had been nicer to me."

"The day I wish that is the day I stop practicing law."

He stood. "That day may come sooner than you think. And get word to Amanda. I want to see her. There's a little matter of some motorcyclists who ran into trouble in Sunland. I'm sure you've seen the reports. You wouldn't know anything about that now, would you, Ms. Caine?"

"Have a nice day, Sheriff."

He nodded, smiled and left me wondering how he'd come by that valuable piece of information. The biker killings were still unsolved. But somehow they'd made an Amanda connection.

Which made them one step closer to me.

CHAPTER TWENTY-NINE

THAT NIGHT I went to Creme, where my friend Sal plays. Salvatore Estanzio had a band I actually helped him trademark. He plays a kind of alt-punk electro-funk that is all the rage in the L.A. rock scene right now. For short he calls it "undeath blues."

Creme has the rep of being alt on the edge of hip, at which point it will begin to die. In L.A., once you get popular, it's over.

Which is why I wanted to stuff a thigh down Sal's throat when he called me up to the stage.

"Hey, I want you guys to give it up for the best dang lawyer in L.A., Mallory Caine!"

The crowd responded with modest applause. Not bad for a criminal defense lawyer.

I stayed seated.

"No, come on up!" Sal said.

Up?

"Mallory used to play a pretty sick guitar before she went all legal on us. And she can sing."

I hadn't done that in years.

Why was he wanting me up there now?

I tried to get out of it but he kept prodding the crowd. I'd have to get him back for this. But truth be told, there was a part of me that missed the music.

I had not picked up a guitar or sung a single note since I was undead. I wondered if I still had any music left in me.

More cheers. Sal could get a crowd behind him, that's for sure.

So I went up. Sal handed me his pride and joy. You know, when I put the strap over me, I felt almost human again.

If I hadn't gone into law, I would have tried to be Joan Jett.

So I led the kids back to the classics, to "I Love Rock 'n Roll" and had my moment. Almost human, almost alive. A zombie getting a club on its feet and rockin'. After the set I went back to my table, getting pats on the back and all that. I tried mightily not to think of the well-wishers as dinner. Talk about a buzz kill. The urge got so intense I rushed out to the back, to the parking lot, stood there among the smokers, trying to compose myself, but knowing I'd eat someone soon.

Smoking. Maybe that's what a good zombie should do to cut down the urge to eat brains. I walked across the parking lot toward Vine, thinking about Jaime, thinking about my father. Thinking about what was going on in my city. The demons gathering and all that.

I didn't want L.A. falling into the wrong hands. But I had enough problems of my own, thank you very much. Sometimes it just gets down to looking out for yourself and the ones you love, like Jaime and Dad.

That's when I realized it. I loved them. In every way a real, live person could. And it scared me.

Then something clamped my shoulder.

It was a hand. It was a big hand. And it spun me around.

It was a guy the size of Disney Hall, with a face like the architecture. Jags and bumps, thick lips and broad nose. Nostrils like manholes.

"If you know what's good for you," he said, "you'll come along nice and quiet."

"Who in the name of Bogart writes your dialogue?" I said.

He blinked a couple of times then held up the one thing guaranteed to terrify any zombie: a bag of rock salt.

I was thinking about making a run for it when I sensed another thug behind me.

"There's another thug behind me, isn't there?" I said.

A voice said, "I don't like that word."

"So you come along nice?" Disney Hall said. "Or do we send you to the morgue?"

"What's this all about, if you don't mind my asking," I said.

Disney Hall said, "Turn around and walk to the black car at the end of the lot."

Seeing as how my eternal damnation was so close, I obeyed.

The car was a typical sedan used by car fleets. Disney Hall opened the backdoor and I slid in. The other thug came in beside me. He was a young hotshot with the two-day-growth-of-beard look that went out with Blockbuster Video.

Beard said, "I have to blindfold you."

"No, you don't," I said.

"Don't give him no trouble," Disney Hall said, getting behind the wheel. "I'm not gonna ask you again."

"You haven't even asked me once," I said. "Sheesh, you guys are dramatic."

I snatched the blindfold from Beard. It was a simple white scarf. I put it on myself and leaned back against the seat. "To the club, Jeeves," I said.

The car started to move.

I GUESS IT WAS ABOUT TWENTY MINUTES LATER WHEN WE CAME to a stop and Beard's hands grabbed my wrists. I didn't fight him as I got out of the car. I'd let them play their blindfold game and then I'd figure out a way to eat them.

Fair exchange.

I heard a heavy door of some sort opening up. The two thugs

led me into wherever we were. I sensed a corridor, judging from the sound of our footsteps against the walls.

"You boys can quit with the dramatics," I said.

No answer.

Another door opened, and another room entered.

And then they stopped me and yanked off the blindfold.

I was in a windowless room, illuminated by dim recessed lighting. It was some sort of commercial storage space. There was metal shelving all around with boxes and medical supplies.

The thugs who brought me here stood off to the side, with their arms folded.

I heard a voice say, "Come eloper."

Come eloper?

When I didn't move, Disney Hall said, "You heard the man. Move!"

"Move where?"

"Cloper!" the voice said. *Closer?* I squinted toward the far end of the space and saw something roundish, perched on a shelf. So I walked toward it, until I was close enough to see it was a human head. Sitting on a pad on a shelf, its neck stump ending in a sort of flared, torn flesh outcropping. Some small device was positioned at an angle in front of the head.

The head blinked at me. It had narrow eyes, a broad nose, and dark, thinning hair.

And a tongue sticking out of its mouth. Then I saw the reason for the speech impediment. It had a stylus attached to its tongue tip. A little sucker cup, like a small plumber's helper, held it in place.

Positioned in front of his head, tilted up slightly, was a Kindle. The head was using the stylus to click on the device.

"Take thith thing oth," the head said and stuck its tongue out toward me.

I wasn't exactly going anywhere so I reached up and I pulled the stylus off its tongue. *Thwop.* I've done stranger things, but I can't remember what they were.

"So you're Mallory Caine," the head said.

"Who are you?"

"Ever hear of Mickey Cohen?"

"Hm, not sure."

"You see that?" the head said to his thugs. "You see what happens when they clean up the town and don't care how they do it?"

To me he said, "My name used to mean something around here. Back in the fifties."

"What am I doing here? What's with all the gangster stuff?"

"That's how we used to do it when this town was really alive."

"That would make you pretty old," I said. "How are you still around?"

"You and I share something in common, Miss Caine."

"You're a zombie," I said.

"I used to have a body," Mickey Cohen said, "until some schmuck with a sword cut my head off."

I said nothing, for obvious reasons.

"If I ever get my hands on him," he said.

"You don't have any hands," I said.

"Which is why I have to get me a body," Mickey said. "And that's where you come in."

"Me?"

"Because you're undead, like me."

"So?"

"You know, it's funny. When I made people dead in the old days, they stayed dead."

The two thugs laughed.

"Hilaiious," I said. "Why do you think I'm going to help you get a body?"

"You're a mouthpiece, right? You'll do it for money."

"I don't need money." That was a lie, but I was pretending to have some scruples here. When you're talking to a mobster head, you have to hold some ground.

"You owe me," Mickey said.

"I owe you?"

"Remember that schmuck I mentioned? The one with the sword?"

Uh-oh.

"Your father, right?" Mickey the Head said.

"I don't know from nothing," I said, trying to sound like a femme fatale.

"You hear that boys? She don't know from nothin'. I like this broad."

The thugs grunted.

"I'm not into body procuring," I said.

"You want your father to walk out of jail a free man?"

"What do you know about that?"

"I can fix it for you," Mickey said.

"You don't mind my saying," I said, "you don't look like you can fix much of anything."

"Now don't make me mad," he said. "I know people. I got connections. Mickey Cohen's still a name to reckon with. I'm going to take over this town again, and you're going to help me do it."

"This isn't 1955," I said. "Nobody takes over a town anymore."

"You kiddin'? You been seeing what's been happening here? Somebody's got the drop on the powers that be. Somebody's buying up politicians and judges and cops, just like the old days. So if that's the way it's gonna be—"

"Do you have any idea who that might be?" I asked. "Do you?"

"It might be somebody out of your league, Mickey."

"You can call me Mr. Cohen."

"It might be somebody big."

"Nobody was as big as me," he said.

"But somebody really did cut you down to size. I mean literally."

"You don't want to get on my bad side, Miss Caine."

"I don't want to get on any side of you at all. You brought me here, fine. You made me a proposition, fine. I walk out of here and no hard feelings."

"I wish I could shake my head," he said. "I need a body."

I said nothing.

"You hear what I'm saying? You can help me get a body."

"And how am I supposed to do that?"

"You'll find a way. A body I can get put on."

"Why don't you just have your boys bring you one?"

"It's gotta be one that gets reupped. They ain't got the power to do that."

"Neither do I."

"But you can find somebody. What do they call 'em? A booker?"

"A *bokor*."

"That's it. We find a *bokor*."

"What? Just Google it? *Bokors* in L.A.? I haven't been able to get to whoever raised me up."

Mickey Cohen said, "So maybe I can do you a service, as an investment. Maybe help you out. We can do an exchange."

"How could you help me out? You're a little immobile."

"I deal in information. For instance, I know about you and your father and the whole zombie deal here in L.A."

"There's a zombie deal?"

"I want to run the whole thing. That's where you come in."

"Me? What have I got to do with it?"

"Word on the street is you rep vampires, hookers, down-and-outers."

"I'm a lawyer. It's what I do."

"Ever rep a zombie?"

"Not to my knowledge."

"What about Carl Gilquist?"

That he knew the name threw me for a very big loop. How did he know about that? Carl had been a zombie friend of mine and Sal's, and my father beheaded him and filled his mouth with rock salt and stitched it shut. Then carved a Z for zombie on his head. Yep, that was Dad before he knew who I was.

"Okay, so you can get information," I said. "I don't want you messing with my father's case. I can get him off fair and square, in court. I've never had to bribe a jury or pull any strong-arm stuff."

"Surely there is something I can do for you, Miss Caine, to show you my good faith. Then you and I can cooperate in my little problem here. I need to find a *bokor*, you must need something from me, right?"

I thought about that a moment. Mickey Cohen, exmobster, current bodiless gangster on the rise. What could he possibly—

"Okay," I said. "I want to know who it was who killed me."

"I'll see what I can do," he said.

CHAPTER THIRTY

THE THUG BROTHERS drove me back to my car at the club, blind-folded again. I was nice to them this time because Mickey Cohen said he could help me out, and what did I have to lose?

Not that I was confident in anything. Mickey didn't realize that he was trying to take over the city at the same time Lucifer was supposedly setting up a war headquarters here. That's not a fight Mickey could win. And it was not a fight I cared about, frankly.

I drove home and went up. I turned on the news and went to my window. The city was alive with lights and car exhaust and pedestrian foot traffic and food smells—from the bacon-wrapped street dogs sold from unlicensed carts with wheels, to keep ahead of the gendarmes, to the grilled cow at Morton's on Figueroa. And it reminded me how much I once loved to eat real food, like sushi in Little Tokyo and liver and onions at Musso's.

Now the only liver I can abide is the same kind Hannibal Lecter favored, only I take mine without the fava beans and Chianti.

Wine! Oh, how I wish I could taste wine again, the nuances of it. But blood is my only grape now, and *full bodied* has an entirely different meaning in my vocabulary.

And then there is the pulse of the city, the way the people just are these days. On edge, looking for salvation in something other than a job, if they have one. For the jobs have all dried up except for, suddenly, local government. The cops are hiring and so is the fire department. The county is hiring, too, especially young DAs.

On the news was a story on our mayor, Ronaldo Garza, talking earlier that day about how great it was to live in Los Angeles, how wonderful to be in California.

Oh yes, I thought, how absolutely marvelous!

Ah, California!

The state that votes itself entitlements but can't fund the ones it has.

Where our tab for unemployment benefits is $10 billion and will be $16 billion in a few years—even though we don't have the money to pay for the current system.

California! Where we borrow $40 million a day from the federal gummint to pay for the claims we have.

Free money! That's how you get clowns elected.

Ah, Los Angeles!

Where the city council votes itself raises and the county board of supervisors passes laws against things like, oh my gosh, plastic bags in grocery stores! That is what we want from our county over-lords! Make it harder for people to pick up poop while walking their dogs! Because that makes the world safe. Just that one thing, banning plastic bags in our little corner of the world, will ensure that the earth survives another million years.

Los Angeles!

Where the mayor can say how wonderful it is, and while people can't buy enough food, he can certainly buy enough votes.

Maybe this town would be better off if Mickey Cohen came back to run things. At least then people had order and a sense of civic pride. Mickey Cohen was a gangster, but he was our gangster.

I listened for a moment to our mayor, whose smile has been compared to the northern lights, talk to the reporter, one-on-one. "We are in for some very exciting times here in Los Angeles," he was saying.

Mayor Ronaldo Garza was an American success story, according to the official bio. His parents were illegals from Mexico who snuck across the border in 1965 in time to have little Ronaldo in an Arizona medical clinic, so the lad might inherit American citizenship.

From there it was a struggle against the odds, with Ronaldo coming to L.A. By himself as a teen and falling into the gang life of East Los Angeles. But he was shot and killed ... At least he was pronounced dead, at the age of seventeen.

I know something about that, but we'll let that pass.

After his "near-death" experience, Ronaldo became a new man —again, according to the official biography. He fought for his high school equivalency then got into UCLA, and from there, the LAPD for five years.

He resigned from the force to go into politics, getting elected as a city councilman from East L.A., which includes Boyle Heights.

He vowed to clean up the gang problem.

And for a time, it seemed like he was making progress. He got funding for a ranch in the Antelope Valley where gangbangers could get diverted from the jail system, for minor infractions. His goal was to get to the bangers early, keep them out of jail and prison culture, turn their lives around through discipline and hard work.

The success of the venture led to his run for mayor, where he defeated his opponent, former District Attorney Rebecca Saltzman.

Garza was now in his second term.

But he was not there without help. During the Traci Ann Johnson case I found out he had been keeping her as a little dish on the side. Traci Ann had finally admitted this to me, and that she had been turned into a vampire by someone working for Garza. Or, I later speculated, someone who *controlled* Garza. Dark powers of some sort set up the whole Traci Ann murder scenario in order to keep Garza in line.

If Father Clemente's theory was correct, about L.A. being some sort of war headquarters for Satan, then it could all fit.

I changed the channel to TCM. A Little Rascals short was on. I fell asleep on the couch, thinking of Jaime and how it was tough enough being a kid these days without ancient gods trying to kill you.

CHAPTER THIRTY-ONE

SOMETHING WOKE me up around three in the morning.

It wasn't a sound that did it. More like a presence. I woke up feeling cold and like I wasn't alone. The TV was still on TCM. Some old black-and-white movie. Looked like early '30s vintage.

Maybe it was the movie that woke me, I thought. I blinked a couple of times. Yep. Definitely early '30s. I had the TV on mute but I didn't recognize the actors.

Then a voice in the room said, "Ah, Richard Dix."

The voice was male, rough, and deep. But not unfriendly. I sat up on the couch but saw no one. Ambient light from the TV cast a ghostly gray luminescence over my apartment.

"Don't try anything," I said.

No answer from the shadows.

"You can't kill me but I can kill you," I said. "Count on it."

Someone laughed. Full throated and warm. And then a form materialized about ten feet away. "You can't kill a ghost."

"Who are you?"

"Cary Grant said you might need my help."

"Cary ... are you a ghost?" I reached over to a lamp and flicked it on.

He looked about forty. He wore a light, slightly rumpled seersucker suit and a medium-brimmed straw hat with a black-and-red band.

"I can go through walls, too. It's pretty neat."

"Okay," I said. "So why my walls? What did Cary Grant tell you?"

"Just that. You have some issues I might be able to help you with. Oh, allow me to introduce myself. Darren McGavin."

"Darren McGavin? That sounds familiar."

"Ah, that's the rub for actors, isn't it? May I sit down?"

"Ghosts sit?"

"Marley did." The ghost of Darren McGavin slipped into one of my chairs and pushed his hat back slightly on his head. "You know, there are five stages of an actor's life. First stage is, who is Darren McGavin? Next is, get me Darren McGavin. Third is, get me a Darren McGavin type. Fourth, get me a young Darren McGavin."

"And the fifth?"

He smiled. "The fifth is, who is Darren McGavin?"

"That's kind of sad."

"I can't complain. I enjoyed my life, my work. I was in *The Man with the Golden Arm,* starring Frank Sinatra."

"I don't think I saw that one."

"Played the father in *A Christmas Story.*"

"That's right! Now I recognize you."

"Thank goodness."

"I love that movie."

"A lot of people do. And then there's this character, the one I'm dressed as now."

"And that is?"

"Carl Kolchak. *The Night Stalker.* You can get all the episodes on Netflix."

"I'm sorry I haven't seen any."

"Ever see *The X-Files?*"

"Of course."

"Well, we were there first. We inspired *The X-Files.*"

"What was your show about?"

"That's why I'm here. Kolchak was a reporter who investigated paranormal activities in Chicago. He went out and found those stories, only to have his editor refuse to run them for lack of proof or some such excuse. Fear sometimes. Nervousness. Well, now it looks like there's real stuff like that happening here in our fair city of Los Angeles. And Cary told me you were charming and needed some of my insight."

"Cary Grant told you I was charming?"

"You can die right now, huh?"

"I'm afraid I've already been there," I said.

"You're dead, too?"

"Zombie."

"Oh, that's too bad. We did a zombie episode once."

"You have any advice on how to get out of it?"

"We never went there. You don't look like a zombie."

"There's a lot of misinformation out there," I said. "But I'm not going to start an organization or anything."

"What about this Rakshasa?"

"This what?"

"I heard you had a run-in with a Rakshasa."

"I'm afraid I don't—"

"At the graveyard, with the boy."

"How do you know about that?"

"We ghosts talk shop all the time, especially about cemeteries and graveyards."

"Tell me then. What word did you use?"

"Rakshasa. We did a show about it on *Kolchak*."

"It's a shape-shifter, right?"

"At times, yes. The Rakshasa also has the ability to go into your mind and withdraw the image of a trusted friend or loved one. And then appear in that form."

"Tell me more."

Mr. McGavin crossed his legs. "In our story, the rise of

Rakshasa activity was associated with the oncoming apocalypse. The end of the world."

"You're kidding me."

"Why would I kid about that? When I was shooting that story it got me to thinking. But I never thought I'd live to see . . . actually, die to see it coming to pass. What's happening to this town?"

"Much," I said.

"There's all sorts of activity at the cemetery. I didn't move in all that long ago, and it was quiet at first. Not now. Hattie McDaniel and Rudy Valentino are looking quite concerned. Something's up."

"What else do I need to know about the Rakshasa?"

"Well, they sometimes do ritual killings in graveyards."

"This is too much."

"What is?"

"What you're telling me. That must be what happened. I have charge of a little boy who kept saying that his mother wasn't his mother. If she was one of these Raka-shocka things, that's why she could take on the look of his mother, and why it had him at the graveyard."

"It's entirely possible."

"But why? Why a little boy?"

"Is there anything strange or unique about this boy?"

"He can breathe fire."

"That would qualify."

"Did you ever do a show about that?"

"Can't say we did."

We sat in silence for a moment. I said, "How do you get rid of them, the Raka ..."

"Rakshasas can be killed only by a crossbow."

"A crossbow?"

"You know, the ancient weapon. But the bolts, what you might call the arrows, have to be blessed by a priest of Brahma."

"Oh, that's convenient. Just run out and find me some of those."

"I didn't write the show, just acted in it."

My head was starting to churn with early morning need for brains. "Mr. McGavin, I wonder if you would be up to helping me out."

"It was always a weakness of mine, helping out attractive young ladies."

"Thanks," I said. "The boy's name is Jaime. And I have a court hearing tomorrow on taking custody of him for protection, and I could use an expert witness."

He scratched his head. I didn't know ghosts did that. "Would they allow me to testily?" he asked.

"You leave that to me, Mr. McGavin."

He smiled. "Done! Kolchak's coming back, in style!"

CHAPTER THIRTY-TWO

THE BATTLE for Jaime Gonzalez began the next day, a dismal one in L.A. Cloud cover on summer heat. The city begins to feel like a steam cleaner. It makes everybody extra grouchy, including judges.

Especially if they're old, like Judge Lincoln Blankenship. He was probably seventy, but looked a decade older. Maybe because he handled family law and custody matters for so many years. That'll take the life out of you.

There is nothing nastier than family law.

Today was a little different. It wasn't a couple of spouses battling in a divorce proceeding. It was weirder than that.

I was trying to take legal custody of a child not my own. I was also representing that child against the claim of a mother. Alleged mother.

Who was represented by Charles Beaumont Manyon.

Yes, that Charles Beaumont Manyon. The most famous lawyer in America. The "fixer" for Hollywood celebrities and well-connected politicos.

Who had once offered me a job. Which I turned down. I love poverty.

But I also know that Manyon didn't get to his lofty position by himself. He's got some tie in with the forces of darkness. He's a vampire. He turned one of my clients into a vampire, and he's used his power to control our city's mayor.

He could not control me, though, and that had to get under his fangs.

None of his powers were going to do him any good in court. He'd have to contend with the law—and me. I was going to make sure he knew he was in a fight.

The first thing Judge Blankenship did when he sat on the bench was rub his eyes. He had wisps of white hair over a mottled pate and looked skeletal under his robe. He might have played Ichabod Crane in the superior court judges' production of "The Legend of Sleepy Hollow."

Nick and I took our places at the counsel table. The judge called the matter and Manyon and I stated our appearances. Then the judge said, "Now let me get this straight. Ms. Caine, you are both a counsel and a party in this?"

"That's correct, your honor," I said.

Manyon said, "And we object to that." Manyon gave the impression of a down-home type lawyer. You know, country boy, bushy mustache, cracker barrel philosopher, aw shucks. But he was deadly underneath that brush. "As a party, Ms. Caine has no standing. She is not parent nor guardian. As counsel, she represents a minor who has been kidnapped from his home. She should be arrested, not given audience in a court of law."

"I have addressed that in my motion," I said. "If your honor please, under California law the best interest of the child is the standard. We intend to prove that Jaime Gonzalez is under imminent threat of physical harm at home and needs protection. We want him declared a ward of the court and placed under our care."

"The child has been taken, illegally, from his mother," Manyon said. "This entire hearing is premature and, indeed, illegitimate. The boy must first be surrendered to his mother and then Ms. Caine may make her wild attempt to establish standing."

"Isn't Mr. Manyon correct?" Judge Blankenship said. "If you

have removed the boy from his mother, you have, so to speak, unclean hands."

"My hands are scrubbed," I said. "And Mr. Manyon is incorrect."

"Do you deny that you have kept the boy from his mother?" the judge asked.

"I deny it entirely," I said. "You see, the boy does not have a mother."

I thought Manyon was going to bust a vest button. "That is an out-and-out lie, and Ms. Caine should be sanctioned for that representation to the court."

"It's no lie, your honor. The woman Mr. Manyon represents is not the boy's mother, and we are prepared to so prove."

I love the feel of stunned silence.

One of those silent was the thing that looked like Mrs. Gonzalez, sitting there in court, pretending to be an aggrieved mother. I hoped Manyon would put her on the stand. I wanted to get a rise out of her in front of the judge.

Finally Judge Blankenship said, "We might as well get this over with. Ms. Caine, call your witness."

CHAPTER THIRTY-THREE

"MY FIRST WITNESS IS LEON JONES," I said.

Leon "Cool Train" Jones came through the gate, looking spruced. He wore a Dodger blue sport coat and gold tie and a big smile.

He was given the oath and sat in the witness chair. "Mr. Jones," I said, "You are currently the caretaker of the grounds at Saint Athanasius Orthodox Church, is that correct?"

"That's right."

"And how long have you been so employed."

"Let's see now, going on ten years."

"What was your employment before that?"

"Ambassador."

"Ambassador?"

"Of the good game of baseball. Before that I played in the Major Leagues, five teams, but my favorite was the Los Angeles Dodgers. After I retired I came back here to settle down and did goodwill work at the stadium. That is, until Mr. O'Malley sold the team. Then it didn't feel so much like home anymore."

"I see. In your work at the church, what are your duties?"

"Keeping up the grounds, you know, the grass and such. I do handiwork, too, all sorts. You see, I was a utility infielder most of my career. Means I could start at any position around the bases. I'm sort of a utility man for the church."

"Do those duties include the care of the graveyard?"

"Especially that. You know, dead folks like their house clean."

Some laughter from the gallery. The judge pounded his gavel.

"Mr. Jones, taking you back to the night in question, did you have occasion at any time to investigate some bizarre—"

"Objection," Manyon said. "Leading and suggestive. And characterization."

"Sustained."

"Mr. Jones, tell us in your own words what happened that night."

"I was in the vestibule of the church, doing a little last cleanup before heading off to bed. I opened the back door of the church to sweep out some dust and that's when I heard something. I thought it was an animal or Lou Brock."

"Excuse me, Mr. Jones?"

"Well, when old Lou Brock used to steal a base, he'd come in right hard and you darn well better be out of the way of his spikes. And he'd growl. I didn't think Lou was out there, so I figured it was an animal of some sort. Maybe a dog."

"What did you do in response to the sound?"

"I took a couple of steps out and kept my broom ready. I was gonna swat whatever it was into right field for a double, if I had to."

"Was it a dog?"

"Didn't see no dog, but I did see some folks out in the middle of the yard, and there was a scuffle going on. Sort of like when Juan Marichal took off after Johnny Roseboro with a bat. You remember?"

"Mr. Jones," Judge Blankenship said, "please confine your answers to the question asked."

"Thought I was," Leon said.

"Proceed, Ms. Caine."

"What did you do in response to the, as you call it, scuffle?"

"I went out to see what was goin' on. That's when you warned me, Ms. Caine."

"Let's hear about that," the judge said. "What did Ms. Caine say to you, sir?"

I hate it when a judge takes over the questioning, but that's their prerogative.

Leon Jones said, "She told me to stay back, and next thing I know, I'm looking at Sandy Koufax."

"I beg your pardon?" the judge said.

"You know, Sandy Koufax, looking in his prime. When I played with him."

"But how could that be?"

I said, "I am laying a foundation for that, your honor."

The judge ignored me and said, "What happened next, Mr. Jones?"

"She got me on the ground. I tell you, Judge, she's got some wrassle in her."

"You ended up on the ground?"

"Sure did."

"Was your face down?"

"Down in the dirt, judge, like a headfirst slide into Brooks Robinson."

"Go on. What happened next?"

"I felt a little oomph on me, then got the pressure released. I guess Ms. Caine got off me after that—"

"Do not guess, sir."

"Well, all right then. She did get off me and I got up with a mouthful of dirt. But I saw Ms. Caine and a boy and a short little guy, reminded me of Eddie Gaedel."

"Who?"

"He was a midget hired by Mr. Bill Veeck of the White Sox, to go up to the plate and get a walk because his strike zone was so small."

"Back to the graveyard, please."

"That's all, your honor. Ms. Caine told me I needed to be a witness."

The judge looked at me. "A witness of what, Ms. Caine?"

Stupid judge. He'd taken the legs out of the testimony. I'd have to prop it back up.

"If I may continue to question my own witness?" I said.

"Don't take that tone with the court," the judge said.

Manyon sat back with a half smile on his face.

I said to Leon, "You saw a figure before I took you down, isn't that true?"

"Yes. Sandy."

"Only it couldn't have been, because he was too young?"

"Well, yes."

"Did this figure change shape as far as you know?"

"Objection, your honor," said Manyon. "Assumes a fact not in evidence. The witness just said he thought it was Sandy Koufax. That's all. We have no evidence of something changing shape, whatever that is supposed to mean."

"Agreed," said the judge. "You will have to rephrase your question, Ms. Caine."

"What did you see after you got up from the ground?" I asked.

"Well now, I thought I saw something fuzzy with long nails. Not that I was shocked. My ex-wife looked the same way—"

"Your honor, if you please," Manyon said.

"Just answer the questions without your color commentary," the judge said.

"I'm tryin' to, Judge, it's just the way I have of speakin'."

Judge Blankenship rubbed his eyes.

"What about the nails?" I asked.

"Long. Really long. I wouldn't want to be scratched by those things ... Sorry, judge, that's the way I feel."

"Go on," Blankenship said to me.

"Anything else?" I asked.

"The eyes," Jones said. "She had terrible eyes."

"Object to the word *she*," Manyon said.

"Sustained."

"What do you mean by terrible?" I said.

"Mean. Deadly. Like Bob Gibson."

"Who?"

"A pitcher you never would want to face, I can tell you. He'd—"

"Mr. Jones," the judge said, "that will do."

"May we approach the bench, your honor?" Manyon said.

Up to the bench we went. Manyon said, "Your honor, the testimony of this witness is irrelevant and immaterial. There has been no proof offered that whatever this man thinks he saw on some given night is the boy's mother. This testimony has nothing to do with custody and everything to do with Ms. Caine trying desperately to cloud the issues."

"I have to agree," the judge said. "Unless you can provide a connection to the boy's mother, Mr. Jones's testimony is not germane to these proceedings. Can you provide such proof?"

Fake it till you make it. "Yes, your honor. If I can call an expert witness."

"Is he here?"

"In a way."

"What's that mean?"

"You can't see him yet. He'll manifest himself."

"Ms. Caine, if you—"

"Let me bring him in."

"Then do it. Mr. Jones will step down, subject to recall. But until you provide a foundation for his testimony, I will not consider it in the slightest."

CHAPTER THIRTY-FOUR

"Cool Train" Jones looked disappointed as he left the stand. I'm sure he had more baseball stories to tell.

Then I said, "I call Darren McGavin."

Eyes turned toward the courtroom gallery. Darren McGavin, dressed as I had first seen him, came forward. Until that point he had been invisible. He'd told me he preferred it that way. No need to cause a fuss, he'd said. Some people still remembered Kolchak.

However, it did look like he popped out of nowhere.

"What... just happened there?" the judge said.

"Mr. McGavin is ready to be sworn," I said.

"I mean, I mean. I don't know what I mean. I thought I saw. Never mind. Swear the witness."

"One moment," Charles Beaumont Manyon said. "I believe I can help your honor with the confusion."

"That'll be the day," I said.

Without any warning, Manyon picked up a copy of the evidence code from his counsel table, walked over to Darren McGavin, and tossed it at him. The book passed completely through the ghost and thudded to the floor. The people in the gallery gasped. One woman screamed. The poor bailiff looked like he didn't know what to do.

"This is a specter," Manyon said. "A ghost. A dead person. Dead people cannot testify in court."

"And where does it say that?" I asked. "There is no provision against dead people testifying. The test is *competence,* and Mr. McGavin is certainly competent to testify. I would remind Mr. Manyon that a witness is *presumed competent* under the evidence code itself"—I dramatically picked up the tome from the floor and held it aloft—"unless there has been some showing of an inability on the part of the witness to perceive, remember, communicate, or appreciate the oath. Mr. McGavin, despite being a ghost, meets all the tests."

Blankenship's lips were moving. Little spitballs were forming at the corners of his mouth. His eyes shifted back and forth as if on involuntary status.

"Somebody get the judge a glass of water," I said.

His clerk, a lovely but confused young woman, attended to the water.

Manyon glowered at me. I don't take to glowering.

We all waited for the judge to gather himself. When he finally looked up, he said, "I'm not going to make my decision yet. I will hear the testimony and then decide."

"But your honor," Manyon said.

"Who is the judge around here? Swear him in and let's get on with it!"

"Mr. McGavin, you were an actor, is that correct?"

"Yes, I was. Loved it. It was fun."

"You performed on stage, screen, and television?"

"That's right."

"You appeared on a series called *Kolchak: the Night Stalker,* is that right?"

The court reporter asked me to spell it, so I did.

"That's right," Darren McGavin's ghost said. "It appeared on the ABC network, for one season in the 1970s. Should have run longer."

"But the series has caught on with new fans, is that right?"

"Wonderful things, the DVDs, the Netflix deal. Wish we'd had 'em back when I was doing the show."

"What was the premise of this series, Mr. McGavin?"

"Well, Carl Kolchak, he was a newspaper crime reporter, you see, and he would investigate these stories and find out there was something strange going on each time. A different sort of supernatural explanation for things. You know, vampires, werewolves, and the like. We got into some of the more obscure monsters, like the Indian bear spirit. And so on."

"And the Rakshasa?"

"Yes, that was one of our more popular episodes. The Hindu demon."

"Now, Mr. McGavin, during the course of these episodes did you do any of your own research into the substance of the show?"

"Yes, I did. I took a great interest in each of them."

"Please tell the court what you discovered about the Rakshasa."

"Certainly." He turned toward the judge, whose ashen face was frozen in a state of imperial unbelief. "Well, your honor, it seems these Rakshasas are very ugly in their native form, with long nails and flesh-eating tendencies. They are the souls of extremely wicked people. Being a Rakshasa requires something more than just normal, everyday evil. You have to be like a Genghis Khan or a Nero."

"Now," I said, "what can a Rakshasa do to confuse us?"

"They can appear to you to be someone you absolutely trust. They can go into your mind and take out a picture of that person and become that person in your eyes. They use this ploy to get you to approach them, you see, until they can reach out and kill you."

"So, hypothetically speaking, if someone had been a professional baseball player, would the Rakshasa be able to appear to him as a former teammate?"

"Quite easily."

Manyon stood up. "Your honor, we've had quite enough of this. There is no relevance here, no foundation for these questions. If Ms. Caine is trying to lay a foundation to assert that Mrs. Gonzalez is a Rakshasa, she cannot do it through this witness."

"I don't think I care anymore," the judge said.

"Excuse me, your honor?"

"Is she here? The mother?"

"Right here, your honor, ready to testify if need be," Manyon said.

"There need be," the judge said. "Oh my, but there need be right now."

"I'm not yet finished with Mr. McGavin," I said.

"The court is finished with him! Where are my pills?" His clerk brought him a little container of pills. The judge popped one in his mouth and drank it down with water from a bottle. Some of the water dribbled down his chin.

"Am I really finished here?" Darren McGavin's ghost whispered to me.

"I think so," I said. "But if I need to get in touch with you?"

"Anytime around midnight at the cemetery. Just walk by and call my name."

He got up and doffed his hat, and then passed through the window of the courtroom and was gone.

CHAPTER THIRTY-FIVE

CHARLES BEAUMONT MANYON said this whole thing could be settled with one witness and called the alleged Mrs. Gonzalez to the stand.

The judge was doing his best to contain himself. His eyes seem to have sunk deeper into his skull.

I sat alone at counsel next to Nick.

Manyon began the questioning by asking her name.

"My name is Ramona Esperanza Gonzalez," the alleged Mrs. Gonzalez said.

"And what is your occupation?"

"I am in the food services."

"Where are you employed?"

"At the Grand Central Market, on Broadway."

"I see. And how long have you been so employed?"

"For the five years. When we came to Los Angeles, my Jaime was only five years old."

"Your son is Jaime Gonzalez?"

"Yes."

"And where is your son now?"

"I do not know!" She pointed at me. "She has taken him."

"Let the record show that the witness has identified counsel, Mallory Caine."

"Objection, your honor," I said. "This witness has no knowledge of the taking or whereabouts of Jaime Gonzalez."

"So freaking what?" the judge said, then buried his head in his hands. He looked up. "Overruled. Continue, Mr. Manyon."

"When did you first encounter Ms. Caine?"

"She come to my apartment. She say Jaime has come to her and is afraid of me. I try to explain that Jaime he has the problems and has seen the doctor. And she bring him back to me, but she is very angry to do it. She is yelling at me and calling me names."

Liar. Rakshasa liar.

"Well, knowing Ms. Caine as I do, I cannot say I am surprised," Manyon said.

I objected, but what I really wanted was to eat Manyon's head. This time out of anger, not hunger. He was a vampire and not very nutritious. But that didn't matter to me now. I kept the feeling to myself, as a good lawyer must learn to do. If I ate every lawyer I got mad at, the DA's office would need to go on a recruiting binge.

The judge told Manyon to keep out the personal stuff and continue.

"Now, Mrs. Gonzalez, there came an occasion when Ms. Caine had another interaction with you?"

"Yes! She follow me on the street. I am walking with Jaime at night. I take him to see a movie. We had a good time. We laugh and ate the popcorn. But then the Caine, she came to us with her little man—"

"You mean her investigator, Nikolas Papadoukis?"

"I do not know his name. But he is little and he is scary."

Nick, sitting next to me at the counsel table, vibrated. I put my hand on his arm, calming him. "Our time will come," I whispered. We had brought a little something with us into court. A surprise for later.

"What happened next?"

"I tell the Caine to go away, that we do not want to see her.

And as I am talking, the little man, he grab Jaime and ran away. And that is the last I have seen of him."

"Did you call the police?"

"*Sí,* I mean, yes."

Oh brother.

"Your son, he means everything in the world to you, doesn't he?"

"Yes. Oh yes."

"And you in no way have given permission, express or implied, to Ms. Caine here to have anything to do with Jaime, in any way whatsoever, correct?"

"Correct, yes."

"That's all."

"Cross-examine," Judge Blankenship said.

"YOU UNDERSTAND THAT YOU ARE UNDER OATH?" I ASKED THE Gonzalez-thing.

"Yes," she said.

"That means you have to tell the truth."

"I always tell the truth. It is what God wants."

"Which god?"

"Why, the only God, of the Bible and the church."

"What about Brahma and Vishnu?" I said.

The Gonzalez-thing's eyes narrowed just a bit. "I no understand."

"Your Hindu gods."

"I am no Hindu."

"You are a Rakshasa, are you not?"

She paused a moment, and a little bit of hatred flashed in her eyes.

Manyon stood. "Your honor, this is outrageous. One has to question the competency of Ms. Caine. She appears to be having a breakdown."

The judge said, "Ms. Caine, what are you talking about here?"

"If you'll just give me a moment," I said.

"No, I will not give you a moment. You give me an offer of proof right now."

"Certainly," I said. "The Rakshasas are Hindu, demonic beings."

"Is that what you are accusing this poor woman of being?"

"I am."

"Then you are incompetent," Judge Blankenship said. "I'm going—"

"Allow me one more question," I said.

"No—"

"You've come this far. One more question, please."

"I object," Manyon said.

The judge threw up his hands. "If that's all it's going to take, then all right. Ask your question, Ms. Caine. But be aware this may be the last one you ever ask in a court of law."

"Then I'll make it a doozy," I said. To the witness: "I will now ask you a hypothetical question, madam. Listen very carefully. Suppose I were to tell you that my associate, Mr. Papadoukis, has in his possession an ancient weapon, a crossbow, and in that crossbow is a bolt, an arrow, that has been blessed by a priest of Brahma. Would that be of any concern to you?"

There was a long moment of hesitation this time. The little demon was thinking. And then called my bluff.

"I do not know what you speak of," she said.

"Then that's that," Judge Blankenship said.

"Now Nick!" I shouted.

Nick sprang into action. It would either be my salvation or my undoing as a lawyer. I'd pulled some fast ones in court, but never anything like this.

The night before Nick, at my instruction, had made up a crude crossbow, out of wood so it would get through security. The bolt was also wood. The weapon was not functional, but it didn't need to be. The Rakshasa—and this was the hard part—would have to believe it.

And when Nick ran to my side and pointed the crossbow at the witness, I had my answer.

THE FIRST TRULY DRAMATIC EVIDENCE DEMONSTRATION PULLED in a court of law in Los Angeles happened back in 1899. The one who did it was maybe the best trial lawyer who ever lived.

It happened this way. A man named Jay Hunter, a handsome aristocratic southerner, came to L.A. to make his fortune, and did. High society, well dressed, carried a cane, all that. Hunter hired another southerner, one William Alford, who had come dirt poor to L.A., and was making a living as a handyman. Alford did plumbing work and sent Hunter a bill for $102.

Hunter refused to pay. Alford sued in municipal court. Hunter didn't show up, and Alford got the judgment. Now he had to collect.

Hunter refused. So Alford made up handbills that said *Jay Hunter Refuses to Pay His Debts*, with details of the court decision, and he was going to post them all over town.

He came one last time to confront Hunter, at the Stimson Building, where Jay Hunter had an office.

No one saw what happened next, though they did hear Alford raising his voice and then a gunshot.

When witnesses came out, they saw Alford standing with a gun over Hunter, who was on the ground with a gunshot to the belly. His cane lay shattered next to him. Hunter was taken to the hospital and later died of peritonitis.

Alford was charged with first-degree murder, and high society wanted him hanged. They even saw to it that a special prosecutor, a former U.S. senator, was appointed to handle the trial.

An unknown young lawyer took on Alford as a client for a fee of $100. His name was Earl Rogers. He was young, handsome, brilliant, theatrical, and ambitious. He had Alford enter a plea of self-defense and assured the press his client would be acquitted.

The trial was the talk of the city. And as it unfolded, things looked bleak for Alford. The prosecution's expert testified that the bullet entered on a downward trajectory, indicating that Alford shot Hunter while facing him.

In cold blood.

When it was Rogers's turn to present evidence, he did something unprecedented. He demanded the intestines of the deceased from the coroner, in a jar. In they came. One woman in the courtroom fainted.

Rogers put a doctor on the stand to testify, and the doctor used a pointer to show that the holes made by the bullet could only have been made if Hunter had been hunched over Alford, hitting him with the cane.

This was consistent with Alford's story. Hunter had knocked him down with his cane, hitting him so hard the cane shattered. Hunter was standing over Alford ready to cane him with the remains of the walking stick. Alford drew his gun and shot upward to defend himself.

Rogers also pulled a famous fast one. It was common for the lawyers to fraternize, and the prosecutor, Senator White, was taking his lunch at a local saloon. Rogers met him there and joined him in a drink. He knew White's reputation as a cross-examiner. Rogers said he would be calling Alford to the stand late in the day and bought White another drink.

But then he rushed back to court and called Alford before the chief prosecutor returned. Alford quickly recounted Hunter's attacking him with his cane, and how he shot in self-defense. The assistant prosecutor asked the judge if cross-examination could be delayed, but the judge said no, get on with it.

There was no one there to get it on. The senator was across the street, in his cups.

Alford was found not guilty.

And the legend of Earl Rogers began.

Because sometimes you have to do something cheeky in court. You may call it courtroom tricks, or antics, and I don't care.

What I care about is the truth, and especially the fate of a kid Rakshasas were trying to kill.

Which is why I had Nick pull out that little wooden crossbow.

OF COURSE, MANYON AND THE JUDGE SHOUTED SOMETHING, and the court watchers gasped the way they sometimes do in old movies about courtroom trials.

But my eyes were on the Gonzalez-thing in the witness box.

Her reaction would be all.

Her reaction would be Jaime's future.

Her reaction would be *my* future.

And it worked to perfection. She turned from a frightened little Mexican woman into what she—it—really was. A furry, fanged, growling, taloned demon.

A demon afraid of being zapped into the abyss right there.

Which left us in a bit of a conundrum. Because now we had this monster unleashed on the courtroom and no real bolts to kill it with.

Sometimes these lawyer maneuvers take on a life of their own.

The Rakshasa started toward Nick, but he bluffed. He held the crossbow up as if to shoot.

The gallery, of course, was a screaming mass of confusion and people scrambling over other people to get out. The bailiff had his gun out but didn't know what to do with it. His eyes were like golf balls and his hands shook.

The demon furball howled and jumped behind the judge's bench.

Poor Judge Blankenship. He grabbed his heart. His face turned gray. His eyes rolled up behind his head and he fell over.

On top of the Rakshasa.

Manyon didn't move. He bared his teeth at me the way vampires do when they want to strut their stuff. I shot him a glare that said, Back off, bitey. I'm not afraid of you.

I heard the judge scream.

It was a pitiful wail of a man about to be consumed. As much as I didn't care for his brand of judicial ineptitude, I couldn't let it end like this for him. I practically jumped over the bench to get to him.

The Rakshasa was about to come down on the incapacitated jurist with a swipe of venomous claws.

I kicked it in the face.

My shoe went into the mouth of the thing, coming out with demonic spit all over it. This was the worst of it. Every time I dealt with one of these things, it was ruining a great pair of shoes. This had to stop.

"Nick!" I wanted the crossbow. That was the only thing that was frightening this thing off. Maybe I could fake it out of the courtroom.

But Nick was not forthcoming.

The Rakshasa took another swipe at me. I ducked the claws.

The bailiff, looking scared and confused—and who could blame him?—came around the bench with his gun drawn.

"Freeze!" he said to the Rakshasa.

It turned on him.

"Back away!" I said, but the bailiff didn't move.

"Dad?" the bailiff said, lowering his gun.

"It's a trick!"

"Dad," he said, voice melting. Tears were starting to form in his eyes.

I jumped the Rakshasa from behind, got it in a headlock.

"Get off him!" the bailiff yelled, and charged forward. And started pulling at my arms.

"Not me!" I said.

"Let go of my father!"

He got my arms loose and I went flying back on top of the judge, who issued what sounded like a life-ending *oomph*.

Then the bailiff screamed. It was the last sound he would make on earth.

Where was Nick?

The Rakshasa ambled away, out toward the courtroom.

I got up and saw Nick and Manyon struggling over the crossbow.

The Rakshasa was moving in on my partner.

The only thing I could grab was the judge's gavel. I gave it a heave and clonked the demon on the head. It was enough to get it to turn around.

Nick had the crossbow in his right hand, was fending off Manyon with his left. Manyon was going to try to bite Nick's neck.

This was new territory. A vampire trying to suck the blood of a Kallikantzaros, while a zombie tried to get rid of a Rakshasa.

Can't we all just get along?

Nick saw me and threw the crossbow in my direction. It hit the front of the judge's bench and clattered to the floor.

The Rakshasa saw it, but before it moved I jumped off the bench and grabbed the makeshift weapon, pointed it at the Rakshasa.

The Rakshasa recoiled.

And then, in a complete surprise to me, the crossbow fired.

Nick had been at it all night, tinkering with the thing, but I had no idea he'd actually made it functional.

But there I was like William Tell, and the bolt zipped right into the midsection of the demonic thing.

With a sickening sound of *goosh* the Rakshasa exploded into a thick, fetid, gloppy cloud of yellowish muck. I got splattered with it.

So did the judge.

He had managed to make it back to the bench, like a climber pulling himself up over the last ledge.

His face was covered with a dripping layer of goo the color of an unripe banana. It was like he'd been hit with a chocolate pie in a silent movie comedy.

With bony, trembling hands he wiped his face so his eyes showed.

"Judgment in favor of Ms. Caine," he said, then fainted.

Manyon said, "No!"

I said, "You lose."

"The game is far from over, Ms. Caine. You will see." And with that he grabbed his briefcase and walked out.

The courtroom was a mess. The bailiff's blood, the Rakshasa's spotty remains. And it smelled like a sewer.

Nick was wiping the goop off his clothes.

"You okay?" I said.

"It's a mess I am!"

"Hey, what was with the crossbow?"

He paused and smiled. "I thought a blessing on it might be good. So I asked Father Clemente. I supposed any priest might be better than nothing. Now, I have lost my only good suit!"

CHAPTER THIRTY-SIX

THE NEXT DAY was a day to celebrate.

We had won. I was now Jaime's guardian. There were forces to be dealt with, for sure. But at least the law was off my back. Manyon was not going to try anything in court now. To have passed off a demon as a mother is something not even a sleazy lawyer can get away with.

Jaime had been cooped up in the church all this time. It wasn't right. It was not good for him.

So we rode the subway from Highland station to MacArthur Park. It was time he saw more of the city, the city I call home. MacArthur Park is named for the World War II general, and is the place where somebody's cake got left out in the rain—a lyric no one in the Western world has ever been able to figure out. It's a square of property off Alvarado Street, bisected by Wilshire in the heart of Los Angeles. Surrounded by neighborhoods stuffed with immigrants from Central America.

We came out of the Metro and into a street scene of Latino music and sidewalk fare, of a bright sun and humming activity.

Jaime held my hand as we crossed Alvarado and entered the park. It had a mix of old people and young, the old sitting on benches, passing the time or letting it pass them.

I saw a flock of white ducks in the lake, paddling around. I bought a churro for Jaime and one for me, and we went down to the lake's edge and tossed a few crumbs to the ducks.

Jaime and I sat on a patch of grass and watched the waterfowl for a while.

Son.

The word popped into my mind and I let myself think it, even though it was wrong. Even though it could never be. For just this moment, I let it go.

"Why am I not like other boys?" Jaime asked.

"What do you mean?"

"Why do people want to hurt me?"

"We don't know that yet," I said.

"Why does fire come out of my mouth?"

"That's what we are trying to find out."

"I am afraid."

"Try not to be. You have friends. You have me, and you have Nick."

"I like Nick."

"Nick likes you, too," I said.

"But I'm still afraid," Jaime said. "Am I a dragon?"

"No, you're no dragon. You are a boy just like any other boy, except that, well, yes, breathing fire is not a normal thing. But you know what? I wasn't normal as a kid, either."

"You weren't?"

"It always seemed like there were people wanting to get me, too. But they never did. You know why?"

Jaime shook his head.

"Because there was somebody watching out for me. Somebody I couldn't see. His name is Max. And he says that there are angels who look out for people, especially children."

"Are there angels?"

"Yes. And they fight. They kick the butts of demons and other angels who are bad."

"Really?"

"They are like the team of Chuck Norrises."

"Who is Chuck Norrises?"

"You mean to tell me you have never heard of Chuck Norris?"

Jaime shook his head again.

"I guess you are rather young at that," I said. "But in the whole history of the world, where there has been butt kicking going on, no one has done it better than Chuck Norris. They used to say he was so fast he could run around the world and hit himself in the back of the head."

"Wow."

"Wow is right. And you know what? I think someday you're going to grow up and be able to do that when it counts. You're going to have people tell you that it's not okay to fight, ever. You should tell those people they aren't Chuck Norris. No, tell them they aren't Jaime Gonzalez!"

He smiled widely and I kissed his head.

"How did it feel to you, when you breathed fire?" I asked.

He rested his head on his knees, his arms around his legs. "I don't remember."

"You were frightened, yes?"

"I guess."

"Or was it more?"

"I don't know," he said. "It just happened."

"Do you think you could do it now? I mean, do you think you can do it anytime you want to?"

He thought about it. "I can try."

I looked around. There were a ton of people walking around. I didn't want Jaime to set anyone on fire. "Maybe we better—"

But he already had his mouth open and was breathing out toward the lake.

Nothing came out, except a few churro crumbs. No flame, not even a spark.

"Maybe it only happens when you're scared," I said.

"But why?" he said. "I don't want to be a dragon."

"You're not a dragon, Jaime. You don't have scales or wings.

You're a good boy who has this ability sometimes. That's a good thing, to have abilities."

"Do you have those?"

"Have what?"

"Abilities."

"Maybe in a courtroom," I said. "I can breathe some fire in a courtroom. Not real fire, just the kind you make with words."

"Cool," he said.

A little white duck was waddling up toward us, no doubt looking for more churro. But we were fresh out.

"Do you know what you'd like to be when you grow up?" I asked.

He thought about it a moment. "A lawyer," he said.

"What?"

"I want to be like you," he said.

Zombie heart, swelling. At that point I don't think I could have loved anyone as much as I loved this kid I'd just met.

The white duck was at Jaime's feet. Head cocked. Cute little thing. Orange bill, webbed feet. Built for water.

But then—

The duck clamped down on the cuff of Jaime's jeans. And started dragging him toward the lake.

Jaime screamed. A little bit of flame shot out of his mouth. He was heading toward the water fast.

This was one strong duck. Backing up with webbed feet, pulling its prey.

I got up as fast as I could.

Jaime was about ten feet from the water's edge. Another fire spurt issued from his mouth. It went out into the air and disappeared in a puff of black smoke.

I got to the lake just as the duck's rear touched water.

I gave the fowl a swift kick. A little explosion of feathers and the duck released its grip and flew about ten feet.

I picked up Jaime and held him.

The duck recovered and flapped wings back at us. Dive-bombed.

I managed to duck the duck and put Jaime on the ground.

The feathered menace came back again, and this time I socked it in the beak. Hurt my hand. But it stunned the duck, which shook its head like a punch-drunk fighter.

It hovered there, a few feet from my head.

Then it spoke. "This is your last warning, zombie. Stay out of it. Give back the witness!"

"What's your name?" I demanded, knowing that if it was a demon it had to answer.

"I am Marduk," it said, "and you know you will be dealt with as I see fit."

Marduk! I'd tangled with him before. He was the chief god of Babylonia, and he was setting up shop here in L.A.

"You're pretty pathetic in that feather suit," I said. "Why don't you come down here and fight like a demon?"

"You are common scum," Marduk the duck said.

"Orange sauce!" I said.

The duck backed up.

"The Name above all Names!" I said, remembering the incantation Father Clemente had once taught me. Demons can't take it.

The duck hissed. Then flapped its wings and flew away, faster than any duck I'd seen before. Like a duck out of hell.

I attended to Jaime.

"What is that happening to me?" he said. "Who wants to hurt me?"

"No one's going to hurt you as long as I've got something to say about it."

I was brushing him off when somebody tapped me on the shoulder. I spun around. A somber-looking woman of about forty glared at me. She had the severely short hair of the severely serious personality.

"How dare you," she said.

"How dare I what?" I said.

"Harm that duck! Don't you know they are protected?"

"Oh," I said. "I'm sorry. I should have let it drag the boy into the lake."

"That's right," she said. "We must let them act according to their own instincts."

"Does that apply to humans, too? Because my instinct is to toss you in the lake so you can talk to the rest of the ducks."

"You're harassing me now."

"I consider that a moral duty, lady."

I grabbed Jaime's hand and got out of MacArthur Park. Was there anyplace in this city we could ever go without some dumb demon-god making trouble?

CHAPTER THIRTY-SEVEN

I GOT Jaime back to the church and Father Clemente. While Jaime was in a bath I sat with the priest in a pew at the front of the church and told him what had happened.

He waited a long time before answering. "Things are moving much faster than I expected. It is very important that you choose."

"Choose what?"

"Sides."

"I told you before, I don't give a rip one way or the other. I'm on Jaime's side."

"But you must, as you say, rip."

I shook my head. "If God and the devil have a beef, let them duke it out on their own."

"That is not how it goes. We are part of the fight, too."

"I thought God was all powerful. Why doesn't he just kill the devil and be done with it? Either he's powerless to stop all this or he's just plain vindictive. Look what he did to me."

"*You* say he did it."

"Didn't he? Isn't that basic theology 101?"

The old priest said, "No, my child, that would make God the author of sin and evil."

"Well, who else is?"

"Lucifer, who used his free will to rebel. That was the start, the spontaneous generation of sin and evil. It all comes down to choice. That is what God has sovereignly granted to mankind."

"It wasn't a very good plan, now was it? Look around you. Vampires and werewolves and zombies and Rakshasas. I mean, this place is a freaking zoo. And innocent people getting chewed up right along with the slimeballs."

"There was an outbreak like this about eighty years ago," Father Clemente said, "in what was then called Persia. The site was a temple dating back to the first Elamite empire. An archaeologist from the University of Manitoba was there alone one twilight and reported seeing a line of webby-winged figures, maybe twenty of them, marching past the temple ruin in what looked like a military formation. They were followed by a company of what the archaeologist described as wolf-like creatures, but walking upright. He followed this brigade to a hillside where a group of British soldiers was holding maneuvers. Over the next twenty minutes he watched as the soldiers were completely overrun, torn to shreds, some killed, some running screaming into the night. This archaeologist was later found in an insane asylum. No one believed his story, except one young doctor who recorded the observations. The archaeologist had only one arm. The other had been chewed off by some set of mighty and deadly teeth. The young doctor's report was suppressed. Very few have ever seen it. I'm one of them."

"But why does God let it happen? Why all the pain and suffering? Couldn't he have done it some other way?"

"Perhaps by making us less than human, unable to freely offer love and kindness. Perhaps if we were created without choice, we could have existed but not truly lived. Perhaps that is the reason we go through this."

"War? Spiritual darkness?"

"There was a time when people conceived of this world as a battleground and believed in sin and the devil, believed in hell, believed the stakes were that high. They believed that God opposed Satan and that this was a real war, a war from the beginning of Lucifer's fall. And they also believed there could be no neutrality in such a war. Trying to sit it out was to be in league with the enemy. It was a cause worth fighting for, they thought once. And if they should die in the effort, well, heaven waited for them, the place of peace where they could finally lay down their arms. But what is it like today? We are still in the war—that has not changed. But people do not see the world as a battleground. They see it as a playground. They think we are here to frolic, not fight. And that only empowers the enemy. This is war. We are in a war zone. The enemy is mobilizing. There is no sitting this out. Not to choose is to choose. Death."

"Death has already been chosen for me, Father, so I don't want to hear about it."

"You must—"

"Stop." I stood. "Just watch the boy. He is what it's all about now."

CHAPTER THIRTY-EIGHT

A LITTLE LATER I LEFT, even though Jaime wanted me to stay. I explained that we needed to make arrangements and this was the safest place for him at the moment.

What arrangements would those be? Was I really going to be his mother? In a loft apartment?

Was I prepared for this?

Was I even the right one? A zombie criminal lawyer?

Maybe I was just being selfish about it. Trying in a pathetic and desperate way to get what I knew I'd missed out on life. But at what cost to a scared little boy who breathed fire?

And as I walked to my car, Father Clemente's words kept clanging in my head. *You must choose. You must choose.*

They reminded me of the words of my own father, who had told me once that I was "the one."

Forget that noise!

I did not sign up for this duty and wasn't going to take it. Not until my own soul situation was secured. If God wanted me on his side, then let him turn me back into a real human being and then we could talk.

What if there really was a God, but he wasn't good?

Did that ever occur to anybody? What if he was a giant version of the nasty kid who pulls the wings off butterflies?

So here we all were, trying to fly around, but without wings. Just a bunch of creatures bumping into each other for the amusement of a sick deity?

But then I thought, where am I getting these ideas of good and evil? If there was evil, didn't there have to be good, too?

I'd had a smattering of philosophy in college, enough to know that you can think your way into believing just about anything.

Maybe that was the deal. We choose our delusions, then justify them.

I couldn't think about that now. I had enough on my plate.

There was my dad, sitting in jail, awaiting trial on the charge of murdering a police officer with a sword. That was going to be hard enough.

There was Jaime, my ward, a kid being tracked by monsters and pagan deities. Was this also part of God's plan? Why did he have to pick on kids?

I got back to the office and rapped on Nick's door. He let me in. His office is a dingy, windowless box without much decoration on the wall. A big poster of Anthony Quinn in *Zorba the Greek* hangs behind an old desk. Nick had sawed off the desk's feet so it would be closer to his size.

"Let's talk about Jaime," I said.

"Exactly what I have been thinking," Nick said, sliding into the little chair behind the desk.

"What have you been thinking?" I asked.

"Ah. The fire. What kind of creature breathes fire?"

"A dragon," I said. "But he's no dragon."

"Agreed. Dragons are not known for shifting their shapes. They are known for their scales and wings. I've met some, back in the old country. I don't like them at all. They're not friendly in the slightest, even when you bring them up in captivity."

"What else?"

"There is the Chimera," Nick said.

"Tell me about that."

"From Greek mythology. Mentioned in Homer's *Iliad*. The body and head of a lion and a snake behind. Fire breathing may be traced to a volcano on the southern coast of Turkey, a place of alleged chimeric activity."

"Hm," I said. "What about Mothra and Godzilla—Japanese monsters. More likely Godzilla emitted radiation. Those were cautionary tales. I don't think any basis in reality."

"Let us hope not," said Nick. Then, quietly, he added, "What if he is some kind of spawn of one of these creatures?"

I didn't answer.

"Well?" he said.

I still said nothing.

"We have to consider it is possible. That this boy is of the devil and he somehow escaped, and they want him back."

An icy arctic blast went through me. "No, there is no way."

"Why not? Did you not see *The Omen*?"

"Will you forget movies and talk about real life?"

His face saddened. "Mallory, this *is* real life. Look about you. Look at what is happening here. Is it too much to assume that the devil himself has placed his own child among us? That our taking him upsets his master plan?"

"I cannot believe that about Jaime. Nor can you. He's a vulnerable, loving boy."

"But that is the deception, don't you see? The Bible does not describe Satan as an ugly, evil-looking thing. It is said he may appear as an angel of light! Is that not how Jaime appears to us?"

I hit one of Nick's chairs with the palm of my hand. It crashed over. "I can't believe that. I won't believe that."

"But the fire. From his mouth. When under stress, it came. Something he could not control. Who is the master of fire but the devil? Jaime is perhaps not even aware of who he is."

"But the Rakshasa who had him in the graveyard, wasn't it trying to kill him?"

"Maybe not. Maybe it was trying to *initiate* him. And if that is so, he is doomed."

"No," I said. "We don't give up."

Nick did not answer. He slid off his chair, his head disappearing behind the desk for a moment. He emerged on the other side and walked slowly to his window. He stepped up on a stepladder so he could see outside. "I hate that I must know these things," he said. "But there is no saving of the devil's spawn. He must be destroyed."

"Now hold on there, shortstack. We are a long way from being certain he is of the devil."

Nick whipped around. His eyes were on fire. "And what if we do? Will you have the guts to do what must be done? Could you kill him if you had to? *Could you?*"

CHAPTER THIRTY-NINE

Darn Nick's stinking Greek logic. Darn his pointy troll hide.

That was the worst possible thing to be thinking. My heart, what there was of it, said it just couldn't be true.

But facts are facts.

There's an old lawyer saying. If the facts are against you, argue the law. If the law is against you, argue the facts. If both are against you, pound the table and cry for justice.

I was pounding on the cosmic table now, in my head, demanding justice from a God I did not see or know.

The whole thing made me viciously hungry and wanting blood. Wanting to take it out on somebody. Not logical in the slightest, but I didn't care.

I dressed as Amanda and went clubbing. It's not something I do often. I prefer the street to the crowd. The darkness of the corner where I can get a pickup without incident—unless it's a cop.

But lately I've found myself feeling sorry for the poor slobs who come by. Family men who have kids that need a father.

So I went to scope out the crowd at Creme. This night, as Amanda, I was into more than just music. Sal's band was off this night, so I could be alone and watch for my dinner. I wanted it to be something dangerous. Maybe there was a little bit of self-hatred going on. I don't know. All I know is that I was totally pissed off at everything and needed to eat a brain fast.

Imagine my perverse delight when an actual celebrity walked into the room.

Jimmy Honeymoon was the start of the hit CBS series *Four Guys and a Babe*. He was also the town's most notorious egomaniac since Charlie Sheen. And he didn't mind holding that crown one bit.

I would have considered him just another annoying boil on the bottom of culture, but he was in everybody's face these last few days.

It seems one of what he calls his "dainty deities" accused him of beating her up. He had his team of high-powered lawyers on the job, planting stories about her rabid drug use.

He was not, to put it mildly, a contender for citizen of the year.

So it surprised me when he came into the club with his entourage and, after a few minutes of chatting up some old friends, approached me.

"Don't be shy," he said. "Ask me out."

I gave him my standard cursory look, as if checking out the bagel window at the deli. "Okay," I said, using my Jersey-Amanda voice. "Get out."

He smiled. He had an awesome set of white teeth, caps, no doubt. He had a full head of blond hair and his eyes were crystal blue. But he had a few wrinkles sneaking away from the comers of his eyes, like field mouse tracks in soft dirt. There was a bit of baggy mess under his eyes, too. His cheeks were the slightest bit gaunt. The effect suggested drug use. He was not shy about advertising his capacity for ingestion.

"Can I buy you a drink?" he said.

"I'd rather have the money."

"Come on! We know we're both here for the same reason."

"Right! Let's pick up some chicks!"

"I like that."

"Like what?"

"A little attitude. I don't like women who just lay down. I get a lot of that."

"What was your name again?"

"You don't know me?"

"Should I?"

"You don't watch TV?"

"Only good shows. Why?"

He nodded like a Dodger bobble-head figure. "I like that. Oh yeah. Come on, we got a bottle of Cris coming. We'll pop and we'll talk."

"No thanks."

"I'm Jimmy Honeymoon. You know, I have that show."

"What show?"

"You know, with the four guys that live in a chick's apartment?"

"Oh, was that based on the Proust novel?"

"The who?"

"Did you go to college?"

"Of course!" he said.

"You must have graduated *summa cum lager*."

"Come to my place. Just the two of us. I got a view that will knock your eyes out. I got an infinity pool and I got more of the good stuff on ice. I got some rock, so we can roll."

"How many times have you used that line?"

"Only a couple. Come on. What hot-looking woman can't go for a little of that?"

"You're looking at her."

One of the bimbettes from his entourage shouted, "Jimmy!" Her voice sounded like an untrained seal's.

"You have plenty of company to choose from," I said.

"I won't be able to think about anybody else tonight, maybe not forever."

"Save the lines," I said. "You say you got rock?"

"You into that?"

"Private party?"

"Just the two of us," he said.

"What about your dumplings?" I asked.

"You mean my deities?"

"Whatever."

"They'll stay here. We got a deal. They know me."

Yeah, and by now they knew me, too. At least, the Amanda me. I'm not sure how coherent they were or how much they'd be able to remember considering my wig and shades. I was due for a change anyway. A new color up top.

Besides, I was hungry.

And I like nice views of the city.

HE DROVE A FERRARI, YELLOW, AND TWISTED ME UP TO THE TOP of Benedict Canyon Road. His place was indeed one of those you dream about if you're into upward climbing in Hollywood.

It was behind a big wall and a gate but in the back it was on a hill overlooking the Beverly Hills and points east.

We were alone in a nice big house with a kitchen that had all sorts of cutlery.

Things were looking up.

He had me sit on a big white sofa, covered with some sort of fur, and flicked on a wall-mounted TV the size of a billboard.

"You have to see one episode," he said. "I can't stand thinking that you'd die never having seen my show."

Die?

The screen came alive with the sight and sound of the vapid sitcom, which may be redundant.

Jimmy laughed as he sat next to me. "This is a really good one," he said. "I was robbed of an Emmy nod."

He opened a box on the coffee table and pulled out a glass pipe, the straight shooter kind, and started preparing a hit of rock cocaine.

"Now watch me," he said.

I didn't know if he was referring to the TV show or the prep.

But when he looked up at himself and laughed again, I knew it was the show.

I tried to watch. It was painful. In this episode, the character played by Jimmy Honeymoon is trying to get the girl he lives with into bed.

"I try to get her into bed," Jimmy said. "I do that on every show."

"Original stuff!" I said.

"Glad you like it," he said. "Lemme fire us up."

I put my hand on his arm. "Would you mind if we didn't just yet?"

"What's up?"

"We need to get to know each other a little." In truth, I didn't care a bit about knowing any more about this guy. What I didn't want was his brain all jacked up on coke.

Those taste terrible and also give me a rash. In my condition that's not a good thing to have.

"I got to have some," he said. "We're gonna be here awhile. And you'll have a chance to make the Hall."

"The what?"

"Hall of Fame. They got the Walk of Fame down there in Hollywood. Up here I have my own Hall of Fame. You want to see?"

"No."

"Lemme show you." He picked up the remote and clicked off his own show—for which I was thankful—then brought up another screen, this one showing the headshot of a beautiful young woman, Caucasian. She did not have a happy expression on her face.

"This was the first inductee," Jimmy Honeymoon said.

"She looks real pleased at the honor."

He clicked and another headshot came up. Another not-so-happy-looking woman, African American.

"She was the first black chick," he said. "The Jackie Robinson of my deities."

"I've seen enough—"

Click. Click Click. He kept running through more faces.

"You can stop now," I said.

Click Click Click

I was ready to end it right here. Get down to the nitty brain-eating gritty, when my breath left with a *whoof*.

"Go back," I said.

"What?"

"Go back to that last one."

"You mean her?"

Back he went, and sure enough it was who I'd thought. The girl. The teenaged Latina I'd taken to the hospital. The one the bikers had captured.

"Under age," I said.

Jimmy looked at me, scowling. "Why do you say that?"

"Where'd she come from, Jimmy?"

"Why are you so interested?"

"You like them young?"

"Why is that your business?"

"Who procured her for you?"

Jimmy threw the remote on the coffee table and got to his feet. "Who are you?"

"Relax, honey. I'm not a cop."

His arm shot out fast as a whippet and grabbed my hair. He came away with a handful of wig.

"Well, well," he said. "This is getting interesting."

Now I got up. "Listen to me, Jimmy. You have one chance here not to get messed up. Tell me who got you the girl."

The Jimmy Honeymoon eyes narrowed into slits. He showed his white teeth but the smile was malevolent, not charming.

"Now I'm going to have to slap you around," he said.

"Do you want to lose your arm?" I said.

That got those slits to blink.

Then he struck. A punch to my cheek with his right fist. I felt no physical pain, but the jolt snapped my head to the side.

Which gave him a chance to jump me.

He was strong in a willowy, work-out-with-a-trainer sort of way. He tried to pin me to the sofa. His hands were on my shoulders. Then he slapped me with his right.

"You want to mess with me now?" he said.

He gave me another slap.

I reached over with my left and grabbed his wrist with an underhand grip. That dislodged his arm and brought it forward to my face.

I took a nice, healthy bite out of his forearm.

Jimmy Honeymoon screamed and jumped back. Blood was spurting all over me and the white fur sofa.

I chewed the bit of arm I had in my mouth. It was a little tough, but not bad. Sort of like octopus sushi.

Meanwhile, Jimmy was cursing and crying and running into the kitchen. I followed.

He got a dishtowel and wrapped it over his arm.

He continued to curse and then took out a large knife from a block. He screamed and lunged at me.

The knife plunged into my stomach.

I hate it when that happens.

When I didn't scream or fall—or bleed—Jimmy did all three for me. He slipped back on the floor, his arm spurting blood under the towel. And he screamed.

The knife was still in me so I took it out and tossed it on the floor. Zombies do not leave human DNA and our fingerprints change daily with the skin transmutations. I was never worried about getting caught in that CSI way.

I stepped over to Jimmy and put my stiletto heel into his chest, pinning him against the sink cabinets.

Once more he screamed.

"You sound like a little girl," I said. "Stop it."

"What do you want?"

"I want the name. The name. Now—or you lose more arm."

"What are you, a freaking zombie or something?"

"Zombie, yes. Freaking, no."

"But you can't be. They don't..."

"They do. And I'm the living proof. Or should I say, the nonliving proof. Whatever. Give me the name."

"There's no way."

I jammed the heel in further. I think I broke skin. His high-pitched squeal signaled pay dirt.

"A name," I said.

He shook his head rapidly. Part of that, I'm sure, was to try to shake off the nightmare he was in. But I wouldn't be shook.

"Now, Jimmy."

"Bite me!"

"Sure—"

"No, wait! I mean, forget about it! You can't make me talk!"

"That sounds like bad *Law & Order* dialogue."

"I was *on Law & Order*. I killed."

"How ironic. And now you're going to *be* killed."

He started to laugh then, crazy and out of it.

"Come on, Jimmy. Give me the name."

More cackling.

I dropped to one knee and pulled his other arm to my mouth. Another chunk of TV star spurted into my mouth.

And Jimmy Honeymoon screamed again.

This was getting bloody—and getting me nowhere. Except to appetizers. I was lusting for his brain. Even with its chemically soaked components. I need it.

But I wanted that name more. Something rancid was going on in the underbelly of Hollywood (what a shock!) and I wanted to put a stop to it.

Why? Why should I be concerned about anybody else but myself in this condition?

Honeymoon was still wailing.

I spit out his flesh. "SHUT UP! Give me a name now or I am going to eat you piece by piece, and let you suffer! And it will be payback for all the garbage you have dumped into living rooms everywhere! I will eat your eyes first and then your fingers one by one and—"

"Sloan!"

"What?"

"Sloan! Oh please, no more ..."

"Who is Sloan?"

"... no ..." Honeymoon's eyes rolled up and he tipped over. Fell to the bloody floor.

Passed out. I couldn't blame him. The prospect of being eaten by a streetwalker was too much, especially with two big bites of arm missing.

I went to the sink and grabbed a dishtowel and got it wet. I wiped the blood off my face, but my clothes were a different story. They'd have to go.

"Jimmy?"

The voice came from the front door. High and squeaky.

One of his dainties, no doubt.

"Where are you, honey? I got to get some, you know what I mean?"

Slurred speech.

"Yo, Jimmy!" A man's voice.

I backed out of the kitchen into the dining area. It was dark at least. But I had to figure out a way to get out of there.

That, or conduct a mass feeding. Which was not a bad idea for me at the time.

So why was I hesitating? What was wrong with me?

I listened to some more calling and more laughing. The voices got closer and then it came, the inevitable scream.

And voices commingling in a cacophony of shrieks.

At some point the guy said he was going to call 911.

I tiptoed through the living room. The lights were still on from when I was watching Honeymoon's stupid TV show. There was a big window from the kitchen looking out into the living room. If these two birds turned and looked, they'd be able to see me.

But if I got to the door, I could probably slip out.

I didn't make it.

The girl screamed and pointed at me. The guy came running into the living room and got between me and the door.

"Don't go anywhere," he said.

"I know this looks bad," I said.

"I'm calling the cops."

"Jimmy was trying to give himself a couple of tattoos, that's all."

The guy whipped out his phone. I walked over to him and he backed up a step. I grabbed the phone from him and said, "We need to talk this over."

"Give that back!"

"Now listen," I said. "I don't want to do anything to hurt you. You seem like a couple of nice kids. Just go away and forget that your friend was almost eaten tonight."

The guys face went through several permutations of confusion and fear. "What are you?"

As he spoke he darted his eyes toward the kitchen. The girl was probably on her phone now.

Except she wasn't. I heard her stepping around behind me. I turned and saw that she was holding a gun on me, steadily, with two hands.

"Don't you move," she said. "I'll fire this, I will. It's Jimmy's and he showed me how."

"Good work, babe," the guy said.

"You could kill somebody with a gun," I said. "Do you want that on your resumé?"

"Did you call the police?" the guy said.

"Not yet," the girl said.

"Keep a gun on her."

"Now I'm going to have to do this the hard way," I said and ran right at the girl. She screamed. Of course, she screamed.

She also fired the gun. It was an automatic so it kept firing. Six shots.

A couple of bullets made holes in me.

When I didn't go down, the girl tried to scream but this time nothing came out. She dropped the gun and tried to run away. I reached out my leg and tripped her. She fell and thunked her head hard on a table. She was going to be out for a while.

I turned around and saw the guy. He was on the floor going through the last twitches of life. Blood oozed out of his heart area.

They say if life gives you lemons, you're supposed to make lemonade. I say you should make a meringue pie out of the lemons and throw it in the "make lemonade" guy's face.

But you should also take every opportunity to feed if you're a zombie. I wasn't going to let this meal go to waste.

I took out Emily and got to work.

It was a pretty messy deal, but I wasn't complaining. When I feed I don't think about anything other than getting the flesh in my mouth. It's like I'm hypnotized or something.

But as I put the final strand of brain into my mouth I looked up and there was Jimmy Honeymoon. Standing, wobbly, dried blood on his arms. His eyes were open with shock.

I had a mouthful of brain matter. I couldn't say anything. But there was nothing to be said, was there? I mean, this was a rather awkward social situation.

So instead of trying to make small talk I growled like a movie monster. It must've been quite a sight, because Jimmy Honeymoon fainted right there in front of me.

This was all I needed.

It took me a few hearty minutes to remove his head and scoop out his brain. Fortunately I found some Ziploc bags and used one to transport my future meal. I washed up as best I could, then took the car keys from the dead friend's pants. I didn't think it would be smart to drive Jimmy's Ferrari out of there.

The keys went to a silver Mercedes. I got in and drove away from what was surely going to become the greatest tabloid headline of the decade.

CHAPTER FORTY

I DITCHED the Benz in a nice, dark neighborhood west of LaBrea. I walked back to Creme with my baggie of brain in my purse and tossed my wig down a drainage opening in a curb.

I had blood on my clothes so I drove Geraldine back to my building and went up to my loft by the service elevator. Changed clothes and put the brain of Jimmy Honeymoon in my freezer.

But my night's work was not done. I was caught up in it, not just the need to eat, but the desire to see all the slime of the earth taken out of it, the ones who did such things.

I set out to see one Scottie Sloan.

He lived behind a large gate that required me to buzz in. His crackling voice came over the speaker. "Who is it?"

"I came with your package," I said.

"What package?"

"Fifteen years old, Latina."

There was a long pause. "I don't know what you're talking about."

"I'm not a cop. I'm alone. It's not like I'm going to have the package with me. You think I'm nuts?"

"You don't sound like the ... like a courier."

"You interested or not?"

"You've got a lot of nerve coming here."

"Take it or leave it."

Another pause. "You think you can blackmail me?"

"Excuse me?"

"You're taping this conversation. You from TMZ or something? You trying to take me down by getting me to admit to criminal activity? On your way, junior."

"I'll tell Big Spin what you said. I'll tell him in hell." The longest pause.

"You don't move," he said. The communication cut. I stood outside the gate and looked up into the L.A. sky. You don't see many stars at night, but Jupiter was hot and glowing like mad. I thought about the Big Bang and God and all the controversy over how things came to be.

But if God was up there and he was responsible for hanging the stars, what was he doing to us?

I wondered if there was a way to get an answer, a real definitive one. You had all these world religions and mystics and teachers and theologians and crazies who said they were connected. You had all these experiences of the divine, and all these people yammering that they knew what was going on up there. So why couldn't I get it from the horse's mouth, so to speak?

Why couldn't I be the one to get it straight? If what Max had told me was true, that I was chosen somehow, for something, then dammit why was I not getting a clue?

As I was pondering the question of the ages, a car screeched up behind me. No headlights. It braked and burned rubber as it stopped. A dark figure was out in a flash. He came up to me and put a gun to my head. "You're trespassing," he said.

"Nice to meet you, Mr. Sloan," I said.

"I'm going to blow your head off."

"Now would you allow that kind of dialogue in one of your movies?"

"You're not listening to me."

"You're not going to blow any heads off. You want what I've

got, so let's talk. Let's take a meeting. Isn't that how you guys
put it?"

"Give me your purse."

"Now you're a purse snatcher? Movie business slow?"

He grabbed my purse off my shoulder. "Inside," he said. He
clicked something in his pocket and the gate swung open.

HE LIKED THE FINER THINGS IN LIFE, THAT'S FOR SURE.
Paintings that were no doubt originals, expensive woods and rugs
and furnishings. It looked like a caliph's palace, is what it looked
like, if the caliph was an American movie mogul out of Brooklyn,
N.Y.

Scottie Sloan had the rock face of the Hollywood player. Not
as young as he used to be—who is? When he was reviving the
career of Stallone, he still had that hungry, devouring look of the
great Hollywood success. Which usually came with trouble behind
the eyes and ulcers. He no doubt had those things, too.

Which is why he was into what he was into, I gathered. Power
is addictive, and you never have enough of it. Accumulation, living
in the danger zone.

Or he could just be one sick puppy.

"Sit," he said, motioning with the gun toward a leather chair
that might have been an antique. Maybe Adolphe Menjou sat here
once.

"You know I would be within my rights to shoot you first and
ask questions later."

"But you won't. You want what I have."

"Maybe you want what I have."

"This stuff? Nah. Say, why don't you make a new Rocky movie?
In this one, Rocky could fight his HMO."

"I'm about out of patience. You said something about a guy
named Spin."

"You know who I mean."

"I don't think I do."

"Look, Sloan, you want the girl or not?"

He looked me up and down. I wanted to take a shower.

"All right," he said. "You're going to talk now. Big Spin is dead. He died in a very bad way. What do you know about it?"

"Little old me? Why would I know anything about that?"

"Because you're here, you know about the deal, you know more than you're telling. And what I'm telling you is I don't care about the package, if you don't give me some answers. I'd rather get rid of you than listen to your lying voice."

"You really do need to hire a good screenwriter."

"Do you see this gun?" His face flushed.

"Your pal Spin and his boys got what they deserved," I said. "That's all I'm going to tell you about it. If you want to think I had something to do with it, go ahead. Me against a bunch of bikers? You really think so?"

"Then how'd you get the package?"

"That's for me to know and for you to dance on the head of a pin."

He shook his head. "What does that even mean?"

"It's called rewriting a cliché. That's how it's done."

His tone changed. It was even somewhat admiring. "Who are you?"

"Just a gal trying to make a buck."

"You're something else. You know what? You are making me very hot."

"Oh please."

"You attached?"

"Sloan, come on, let's get down to business."

"You see what I got here? You want a part of this? Because I think you do, no matter what you say. Everybody wants, as you put it, to make a buck. You can have bucks dropped right in your lap."

"What about your predilection for little girls?"

He smiled and shrugged. "That's just to take the edge off, you know? Some men drink martinis, some do coke. I do other things."

"And you expect me to be turned on by that?"

"Don't knock it till you've been with somebody like me. Now tell me how to get this package. I won't pay more than what I promised Spin."

"Before I do, I want to know where I can pick up more clients. Clients just like you."

"I don't know what you're talking about."

"I think you do. Guys who are into what you're into—you got networks. I'm taking over Big Spin's business, you see, and I want leads."

"You got to be kidding me."

"We talking or not?"

"They'd kill me if I gave out that information."

"You could make the introductions. One at a time."

"Maybe. For a piece of the action."

"You want a cut of what I get?"

"This is Hollywood, baby. That's how we roll."

"I'm telling you, more dialogue like that and I'm out of here."

"You're not going anywhere until I say you can."

I stood up. He trained the gun at my head.

"Ease up there, lightning," I said. "Let's do this deal. But before we do, I just want to know one thing."

"What's that?"

"How long have you been at this, the girl thing?"

"Why's that important?"

"Humor me."

He laughed. "I've lost count."

"What happens to them when you're through with them?"

"Who's going to miss an illegal spice girl?"

I wanted to vomit up my last feeding. "I'll deliver, when you give me the name of another client."

"How do I know you even have what you say you have?"

"You can have her in ten minutes. All tied up in a nice little package."

"Bring her first, then I'll give you a contact."

"And how do I know that?" I said.

"It looks like we're at an impasse," Scottie Sloan said.

"I want to see the list," I said.

He shook his head.

"I want to know you have it," I said.

"You want to know I have it? Really? That's what you want?"

"That's it. Then we do business."

He gave me a curt nod, then backed toward a desk. He kept the gun on me.

He reached around and opened a drawer, then pulled out a little black book. He waved it at me. "Here it is," he said. "Old school. I don't want anything on computer."

"How many names in there?"

"Why don't you have a look for yourself?"

He tossed the book to me. I couldn't believe it. I opened it and flipped through it. It was a common, alphabetical address book. There were names scattered in it. One or two I thought I recognized. From the movie business.

"Satisfied?" he said.

"Sure," I said.

"Well, I'm glad. Because you're never going to use that information."

"I'm not?"

"No. Because you're going to be dead. I'm going to have to kill you now. Your story doesn't hold up. You want some dialogue? I'll give it you. Say your prayers."

I shook my head. "I don't like that one."

"Would you mind stepping to the left then? I don't want to put a bullet in the Picasso."

"Oh," I said. "Sure. You need me to get any closer?"

He didn't flinch when I said that. Trying to play it cool to the end.

The gun went off.

The bullet ripped through my chest and out the back. I turned to look. I thought I saw it embedded in the wood of a credenza.

I turned back to Sloan. "That's not going to look too good."

He fired again, and then again, but only hit me once.

His face kicked into *Blair Witch Project* mode. He would have been great in one of his own horror movies.

"What are you?" he screamed.

I started toward him. He screamed again, turned, and ran.

His foot slipped on a fine Oriental carpet. He went down on one knee. That gave me the moment to jump him from behind.

Down we went.

His doughy body and fear made him easy to control, though his squeals were loud and pathetic in my ear.

Wham!

Sloan hit me on the side of the head with the gun. Just like in the movies. I should have seen that coming. It loosened my grip and he squirmed away.

A voice. In my head. It said *Stop.*

Who was it? Max?

Too late. I had the lust for food in me and started after Sloan again.

Stop.

Sloan ran for the front door. To do what? Go screaming into the night? Yes, no doubt. No matter what he'd have to explain later, he'd at least be alive.

I charged and got to the door just before he did.

He fell to his knees. "Please! No! I'll do anything you say! Don't kill me!"

"Stop it," I said.

"I'll give you a deal! We'll do a movie! About you. Whatever you are, I'll make you famous!"

"It's too late, Scottie."

"Please!"

He started crying.

And I started feeling the one thing I could not afford—sorry. Sorry for this miserable bag of flesh, this blot on humanity. I knew what he was and that he would not change. I knew he was only begging for his life so he could have a chance to get away, to deal with me later. Yes, I knew what he was and that his kind just did not get better, that he would repeat his deeds again and again and again.

I knew all that but felt sorry. A man begging for his life at my feet.

Stop.

But there was another part of me that was out of my control. The eating part. The need part.

Stop.

And in that way, I realized with sickening clarity, I was just like him, wasn't I? I could not change, either. I was who I was.

Stop.

And I realized then where that voice was coming from. This time it wasn't from Max or some outside force trying to control me.

No, it was my own voice.

It was me, telling me to stop.

What I did then was grab the gun from Scottie Sloan.

He screamed, "Please!"

I grabbed the gun from his hand and shot him.

And then did what I do.

When I was finished eating I took Sloan's black book with me.

It was not just a list of addresses.

It was my menu.

CHAPTER FORTY-ONE

I WAS ALMOST home when my phone buzzed.

It was Aaron. I was actually glad. I needed familiarity right now.

"We still talking?" he said.

"That's up to you," I said.

"We're still talking."

"You walked out on me."

"You blame me?"

"Yes."

"Don't beat around the bush," he said.

"Okay. Yes, I blame you."

"Step into your lawyer shoes and see me as a client."

"A client?"

"You would try to see my side of it, wouldn't you? I asked you to marry me and you told me no. How do you expect me to take that?"

"I thought I explained myself," I said.

"Look into your heart right now, Mallory, and tell me that you never want to hear from me again, except when we're trying a case against each other. Go ahead."

"Okay ..." I started some smart remark but couldn't finish it, couldn't get it out.

"I'm waiting," Aaron said.

"I wish I could hate you, Aaron. It would make defending my father so much easier."

"But you can't, and there's your answer. Don't give up on us."

I got another call. This one from Father Clemente.

"Let's talk later, Aaron. I have to take this."

"I'll wait."

"Good. Talk to you Tuesday."

I cut him off and took the call.

The priest's voice said, "It's Jaime. He's crying and won't stop. He says he must see you. I know it's late—"

"Tell him I'll be right over."

WHOEVER DESIGNED THE STREETS OF LOS ANGELES HAD ONLY good intentions. They are fairly symmetrical and easy to follow and get you where you need to go in the shortest possible fashion.

Except when there are cars on them.

Traffic in L.A. is as unpredictable as a riot, several of which we've had in our fair city.

There was the Zoot Suit uprising of 1943. The Watts riots of '65. And the riots following the Rodney King verdict in 1992.

When these things happened, part of the city just shut down and it was almost impossible to get anywhere near the hot spots—or out of them.

Tonight there was a snarl on the 101 going toward Hollywood. It was moving at maybe 5 mph. What was up? I check the Sigalerts on my phone and saw it was this way all the way out to the Valley.

So I got off at Alvarado, in Filipinotown, to take surface streets.

And they were clogged, too.

I flicked on the radio to the local news station.

And got a commercial for tampons. Obviously this wasn't one

of those movies where you turn on the news at just the right spot. It was something on how Serena Williams wasn't going to let Mother Nature's monthly gift get her down.

I screamed at the radio and at the night.

Finally the news kicked in.

"Once again, rioting has erupted in and around MacArthur Park at this hour and citizens are advised to avoid the area. We are trying to get a reporter on the scene but obviously this is a volatile situation and we will get you information as it comes in."

Just great.

I called Father Clemente and kept Geraldine going through the snarl.

"How is he now?" I asked.

"Still upset," Father Clemente said. "He keeps saying he thinks he's going to die."

"Will he talk to me on the phone?"

"I'll see."

There was a pause, then the priest again. "No, he wants you here."

"I'm trying, but I'm stuck here."

"In the violence?"

"You heard about it?"

"It has a strange feeling about it," Father Clemente said. "Like the beginning of something."

"The beginning of what?"

"Of the end," he said.

"I don't want to hear about it!" I hung up on the father and gave a frustrated yell out the window.

One minute later an owl flapped through the window and scared me to undeath.

CHAPTER FORTY-TWO

"SUCH A RACKET YOU'RE MAKING!" Max said, perching on the passenger seat.

"So now you show up!"

"You want I should go?"

"As long as you're here, what's going on?"

"You want my guess?"

"I'd like a little more than that, if you don't mind."

"Take it or leave it, kid."

"I hate talking to owls, I just hate it."

"Listen, *Tchotchke,* you gotta dance with who brung ya."

"You haven't brung me anywhere!"

"I'm hurt. Who was there when you were born? Who's been around when you've needed him? Who? Who?"

"Now you sound like a real owl," I said, then stopped at the hurt look in his eyes. "Okay, Max. Let's start over. Tell me what is going on here. MacArthur Park is where a duck named Marduk tried to drag Jaime away. I thought he was trying to kill him. But maybe I was wrong about that. Point is, the park seems like a place where demonic activity is heavy. Is there some connection here I should know about?"

Max said, "All right, kid. I'll give it to you. Only my opinion, you understand. I don't know everything. But it sounds like the unloosing."

"What's that?"

"Do you not know the Good Book?" he said.

"What, the Bible?"

"No, *Huckleberry Finn*. Of course the Bible!"

"As much as the next person, I suppose."

"The next person knows piffle." He folded his wings.

"I did a little time in Sunday School when I was a kid. I know about the Red Sea and Lazarus rising from the dead, things like that."

"Do you know about the unloosing of Satan?"

"Suppose you tell me."

"It is in the Revelation. Chapter 20. An angel comes down from heaven and he has a key to the bottomless pit. And a chain, too. He gets it around Satan and binds him for a thousand years. But then he's unloosed for a little season."

I thought about that for a second. "Okay, so what are you telling me here? What's all that about a thousand years? Isn't that some prediction about the future?"

"That is the soap some people are selling," Max said. "About some future earthly time, lasting a literal one thousand years, to be established after a Rapture of the church."

"Right. The Rapture. I've heard of that."

"Only that's not what the Revelation is about. Why do you think it is called the Revelation and not the Prophecy?"

"Well then, what's it mean?"

"The Revelation is a book of signs and symbols. Dragons. Swords and fire coming out of mouths. Horses in the sky, yet. That anyone should take any of these things literally is a stretch, I'm telling you. And for that reason they miss it."

"Miss what?"

"The message! For the ancient Jews all numbers had symbolic force. The numbers three, seven, and twelve especially. The number one thousand was a number for a long period of time, of indeterminate length. There is not going to be any literal seven-year Tribulation on earth, yet to come. There is not going to be any literal one-thousand-year earthly kingdom established by God. No, no. We are in the thousand years right now! This is the great tribulation, the battle of good and evil, God and Satan, and we are right in the middle of it."

I said nothing.

He said, "So people must choose. To follow good or evil."

"So what's all this thing about Satan and a little seasoning?"

"Season! Satan must be unloosed for a little season. This is a shorter period of time, right before the end."

"The end? Of what?"

"Everything. This. The wrap-up. The last act. The Apocalypse. The Judgment. The fire that will consume everything. Eternal destinies—"

"I get it. It's big."

"The biggest."

"So a little season is a period of time. But what's it mean to have Satan unloosed?"

"He is given full reign over earth once again."

I shook my head. "Well then, what's God doing?"

"He's watching. To see how mankind will choose."

"That's it? He's just watching?"

"He's done that before. Do you know what the oldest book in the Bible is?"

"Um, Genesis?"

"No. It is the Book of Job. It is the oldest, and oy, that poor man."

"I know, the guy lost everything, right?"

"Taken away by Satan who was given permission by God! It was like a bet. Satan bet that he could get Job to curse God. God allowed the test. The Book of Job teaches us many things. It teaches us that Satan is not ruling from hell, as Milton had it in *Paradise Lost*. He is on the earth, but he can storm God's very throne room if he wants. And God gives him permission to roam the earth."

"But why did God do that?"

"To give Job a choice. Now he is doing it again, only on a world scale. He has given Satan permission, for a little season. He is unloosed, and all mankind must choose. You must choose."

"Choose how? Or what?"

"You will know when the moment comes."

"Come on!" I said. "No more of these mysteries."

Max flapped his wings and shot past my face and out the window.

"Max!"

The owl turned back toward me, hovering. "I don't make the rules," he said, "but if there ever was anybody I'd love to break 'em with, it'd be you."

And with that he flew off into the night.

IT WAS WELL PAST MIDNIGHT WHEN I FINALLY GOT TO THE church.

Jaime attached himself to me. His face and eyes were red.

"Okay, now," I said. "I'm here. You don't have to cry."

"I am going to die," he said.

"What gave you that idea?"

He spoke into my stomach. "I see it. I see it in my dreams."

"That's just a nightmare. It's not real."

He pulled his head away from my body and looked at me. His poor little eyes were frightened beyond anything I've ever seen in them before. "I see it when I am not asleep, too. I see it in the day. I see my body on the street."

"Is it always the same?"

He nodded.

Father Clemente was listening closely, his forehead a row of furrows.

"Jaime," I said, "you're not going to die for a long time. You have to grow up first. You have many things to do and I'm going to make sure you do them."

I had no idea what that was supposed to mean, but it felt like words I was supposed to say. Now I would have to make them stick. I wouldn't let him die, not as long as I was alive.

Or dead.

Or whatever it was I was.

I stayed until Jaime fell asleep. And I didn't leave him until I was sure he wasn't dreaming.

PART THREE

ROLL OUT THOSE LAZY, HAZY, CRAZY BRAINS OF
SUMMER

CHAPTER FORTY-THREE

ONCE AGAIN THERE was a lull in the demonic activity in the city.

It was almost as if the MacArthur Park riot, as it was now known, had been the pressure release.

For all anyone knew, it had been a spontaneous eruption of violence.

I had my doubts.

Because there was the convenient heroism of our mayor. Right before election season was going to heat up.

I found it more than a little odd that only one videographer, who seemed to know exactly where to go to capture the most dramatic moments of the rioting, got the only footage shown on the nightly news.

The nightly news gave it the following treatment.

We see Mayor Ronaldo Garza, his shirtsleeves rolled up like the man of the people he never was, entering the park from the west gate at Park View Street.

He continues to the bottom of the grassy hill, takes in the sight of the rioters. He's got some people with him, of course, one of whom has a bullhorn. Good planning, that.

Garza then goes back up the hill on the south side of the park.

He takes the bullhorn. And then begins what can only be described as a sermon on a mount.

"My good friends," he said, "this is not the way! The city of Los Angeles is better than this! Listen to me!"

The crowd begins to drop their bats and beer bottles.

You remember those deals where people in Grand Central station, at the right time, just freeze? To see what the reaction will be?

It seemed just that way here, only the people stopped rioting to listen to the mayor of Los Angeles.

That's what really raised my suspicions. When was the last time anyone dropped a good riot to listen to a politician? I got the feeling the whole thing was staged to make Garza look like a hero.

There were powers behind his throne.

But all that was over now and in the relative quiet of the city at rest I myself could not rest. Because once again I'd be facing Aaron in court. And once again I was going to make sure I kicked his butt around the room.

The killing of Jimmy Honeymoon was still all over the news, of course. Wild speculations were rampant over who did this. Was it some former girlfriend? That only meant about 20,000 suspects.

A weird religious cult? Take your pick in Los Angeles.

Or could it have been a real zombie, of which there were increasing reports?

And then there was the still unsolved "ritual" killing of the biker gang in Sunland. There was one blog that kept insisting the biker killings and Jimmy Honeymoon were linked in some way.

It was, in fact, a blog run by an anonymous member of law enforcement. No one truly knew who it was, but there was a rumor that the author was connected to the L.A. County Sheriff's Department.

They said it might even be Sheriff Geronimo Novakovich himself.

CHAPTER FORTY-FOUR

THE NIGHT before the trial of my father I wanted to make sure I ate well, and so I went clubbing, on the hunt for a man named Garth Capra. He was the last name listed in Sloan's book.

For the last two months I'd made my way through the names, ten in all, who had a special code attached to their listings. The first name confirmed to me, just before I ate him, that the code meant those who were part of the ring that trafficked in young girls.

This was my justification. I was a vigilante now, a zombie doing her part to make the world a better place. As if being more selective made it all right.

Judge, jury, executioner, gourmand.

Only in L.A.

I waited patiently in line until I was finally let through the velvet rope. Inside the club was hopping with the hipster crowd. I immediately made out Garth Capra, from his picture on the Internet, and from the way he was going on and on with a couple of hotshot types. I got myself a Beefeater martini to sip, then sidled up alongside the table, pretending to be listening to the music. What I picked up was Capra, loud and long, on the latest Brad Pitt film.

"He can't act anymore. He's mailing it in. Ever since Angelina, he isn't the same guy. I can see that. The guy was good back in *Thelma,* that guy, what happened to him?"

"He still makes a lot of money," one of the other guys said.

"Not like before. Not like when he could open number one. He's not doing things like Depp is doing. Depp did that movie with Angelina. Why didn't Brad? I'll tell you why. You don't wear the pants no more, like the fella said."

"Hey, why aren't we talking about it?"

"Talking about what?" Capra said.

"You know."

"No, I don't know. You want to tell me?"

"Scottie, man. How's a guy die like that?"

"This town," Capra said. "Let's talk about something else."

I said, "Ed Wood."

The guys at the table looked at me. I took a sip of my martini and bobbed my eyebrows.

"Excuse me?" Capra said.

"Ed Wood. The guy Johnny Depp played in the movie. That's the kind of thing Brad Pitt should be doing. I wish there was somebody around here would make a movie that took a risk. Not just the same old, same old."

This seemed to amuse everybody at the table.

"You some kind of film critic?" Capra said.

"Just somebody who would like to see a good movie again. I mean, can you believe the stuff they are making? Have you seen that gladiator movie that just came out? Did we really need to see that? I mean if it was well written, or well directed, then maybe. But somebody dropped the ball on that stupid flick and I'm out twelve bucks."

"Who put you up to this?" Capra asked.

"Up to what?"

"Who told you to come over and say that? Was it Brock Norman? Is he here?"

"I'm sure I don't know what you're talking about," I said.

"Right. You didn't know that I was the producer of that movie, did you?"

I pretended to blush. I put my hand over my mouth. Then I said, "Oh my. I put my foot in it this time, I guess."

"You want to have a seat and tell me all about my movies?"

"I don't even know your name."

The other guys at the table laughed. There were three of them, a fat guy, a guy with a beard, and a guy in a porkpie hat.

The fat guy said, "She doesn't know your name, Mr. Spielberg."

"Sit down," Capra said, sliding over. "Forget about these slobs. I'm Garth Capra."

"Any relation to Frank Capra?"

"I get that all the time. Unfortunately, no."

"Call me Amanda," I said.

"Where you from, Amanda?"

"Jersey," I said.

"And you so want to be in the movies, don't you? And that's why you engineered this whole ruse, am I right?"

"Let me tell you something, Mr. Capra. I don't want to be in any movie, least of all one of yours."

The three other guys *oohed*.

Capra tried not to look served. "I invited you to sit and I can uninvite you."

"But you won't," I said. "Because I fascinate you. And you know it's really too bad about that other producer. What was his name again, Scottie ...?"

"We're not talking about it," Capra said.

"I mean, considering what he was into, are you surprised?"

Garth Capra stiffened.

The guy in the hat said, "What was he into besides money?"

"Maybe Mr. Capra knows," I said.

"I'm not finding you amusing anymore. You can leave now."

"What, when we just started this conversation?"

Mr. Beard said, "What is she talking about, Garth?"

"Yes, what am I talking about, Garth?" I said.

"Excuse me," Garth Capra said to his friends. To me he said, "Let me buy you another drink."

"Sure," I said. "Nice meeting you all."

AT THE BAR, CAPRA SAID, "WHAT'S THIS ALL ABOUT NOW, honey? You playing some kind of game with me? Because I like games."

"I know you do."

"How do you know? That's what I want to know. How do you know I like to play games?"

"Scottie told me."

"Scottie? Why would Scottie tell?" His eyes did an Oscar worthy dance in his head. "Did you have something to do with ... ?"

"I'm just a simple girl doing some business, that's all. This ain't no game, Mr. Capra. This is some serious stuff. I mean, when you're into the sort of thing that can send you to prison for life, well, wouldn't you call that serious?"

"I don't know what you're talking about here, sweetie."

"Let's suppose I had some information about a few powerful types who were into sharing a certain commodity. Let's say this commodity had to be brought in on the down low and was in fact not a thing, but a person. Let's suppose I had the names of the people involved. Would that make a good movie?"

He stared at me for a long time. I could tell he was starting to get nervous. And trying very hard not to show it.

"If you had a concept like that," he said, "I'd say it'd make a pretty good movie. Pure fiction."

"I like movies based on a true story."

"Then go find one."

"I have."

"If you have, why come to me? Why don't you go to the cops or something?"

"Maybe because I like the color of money."

"You want money?"

"Doesn't everybody?"

"Maybe so, honey. Maybe so."

"Is there a place we can talk business? Alone?"

"There might be. How about if I pick you up in ten minutes, right out in back?"

"I wouldn't miss it."

CAPRA HAD A BENTLEY. OH, VERY NICE. HE DROVE UP Highland and just before the freeway turned into the driveway of one of the Hollywood Bowl lots. It was empty and dark. That's when he opened the glove compartment, leaned over me, and pulled out a handgun. A big one.

He waited for me to freak. I just sat there, like Jabba the Hutt.

Slimmed down, of course.

"You see what I have here?" he said.

"You're holding a gun," I said.

"You don't want to be with me when I'm holding a gun."

"You going to shoot me here? In your nice car?"

"I don't want to shoot you at all."

"Want?"

"Just do what I say," he said. "Slide over me. You're going to drive."

I slid over. I wasn't going to eat him right here on Highland. "Where to, Chumley?" I said.

"Just drive and I'll tell you when to turn," he said.

I backed out of the driveway and he had me get on the 101, north.

After we were in the flow he said, "Honey, I want to hear you tell me all about my movies again."

"Really? Now?"

"Oh yeah. All about it. I want you to tell me just what good taste you have."

"I don't think you really want me to tell you that."

"I do. Because I want that to be the last thing I hear from you."

I waited, pretending to be scared.

Capra said, "You hear what I said? The last thing?"

"You really haven't thought this through. Just like you didn't think through your last movie. What were you thinking casting Ray Romano as Caesar?"

"It was a comedy!"

"But comedies are supposed to make you laugh, aren't they?"

He said nothing.

"Why can't you make a movie like *It's a Wonderful Life.* Like the good Capra?"

"Why don't you just shut up and drive now?"

"Of course, you'd have to find someone like Jimmy Stewart. I don't think there are actors as good as Jimmy Stewart anymore."

"You're really messed up. You know you're going to die, don't you?"

"Garth, I've been trying to tell you—"

"Don't you see the gun?"

"But I'm driving the car."

"So?"

"So what if I drive to a police station?"

"I won't let you."

"So you'll shoot me? I'm doing fifty right now. You're in the car with me. You think that can have a happy ending, as they say?"

Capra said nothing.

"This is your problem," I said. "Your endings suck. You don't know how to write a story with a satisfying ending. You're all high concept and no finish."

"I can make this very hard on you."

"I don't see how. I'm sorry, I really don't. Why don't you tell me, Mr. Pedophile?"

"Don't call me that."

"It's true, isn't it?"

"It's only because of a quirk in the law," he said. "Why

shouldn't a girl who's thirteen give consent? They can do everything else, pretty much. We treat them like adults. Why not?"

"Maybe it's just wrong. Maybe there are some things that are wrong just because they are."

"You can pull off at the next turn," he said.

"Oh, yes," I said. "We're going up into the hills?"

"You're going where I tell you to go."

He told me. It was up in the hills of Studio City, all the way to the top.

It's pretty up on Mulholland Drive, at night. The lights of the San Fernando Valley on one side, the sparser yet still glittering lights on the canyon side. It's like Christmas one way and lodging for a weary traveler the other.

Along the rim on the Valley side, it's packed with homes. Old style, but with killer views. The canyon side has homes some of the time, but there's a big undeveloped run, too.

Which is what we were approaching.

"I'm not stopping, Mr. Capra. You're going to shoot me, so I'm going to keep on going."

"I'm putting the gun away. I'm going to let you out on the road. No one will ever know about this. You can't prove anything, and I can't prove anything. But if I ever see you again, you'll regret it."

"Bad dialogue again."

"Shut up!"

I gave the car more gas. We were heading toward a long area of Mulholland with a severe drop-off and no homes.

"What do you think you're doing?" Garth Capra said.

"I'm driving," I said, impishly.

"I said stop."

"I'm not going to stop. I'm going to drive us off the cliff."

I gave him a quick look. I wanted to see his eyes. It was worth it. Fear engorgement is its own punishment, and this guy deserved punishment for what he'd been getting away with.

"Stop now!"

I didn't stop. I turned hard right and popped the front tires over the curb. *Then* I stopped. One push on the accelerator and we'd be hurtling toward certain death. One of us, anyway.

"Don't!" Garth Capra said. And then he called me crazy, and a couple of other names.

"That's not going to win you a reprieve," I said. "Why don't you shoot me?"

"Who *are* you?"

"Your worst nightmare. A film critic who eats flesh."

Garth Capra opened his door and jumped out.

Gack! I hate it when that happens.

Now I had to track him.

Where did he think he was going to go? He chose north and ran along the street. Holding the gun.

I hate running in heels.

No time to kick 'em off, and even so the asphalt would wreak havoc on my zombie-skinned feet.

You just have to know how to do it, and what you do is imagine you are in heels an inch higher than you're actually wearing. I had two-inch heels on, so I was light on the heel and heavy on the balls of the feet—and mad at this guy for making me run.

Yes, zombies can run. Be very afraid.

Garth Capra's miserable brain was consumed on the side of a hill as I looked at the stars. If there had been some nice music it could have been a picnic at the Hollywood Bowl.

CHAPTER FORTY-FIVE

I WAS FEELING WELL FED the next morning and excited to be heading back to trial.

If there was one thing that could get me out of my zombie angst, it was doing battle in the courtroom.

Only this time the stakes were the highest they'd ever been for me. My own father on trial for murder. And Aaron Argula on the other side, again.

But I loved it. I lived for it, if you can put it that way. A fight in a courtroom is a microcosm of society, and it goes back to the ancient practice of jousting. Whoever is left on the horse, that's the winner.

We were in the courtroom of Judge Armand Hannad, a serious-looking former prosecutor in his forties. He called the case and we started picking a jury.

It went on for two days, Aaron not giving an inch to me, challenging the jurors he knew I wanted.

I did the same thing to him.

He seemed to be taking it all so personally now.

He really, really wanted to clean my clock.

Wasn't going to happen.

. . .

On day three we had our jury and the trial was set to begin.

Harry Clovis seemed calm all the way through. He said he'd been having visions of a tremendous victory.

And something strange. He said he kept seeing the body of a little boy dead in the street.

Jaime had stopped having those dreams. I was seeing him almost every day. Father Clemente was overseeing his education, giving him private lessons and readings. We had decided Jaime would be educated by us, and not enroll him in the public schools. Here in L.A., that's almost an intellectual death sentence.

An opening statement must be delivered in such a way that the jury does not think you are trying to manipulate them, even though you are. This is a persuasion business, after all.

And juries today are more cynical than in the past. A hundred years ago, they thought of the lawyers as learned and professional, as being smarter than they.

Today that's been flipped around. After decades of trials on TV and shows and movies about the so-called sleazy lawyer (if I never hear those two words used together again, I will be a happy zombie), today's juror is skeptical and suspicious.

Not only that, today's juror doesn't even want to be a juror. No one likes getting called out of their busy lives to come down to the jury room and sit around, waiting to have their name selected.

And when it is, when they have to trudge up to a courtroom, they silently pray they won't be picked.

The ones who want to be picked, those are the jurors you have to watch out for. They usually have an agenda. They try to take over the deliberations. They are the monkey wrenches in the fine gears of the justice system.

So now they have been selected, and you stand up to address them formally. They've gotten to know you a little bit during *voir dire*, the questioning of the jurors. And they've been sizing you up ever since they first laid eyes on you.

It is a rule that there is always one juror, at all times, watching you.

I remember one prosecutor I went up against, an older guy who'd joined the DA's office after years in private practice. He wasn't cutting it on the outside, so the DA took him on and started him in misdemeanors.

It was a shoplifting case, and my client was caught dead to rights. But I love those cases. Undead lawyers never take "dead to rights" all that seriously.

This poor, hapless baby DA had the habit of scratching his nose. He tried to do it surreptitiously, turning his head and the like. There was, as from the old *Seinfeld* show, some nostril penetration. Even though it was incidental, the jurors started talking about him outside the courtroom.

They called him "Picky."

It is an unbreakable law of trial law that if a jury calls you "Picky," you are bound to lose the case.

And he did. I won. My client walked.

The jurors watch you.

And if your client is accused of slicing off the head of an ex-cop, you've got a real hill to climb.

On a muggy morning in downtown Los Angeles, I started my ascent.

"Ladies and gentlemen of the jury, as I told you when you were selected, this is not going to be an ordinary trial. What the evidence will show is that my client, Harry Clovis, in an act of pure self-defense, put an end to an undead life. What I mean by that is the alleged victim was not a victim at all, but a zombie looking for flesh to eat. The evidence will show that this activity has been on the increase in Los Angeles, and that the alleged victim's own activity was part of a larger conspiracy."

Aaron was on his feet, shouting an objection. It is usually

frowned upon to object during an opening statement. The jury doesn't like that, thinks the objecting lawyer is trying to keep something from them.

Which is exactly what I wanted them to think. About Aaron. I was playing him like a trout.

And he knew it, I'm sure. He had his own strategy. Paint me as an out-of-control spinner of lies.

Once a jury believes that about you, it's over.

Judge Armand Hannad wasted no time in sustaining the objection and calling us up to the bench.

He said, "Ms. Caine, unless you give me an offer of proof on this conspiracy theory, you will not mention it again to the jury. And I will not allow you any witnesses on it unless and until you can show me a likelihood of such conspiracy existing."

"You mean," I said, "I can't offer testimony until I prove it, and can't prove it by testimony?"

"Something like that," the judge snapped.

Which would mean I would have to be very clever indeed.

But that's just my natural self, don't you know?

AARON'S FIRST WITNESS WAS A COUNTY MEDICAL EXAMINER named Clifford Moody. A shifty-eyed old-timer with thinning gray hair and sallow skin, he'd been in his office since the discovery of penicillin. I knew his rep, too. He had always been suspected of being less than objective and skewing things toward the prosecution.

A county hack, in other words.

After getting out his background and employment history, Aaron began the direct examination in earnest.

"Taking you to the murder scene, did you have occasion to examine the body of the victim, Cruz 'Bud' Bracamonte?"

"Yes, I did," Moody said.

"And what was your conclusion?"

"That he died as a result of exsanguination, or massive loss of blood."

"And such loss was the result of what?"

"Of irreversible torsal-cranial disaffiliation."

"In laymen's terms, if you please, Doctor."

"His head was chopped off."

"And what was your conclusion, if you have one, about the implement used to remove said head?"

"A large, sharp-edged weapon."

"Such as a sword?"

"Yes."

Aaron went to his counsel table and removed the tagged sword. "Showing you what has been marked as People's Exhibit 1 for identification, can you tell me, Doctor, what kind of sword this is?"

"I believe it is commonly called a samurai sword."

"It has a curved blade, is that right?"

"Yes."

"Now can you tell us if this weapon meets the criteria you established and would be capable of cutting off a head?"

Moody gave the sword a quick scan.

"Absolutely," he said.

"Your witness," Aaron said and sat down.

"GOOD MORNING, DOCTOR MOODY," I SAID.

"Good morning." Clipped and careful. I'd tangled with Moody before. I'm sure he remembered. It was not a pleasant experience for either of us.

"You testified that the victim died of blood loss, is that right?'

"Yes."

"Where did you first see the body, Doctor?"

"At the scene."

"You were dispatched from the coroner's office?"

"Yes."

"Did someone at the scene request you specifically?"

Short pause. "I believe so."

Bingo. Someone wanted this particular ME to do the exam.

"And when you arrived, you were shown the body?"

"I was."

"I'm curious, Doctor, how far was the head, what was the word you used, disaffiliated from the torso?"

"Thirty-seven and one half inches."

"I'm assuming you measured that."

"Of course, I would never presume to do that by sight."

"But you would presume to declare blood loss where there was no blood, isn't that right?"

"I beg your pardon."

"Isn't it true, Doctor, that there was minimal blood found at the scene?"

"It depends on your definition of minimal."

"Doctor, you have told the jury it was massive blood loss that was the cause of death."

"It had to be. The head was disaffiliated—"

"Yes, yes, but where is the blood?"

"It was there."

I went to my counsel table and took out the police photographs which I had received in discovery.

"Let me show you now three photographs, marked sequentially as Defense's 1, 2, and 3 for identification." I laid the color photos on the rail of the witness box. "Can you identify those for us, Doctor?"

"Yes. These are photographs of the body and head of the deceased, from three different angles."

"And looking at the space between the head and torso, what do you see there, Doctor?"

"Bloodstains."

"How would you characterize those stains?"

"I am not a serologist."

"You're a county medical examiner, are you not?"

"Of course."

"Which requires a medical degree."

"Yes."

"You've seen many bloodstains in your years with the office, yes?"

"Yes."

"So you know what massive blood loss looks like. And this isn't it, is it, Doctor?"

He frowned at the pictures. "It might be. It depends on many things."

"Doesn't it depend on having blood in the veins?"

"Of course!"

"A normal amount of human blood?"

"Yes."

"And isn't it true that what you see in these photographs is not a normal amount of human blood, what you would expect to see in an injury of this type?"

"It may not be normal, but—"

"Ah, not normal?"

"It may not be. But then again, it might."

"If the body did not carry the normal amount of human blood, for instance."

"How could that be?" he said.

"I am asking the questions, Doctor."

The judge said, "Just move on, Ms. Caine."

"You may not be a serologist, Doctor, but you do know that when the carotid artery is cut, slashed, as you claim in this matter, there is significant spurting of blood?"

"Yes."

"Called projected blood in serology, isn't that right?"

"Yes."

"Because human blood travels with some force through the body, correct?"

"Yes."

"Do you see any evidence of projected blood spatter in these photographs?"

"No."

"Might that not mean that whatever blood was traveling through the body was not, in fact, human?"

"Objection," Aaron said.

"Your honor," I said, "this is the People's own witness. Called to render an opinion. This is in fact a consideration. If something does not look human—"

"Objection sustained," Judge Hannad said. "Move on."

How could I move on when I was being railroaded in the opposite direction?

"Then let me put it this way," I said. "There was not the amount of blood you would expect to see from the severing of a carotid artery, right?"

"As I said, a number of factors ..."

"Name one," I said. A dangerous question. Almost always on cross-examination you want to keep to yes and no questions. You don't want to leave the door open for a witness to hit you with something you didn't anticipate.

But I felt confident he couldn't come up with anything that would fit the facts.

"I would have to think about that," Dr. Moody said.

"Seeing as how we don't have time to pause," I said, "I'll conclude my questioning with this. Isn't it a fact, Doctor, that when you examined the head of the deceased it was still alive?"

There were audible gasps in the courtroom. I love audible gasps. They're so rare.

He looked shaken. I knew why. I knew he had to have seen Bracamonte's zombie head moving something. Eyes. Lips. Maybe it even spoke.

But without salt inside it was absolutely sentient.

"That's ridiculous," the good doctor said.

"Is it?"

He did not answer. And I sat down.

. . .

AARON CALLED DETECTIVE MARK STROBERT TO THE STAND.

Poor Strobert. He did not look like the confident, no-nonsense cop I'd first encountered in the Traci Ann Johnson murder trial. Now he'd seen too much. He was trying his best to look like a competent professional. But some of the juice had been sucked out of him.

I almost wanted to hug him and tell him everything would be okay. Me, a criminal defense lawyer, wanting to hug a cop. Strange days indeed.

Aaron walked Strobert through the events, with Strobert repeating pretty much what he'd said at the motion to suppress.

This time, though, I was ready with some new questions on cross-examination.

"Detective Strobert," I began, "this was not the first beheading you've seen of late, is it?"

"I don't know what you mean by that."

"Isn't it true that last year you and your partner, Detective Richards, investigated the death of a Carl Gilquist, a plumber who lived in Hollywood?"

"Yes."

"Isn't it true that the head of Carl Gilquist had been severed?"

Strobert nodded.

"You'll have to answer out loud for the record," I said.

"Yes," he said.

"And isn't it also true that Mr. Gilquist's mouth had been filled with salt and his lips stitched together?"

"Well, yes."

"Do you know what a zombie is, Detective?"

"Objection," Aaron said. "There is no foundation for that question."

"Sustained," the judge said.

I said, "Did the victim, Carl Gilquist, have something carved into his forehead?"

"Yes."

"What was it?"

"It appeared to be a letter."

"What letter was it?"

"I believe it was the letter Z."

"Did the subject of zombies come up then?"

"I believe you brought it up," Strobert said.

"Isn't that because your partner asked my opinion on what had happened?"

"I don't recall."

"I think you do."

Strobert's eyes flashed anger as Aaron objected once more. The judge told me to keep personal animosity out of my questions. That was going to be hard if Strobert kept conveniently forgetting key facts.

"Do you recall, Detective, the term 'zombie' coming up?"

"Yes."

I decided to switch gears. Sometimes you can catch a witness off guard if you change the subject fast enough.

"Detective Strobert, were you aware that Detective Braca-monte was the subject of an internal affairs investigation?"

"I learned that later."

"And that he was not on the force when he died?"

"I learned that, too."

"Because he was a zombie, isn't that right?"

"Objection," Aaron said.

"Sustained."

All right, we'd go in the side door. "Detective Strobert, are you up on the law concerning self-defense?"

"Sure."

"Can you state that law for us?"

"Maybe not in your jargon."

"Any jargon you choose, Detective."

"Well, if someone is facing a threat of force, and it's reasonable that they think it's imminent, they can use equal force to protect themselves."

"Excellent, Detective. You'd make a fine lawyer."

"That'll be the day."

Titters broke out in the courtroom. The judge shut it down with a bang of the gavel.

"Let's stick to the questions," Judge Hannad said.

"All right," I said. "Now, if someone were to be coming at me with, say, a brick in his hand, and I reasonably thought he was going to kill me, I would be justified in killing him on the grounds of self-defense, correct?"

Strobert said, "If the facts made it reasonable to believe he had intent to kill, then yes. But that's for a jury to decide."

"Exactly," I said. "And this jury will do just that. So I will ask another hypothetical. If it is reasonable to believe that a zombie is about to try to kill you, wouldn't it be justifiable to kill the zombie?"

"Objection," Aaron said. "Again, no foundation for this wild speculation."

"May I remind the prosecutor that this is a hypothetical question?"

Aaron fired back. "It still requires a foundation. You can't just snatch things out of the air."

"He has a point," the judge said.

And my trap was sprung. Thanks, Aaron, for walking right into it. "I am prepared to lay that foundation now, your honor."

"What foundation?"

"The existence of zombies. Since Mr. Argula has conceded that is the next point to be established, and since that is essential to my defense, I am ready to proceed."

The judge tapped his chin. "Do you have a witness?"

"I do."

"Do you wish to call that witness now?"

"Yes."

"All right. I will allow the defense to call one witness for the sole purpose of establishing a foundation for the question. Detective Strobert, you may step down, subject to being recalled. Understood?"

"Yes, your honor," Strobert said, and got up. I thought his look was slightly admiring as he walked by.

"Call your witness," the judge said.

"I call the head of Mickey Cohen."

CHAPTER FORTY-SIX

BEFORE ANYONE COULD SAY ANYTHING, the judge and Aaron included, I waved to the back of the courtroom where Nick was sitting, holding a Crate & Barrel box on his lap. He came toddling down the aisle with the box and joined me.

"What is this, Ms. Caine?" the judge said.

"My witness," I said. I took the box from Nick and walked it to the witness box, placing it on the rail. The part of the box that opened was facing outward toward the gallery. I opened it.

Mickey's head said, "Finally!"

Gasps, mutterings, and more than a few expletives erupted in the courtroom. It wasn't everyday a head was brought in to testify.

Aaron shouted an objection. He didn't give a ground for it, because there's nothing in the evidence code that requires a witness to have a body. The good people who put together the laws over the course of eight hundred years of Anglo-Saxon jurisprudence did not anticipate the living dead or dismembered heads as competent witnesses.

So Aaron simply told the judge it was "improper" and that I was pulling a "stunt."

The judge didn't look like he was thinking clearly at all, so I decided to help him along. "Your honor, it would violate all antidiscrimination laws on the books not to allow someone to testify just because he doesn't have a body. In California we specifically prohibit discrimination based upon physical handicap. The only requirement is if the witness is able to testify and competent to do so."

Judge Hannad blinked a few times, like a man stepping into the sun after a six-hour backroom poker game.

"Can you hurry it up?" Mickey Cohen's head said. "It's a little hot in here."

"I, uh ..." Judge Hannad said. "I don't see . . ." He swallowed, hard, his Adam's apple a golf ball stuck in his throat. "I can't... oh, let him be sworn."

The clerk said, "Please raise your right hand—" then stopped and cleared his throat. "I mean, do you solemnly swear that the testimony you are about to give in the cause now pending before this court shall be the truth, the whole truth, and nothing but the truth?"

"You bet I do," Mickey Cohen said. "And never bet against Mickey Cohen."

I began the questioning. "Your name is Meyer Harris Cohen, is that correct?"

"Check."

"*Yes* will do," said the judge.

"Check, judge. I mean, okay."

I said, "You were a citizen of Los Angeles in the 1950s, is that right?"

"Still am. Love this town."

"Mr. Cohen, you have been called as an expert in the field of zombies. Please state your qualifications for the jury."

"Just look at me," Mickey Cohen's head said. "I'm born in 1913, and I got no body. How you think I'm still alive?"

"How did you come to be in this condition?"

"Well, it happened like this, see? They thought I was dead and I guess I was, up till about five years ago. Then all of a sudden, I'm back. Out of the grave, you see? I was never in a grave anyways. My boys took my body and kept it from the Feds. So one day I wake up, that's what it feels like, and I got a voice in my head telling me what to do."

"Is this something that is common for zombies?"

"Yeah. Somebody brings 'em back and tries to control 'em. Only some of us don't want to be controlled. I smacked right back at the voice. Next thing I know, somebody cuts my head off. I never found out who, but when I do, boy—"

"Mr. Cohen," the judge said, "that will be quite enough."

"Sorry, Judge. My mistake."

I said, "Is this someone who brings you back to life called a *bokor?*"

"I think so. I never took no foreign languages. Except Brooklyn. I talk good Brooklyn."

"I see. Now, sir, what is the preferred diet of the zombie?"

"A zombie's gotta have human flesh. Simple as that."

Groans and one stifled scream issued through the courtroom.

"Hey, I didn't make the rules," Mickey's head said.

"There is no question pending, Mr. Cohen," Judge Hannad said.

"Sorry again, Judge."

"That being the case," I said, "if a human person were to encounter a zombie on the street, wouldn't it be reasonable to assume that said zombie would have the intent to kill and eat that person?"

"Oh yeah, wouldn't be no doubt about it."

"Your witness," I said to Aaron.

"Mickey Cohen," Aaron said. "You were, or are, what is known as a mobster, isn't that true?"

I objected and asked to approach the bench.

"Mr. Cohen's life is not on trial here," I told the judge. "He was called as an expert witness only."

Aaron said, "I am entitled to impeach a witness if he has felony convictions in his past. His veracity is very much in question."

"I agree," Judge Hannad said. "You may continue."

When we were all back in our places, me steaming at the minor victory Aaron enjoyed, my ex-lover said, "You were a mobster, is that correct?"

"Nothing like that was ever proved," Mickey said. "I got caught up on a tax rap. And I bet every member of this jury had their run-ins with the IRS."

I noticed a couple of the jurors nodding. Nice.

"You were convicted in a court of law of tax evasion?"

"You think the government can do better with your money than you can?"

"That is a non-responsive answer."

"It's a good one though, you gotta admit."

Aaron looked to the judge. "If your honor please, can you direct the witness to answer the question?"

"Mr. Cohen, I'm not going to warn you again," the judge said.

"Or what?" Mickey Cohen's head said. "You going to roll me into the clink?"

The judge closed his eyes and rubbed the bridge of his nose.

"Let me ask you this," Aaron said. "You have offered an opinion that a zombie must eat human flesh, is that correct?"

"You got it."

"Which means, of course, that you eat human flesh, isn't that true?"

Mickey's eyebrows turned downward over an angry glare.

"I ask you again," Aaron said. "Do you eat human flesh?"

"I refuse to answer on the grounds of the Fifth Amendment," Mickey said. "Go fry yourself."

Aaron had what he wanted. A witness who pleads the Fifth always looks guilty to a jury.

But I also had what I wanted. It was a foundation for arguing self-defense. I have to say I was pleased.

. . .

AARON ONLY HAD ONE OTHER WITNESS TO PUT ON FOR HIS CASE in chief, a forensic expert. These days you have to do it. Juries expect to have scientific evidence for every crime. They see it on TV. Prosecutors call it the "GS7 effect." As if that happens in real life.

So Aaron got a county forensics guy to get up and yammer on about blood and DNA and the sword and dead body and put it all together with wrapping paper and pink ribbon.

But since our argument did not dispute that Harry had done the deed, there was no need for me to ask a single question.

Sometimes that's the best thing a trial lawyer can do. Not ask a single question, so the jury thinks, Hey, she's not worried about that evidence at all. Maybe we shouldn't be, either.

So that was Aaron's case. Short and to the point. Not overcomplicating things. Not over-trying. He was right and he was smart. Most observers thought O. J. Simpson, Robert Blake, and Casey Anthony all walked because the prosecutors tried too hard with too little.

Aaron wasn't going to let that happen here.

I asked the judge if we could adjourn for the day and boy, did he go for that.

CHAPTER FORTY-SEVEN

As Nick and I were returning Mickey's head to his thugs, he said, "Oh yeah, meant to tell you. Got a lead on that booker."

"It's *bokor*."

"Yeah, I just can't get that word right. Anyway, one of my boys was looking to rough up a low-level drug dealer the other night, and the dealer said there was nothing he could do to him. If he killed him, the guy said, he'd just come back to life and knew the person who could do it."

I started to vibrate with excitement. "Who? Who was it?"

"The guy didn't say, but we did find out where he was selling his reefer. It was some strange place in Hollywood. The Medical Hindenburg or something like that."

I rolled that one around in my mind, then it clicked. "You mean Med Zeppelin?"

"That's the place," he said.

CHAPTER FORTY-EIGHT

GINNY FINN WAS DRESSED up as Badtz-Maru. She was in the sitting room of the Roosevelt Hotel giving final instructions to the crew there.

"Cainie!" she said. "Glad you could make it. You look too normal, though."

"I'm not here to party," I said.

"You'll miss out. I got some togs you can flog. What do you say? Up in my room."

"Why don't we just step outside for a second, huh?" She gave a final command to a bartender, then put her arm around me and walked me to the doors. "This is gonna blow it out," she said.

Outside on Orange, Ginny reached for a cigarette and lit up. "It's nice to get a little fresh air," she said, blowing smoke my way.

"Ginny, it was you," I said.

"Me who?"

"You who brought me back to life. You reupped me." She looked at first like she was going to deny it, but she knew me. Knew I could tell a liar. I wasn't going to let her off the hook.

"How did you find out?" she said.

"That doesn't matter now," I said. "When did you get into raising the dead?"

"You never knew my parents, did you?"

I shook my head.

"Missionaries. To Haiti. That's where I grew up, until I'm twelve. That's where I learned. I haven't done it a lot, Mallory, honest. But you were my friend."

"That's bogus. Somebody hired you. Somebody who planned to kill me in the first place. I want to know who."

"Cainie, please. Don't ask me that. Can't you just be glad you're still alive?"

"You call this life? What's the matter with you? I would have been better off dead! Better off than crawling around the streets having to kill to eat. Losing my soul. Who killed me?"

Ginny shook her dorky little head. Tears formed in her heavily made-up eyes.

"I can't, Cainie. I just can't."

I took her by the shoulders and shook her. "This is my life we're talking about! Maybe my eternal life! This isn't one of your funked-out raves!"

"Don't!"

I was not going to let go until I had an answer. My grip on her shoulders tightened.

"You're hurting me!"

"Not as much as I'm going to. Talk to me!"

"I can't! Stop it!"

She opened her mouth wide then, her eyes bulging. And then she collapsed at my feet, a dagger sticking out of her back.

I looked up in time to see something at the comer of Orange and Hawthorne, looking at me. A streetlight reflected in one large eyeball.

It was the cyclops.

Then it disappeared.

I RAN AFTER IT.

I've never been one-on-one with a one-eye before. Except for the one who ran me into a wall. Could this be the same clops? Or were there more than one on the streets?

The good thing was he wasn't very fast. He was dressed in jeans and a polo shirt, but he ran funny. I found out later it was because of the hooves.

My gain.

It took me only half an alley to catch him. I jumped on his back and forced him to the ground.

He was wiry but not that strong. All those cyclopes you see in movies look strong because they're big. In reality they're more like giant lizards.

At least this one was. I rolled him over and sat on his stomach and looked down at his ugly face. One horn and one eye is not going to get you the cover of *GQ*.

"Who sent you?" I said.

His response was to spit in my face.

So I stuck my thumb in his eye.

He howled with pain. Then I grabbed his horn and gave it a jerk. It cracked.

He cried out more.

"Talk to me and I'll let you go," I said.

He was pawing at his eye with his scaly hands, moaning.

I slapped him a few times. "Talk!"

"Die, zombie!"

I was about to give him another poke when a couple of hands pulled me off my prey.

On my feet I saw it was a big guy, maybe twenty years old, wearing a University of Oklahoma T-shirt.

"You shouldn't've oughtta done that," he said to me.

What?

Meanwhile, the cyclops was up and running again.

I started to follow but the big ham hands held me back.

"He's just doin' his job, lady," he said.

"What are you *talking* about?"

"A guy in a costume so folks can take pictures with him. I seen Captain Jack Sparrow and Spiderman, too."

"It's not a costume, pal. Now let go of my arm."

"Whattaya mean it's not a costume?"

I yanked my arm away. I was about to chase when I noticed a wallet on the sidewalk. I picked it up.

"That's his wallet," Oklahoma said.

He reached for it. I pulled it away from his grasp. "I'll take care of this, junior. I'm a lawyer."

"Can I take your picture?"

"Just tell the folks back home you met a cyclops, okay?"

"What were you doing hitting him like that?"

"They don't take criticism well."

"Wow, a cyclops! What is that?"

I didn't stay to explain. I got out of there before the cops came and asked about the knife sticking out of Ginny Finn's back.

I GOT BACK TO MY LOFT AND THAT'S WHEN IT HIT ME FULL-ON. I'd been searching for my *bokor*, the one who reupped me, to get her to give me back my soul. And now she was dead. Now what was I supposed to do?

Wanderer in the earth.

Thank you, God! You've been great! Don't forget to tip your waiter on the way out!

I started going through the cy's wallet.

It was a leather job, like you'd find in the back pocket of any construction worker. The clops had a twenty and three ones for cash. And not much else.

Except a business card. From a lawyer. One that looked well thumbed. It had a smudge over the name, as well it should.

It was the card of one Gus Gilboy, sleazoid-at-law.

CHAPTER FORTY-NINE

TRIALS DON'T STOP JUST because a cyclops kills your traitorous friend. Or because the assassin had the card of a lawyer you knew and despised in his wallet.

I had a job to finish, and it was going to finish today. Since this was going to be a self-defense play, I needed to put my father on the stand. This is usually a bad idea, but I had no choice. What was in his mind at the time of the killing was the all-important factor. It would convict him or set him free.

He was sworn and took the witness chair.

"What is your full name?" I asked.

"Harrison Morrison Clovis."

"And you are also my father."

"I like being your father."

I cleared my throat. "Taking you to the night in question, Mr. Clovis—"

"You can call me Dad."

"Not in court, if you don't mind."

"I must make my witness."

Judge Hannad said, "Just answer when a question is posed to you, sir."

"I will make my witness."

The judge threw up his hands.

"Mr. Clovis," I said, "let me take you to the night in question, the night when you defended yourself against Bud Bracamonte."

"Objection," Aaron said. "Object to the word 'defended.' Assumes a fact not in evidence."

"You will have your chance," the judge said. "Overruled."

"You were carrying a sword with you at that time?"

"Yes, like any citizen concerned about zombies."

"That was your concern?"

"Of course! The undead must be eliminated!"

My father realized then he was talking about me, too, and looked apologetic.

I quickly added, "What led you to believe that Bracamonte was undead?"

"I was on his trail because of a revelation from God."

"How did that revelation come about?"

"It was given to me in a dream. In this dream I saw him as the undead, walking on the very street where we found him."

Aaron asked if we could approach the bench.

"Your honor, how much of this do we have to endure? This man is clearly trying to convince the jury that he is crazy. He is coming up with all sorts of wild things to say. Are we going to just let it continue?"

I said, "His state of mind at the time of the incident is what is at issue here. I'm sure Mr. Argula would be happy if my client just confessed to murder. But that's not going to happen. Instead we seek the truth here, something Mr. Argula is pretending to be blissfully unaware of."

Aaron looked like he wanted to strangle me.

"I'm done," Judge Hannad said. "I'm through. I don't want to be here anymore. Heads in boxes. Zombies. I'm going to let the witness say whatever he wants, then I'm going to let Mr. Argula cross-examine to his heart's content, then I'm going to let you give closing arguments, and then I'm going to give this to the jury and take a vacation. So please, get on with it!"

And so we did. I established that my father was fully convinced Bracamonte was a zombie. Aaron tried his best to shake my father up, but he held firm.

Finally I called a clerk at the Hall of Records to vouch for a death certificate Nick had managed to locate. It was the death of Cruz Bracamonte four weeks before my father chopped his head off.

In California the prosecutor gets two bites at the apple at the end of a trial. He argues to the jury first, then the defense goes, then the prosecutor gets the last word on "rebuttal."

Aaron gave his usual sharp closing. He was on his game.

I hate to admit it, but he was almost as good as I am. I watched him and just admired his work as a trial lawyer.

It's like that scene in the movie *The Hustler* with Paul Newman. Newman plays "Fast Eddie" Felson, and all he wants to do is beat Minnesota Fats, the greatest pool player in the world. So he gets a match with him, and they start playing. And Eddie is mesmerized. "Man, he is *great,*" he says to his manager. He watches admiringly.

That's what I did with Aaron. But to be the best you have to beat the best, and that's what I was going to do to the prosecutor.

He sat down.

Now it was my turn.

My dad gave me a pat on the arm before I stood up.

"Remember," he whispered, "the anti-Christ is near."

"I'll keep that in mind, Pop," I said.

Then I faced the box.

"Ladies and gentlemen of the jury, I stand before you as a simple messenger, not an advocate. The message is one you already know. We are at war in this community, this city. We are being overrun by all manner of monstrosities, and you saw yourselves here in court what that can look like.

"Mr. Argula calls it a cheap trick. Let me ask you, ladies and gentlemen, would you rather know the truth through a trick? Or would you be content to live a lie in the quiet of your homes?

"What Mr. Argula calls a trick was something you all needed to see. The very threat you felt is what my client felt that night a zombie named Bud Bracamonte, a former cop, came after the two of us. It was a clear act of self-defense.

"Mr. Argula can give you all sorts of legalese, but let me tell you what he's doing. It's the dark ink of the octopus.

"You know what an octopus does when it's afraid? It issues an inky substance into the water, clouding it, and in the ensuing confusion it hopes to escape.

"That's what Mr. Argula's mumbo jumbo is. The black ink of the octopus. Because he knows if you put yourselves at the scene, you too would conclude this was self-defense. At the very least, there is reasonable doubt. Mr. Argula has not been able to prove conclusively that Mr. Clovis set out to kill Bud Bracamonte. Yes, he was carrying a sword, but wouldn't you walking these mean streets? If Mr. Argula wants to file this as an illegal weapons case, let him. But he wants more. He wants it to be murder.

"It is not. It cannot be. You cannot so find. The law will not allow it.

"Look at Mr. Argula's table over there. You see it? See Mr. Argula sitting there? Well, on the table right in front of him is a huge, three-ton boulder. I want you to see it in your mind. That boulder is called the presumption of innocence. It is the boulder Mr. Argula can only move by proving every element of his case beyond a reasonable doubt.

"If he does not remove every scrap of that boulder, Mr. Clovis must be set free.

"I submit to you, ladies and gentlemen, that Mr. Argula has not even made a chip in that boulder, not one.

"Which means your duty is clear. You swore as jurors to uphold the law, and the judge will instruct you on the law in just a few minutes.

"That will come after Mr. Argula argues to you one last time. I will not have a chance to respond to anything he says.

"But I don't have to. You can.

"Whenever you hear him talk about the evidence, you remember the black ink of the octopus.

"And then clear it all away with your verdict of Not Guilty.

"I thank you."

CHAPTER FIFTY

AARON REBUTTED, then the judge instructed and charged the jury, sent them to the jury room.

A deputy took my dad away, but not before I kissed him on the cheek. Very unprofessional, but I didn't care. Then Aaron came over to me and shook my hand.

"Well done, counselor," he said.

"Back atcha."

"Not that you're going to win, of course."

"Would you like to place a side bet?"

He shook his head and smiled. "I've got plenty of money. But I would like to talk to you one more time, just the two of us. It's important."

"It's not going to end with one of us walking out, is it?"

"I promise. Shall we go up to my office?"

"What? Enemy territory?"

"I want us to have complete privacy."

"You're going to try to take advantage of me, now are you?"

He bobbed his eyebrows. "Your secret dream?"

He didn't know how close he was.

· · ·

Up on floor eighteen of the Foltz building is the lair of
the DAs. Like a hive of hornets, they buzz around in cubicles and
offices, looking to sting defense lawyers.

I knew a bunch of the players and got some good-natured nods
and a few verbal jabs as Aaron walked me to his lair.

It was an office with a view of one side of downtown. Across
the 101 Freeway and into Chinatown. You could write a whole
history of the city just using this view.

I sat in a chair and Aaron sat on the corner of his most orderly
desk.

"What would you think," he said, "if I ran for mayor?"

I said, "Anything would be better than Garza."

"That's not exactly a ringing endorsement."

"Sorry," I said. "I didn't mean it that way. You'd make a great
mayor, Aaron, except for the compassion."

"What compassion?"

"Exactly."

"I have a heart," he said.

And I wanted to eat it and love it at the same time.

"But there's something I don't have," he said.

"What?"

"A wife."

I put my head in my hands. "Aaron, we've been through that."

"I know it sounds crass," he said. "But someone who is going to
make it in politics needs a spouse, and I don't want just anyone. I
want you."

I opened my mouth and heard myself say, "Okay."

"What?" Aaron said.

"Sure. Why not? Let's get married. Let's do this thing." And I
really did mean that. Who cared about anything anymore? Aaron
Argula. We'd get married and then he'd find out, and then he could
deal with me. Maybe there was a way it could work out. Maybe
there was. Maybe I could think of it.

Of course there wasn't, but I told myself there might be. I was
tired of fighting it.

And if worse came to downright horrific, I could eat him and be done with it. I could eat the only man I truly loved and then my soul would be damned even more.

What possesses a girl who says yes to such an arrangement?

I had no idea. But *possessed* felt like the right word.

"I can't believe I'm hearing this," Aaron said. He pulled me to my feet and into his arms. He kissed me and I didn't bite him.

"When?" I said.

"As soon as possible," he said.

"Aaron—"

"This is all so—"

"Don't think," Aaron said. "Feel. Do you feel it?"

I felt it all right. Overwhelmed, in fact. Maybe some psychiatrist who deals with the undead will say this was denial, big-time, and I was worn down too much to resist. I'm not going to argue.

I told him I'd think about it and stumbled out of there and took the elevator down to the ground floor.

When I hit the street, I still wasn't thinking straight. And then I remembered I needed to pay someone a visit.

CHAPTER FIFTY-ONE

IT WAS a law office on Third Street. It was one of those that rents to several lawyers with a shared receptionist.

Who, this day, was a very young intern type who could have had **clueless** tattooed on her forehead.

"I'm here to see Mr. Gilboy," I said.

"Who?"

"Gus Gilboy? It's posted on the front of the building?"

"Oh, Mr. *Gilboy*. Yes." She looked at something on her desk. Maybe a directory.

"I don't see that name."

"Look under the Gs."

"Oh, there it is." She looked at me. "I'm new."

"Really?"

"Would you like me to tell him you're here?"

"I would love that."

"Okay." She picked up the desk phone.

"Would you like my name?" I said.

"I don't even know it."

"Excuse me?"

"I might like it if I knew it, but I don't."

"I mean, to announce me."

"Oh. Yes. Your name is?"

"Mallory Caine."

"That sounds familiar. Are you an actress?"

"Just tell Mr. Gilboy ... On second thought, don't tell him anything. He's in number 202."

"He is?"

"I'll just let myself in. We're old friends."

I walked past the desk and started down the corridor.

"Cool," the receptionist said.

I walked past a couple of open doors and got some suspicious looks. Then I came to 202, which was closed. I heard a voice behind it, though, yakking away.

In I went.

Gus Gilboy had his feet up on the desk but took them down when he saw me.

"I'll get back to you," he said into his phone, then hung up. "Where do you get off coming in here?"

"Hi, Gus."

"What do you want?"

"I want to know why you're hiring out cyclopes."

His face twitched but didn't give much away. Years of lying practice may have had something to do with it.

"Ms. Caine, I don't know what you're talking about."

"Can it, Gus. A cyclops gave me your card."

"Gave you?"

"In a manner of speaking. Now why would he have your card, Gus? You defending him on a peeping rap?"

"You know as well as I do I don't discuss clients."

"If he's really a client. Maybe you hired him."

"To do what?"

"Kill someone."

Gus stood. He was wearing a light pink shirt with a lavender tie and polka-dot suspenders. "You come in here to accuse me of soliciting murder?"

"I don't think you did it directly. But you have a cyclops working for you and I want to know why."

"You're crazy, Ms. Caine."

"Am I?"

"Crazy and stupid."

"Now that's interesting," I said. "What makes you say that?" He'd gone too far. To call me stupid meant he had made an assessment of some kind. Which in turn meant he had some kind of information.

When he didn't answer right away, I knew I was right.

"Spill it, Gus. What am I supposed to be stupid about?"

"Just generally," he said.

"No way you're getting out of it that way, Gus. Or do you want me to press the cyclops thing? I can make life difficult for you."

"You can't do a thing to me," Gus said. "You can't do a thing to anybody. It's over."

"Quit being so dramatic."

"You don't even know. That's why you're stupid. Now leave."

"I'm not finished with you, Gus."

He picked up his phone and hit a button. "Yeah, call security, please ... Security... Look under S ... Not F, S ... *Security*..."

"Never mind, Gus," I said. "Let's leave the poor girl her dignity."

Just before I left, I got a look at some of the framed photos on his wall.

There was one of him with Mayor Garza.

And another of him with Charles Beaumont Manyon. And a third, this one of smiling Gus and that ever-loving center for the Los Angeles Clippers, Rudy "The Roof" Gamboni.

"That's quite a hall of fame you've got there, Gus."

"Get out!"

"I'd say you had some powerful friends in dark places."

"You're done! You're dead!"

"Tell me something I don't know."

"You'll see!"

CHAPTER FIFTY-TWO

GETTING THREATENED by the likes of Gus Gilboy is not the most pleasant of experiences. It ranks just under a gynecological exam from a duck. But he knew something. He was connected to something.

My guess is he was a stooge. For the mayor and for Manyon. Doing petty little things for them like suing enemies or hassling political foes. By hiring one-eyes.

But what was his connection to Roof Gamboni?

And what was Gamboni's connection to Mrs. Gonzalez, Jaime's mother? The pieces all seemed assembled to create a picture, but it wasn't coming through. It was like having a song in the back of your head, and you just can't remember where it came from.

I made my way down Broadway toward my office—but kept right on walking. I need to air out a little after being in the same room with Gilboy.

As I walked, I couldn't help noticing again the amazing amalgam that is Los Angeles. Black, white, Asian, Latino. Hustlers and tourists, drug dealers and evangelists, dreamers and skeptics, heroes and villains, helpers and haters, young and old, male and female and indeterminate, human and otherworldly. You couldn't really tell from the looks who was in the realm of the supernatural, who had come to town for the big takeover plan that was supposedly in the works.

Or maybe it was just a game with these people, these demons and dark spirits. Maybe that's just what they did, create chaos, because there was nothing else they *could* do, just like there was nothing else I could do but eat brains and flesh and stay in this weird netherworld existence.

There was a philosopher once who talked about it all being a dream that recurs, so you're never in a real world. You're only in a dream and it never ends. I guess it's like *The Matrix* or something, only we're not hooked up to anything—though we could be. We just don't know where we are.

I crossed Olympic, still walking, still thinking, drinking in the sun and the sky, and then thought it was too real for a dream. I couldn't prove it. Nobody could. But you just had to take it that the connection you longed for was out there.

I realized then I wasn't very far from Staples Center and wondered if the Clippers were having off-season practices. I wondered if I could get to see Gamboni again. I'd have some more pointed questions for him this time.

Believe it or not, that same rotund security guard was sitting outside the doors. He had earbuds on and could have been sleeping behind those sunglasses of his. Because he didn't move a muscle as I approached him.

So I yanked one of his buds out and said, "Security?"

He jumped like he'd just been awakened from a dream of roast beef. "Hey!"

"Remember me?"

He looked me over. "Yeah, I remember."

"I'm looking for Gamboni."

"It's off-season," he said.

"Thought maybe he showed up for practice or something."

The guard shook his head. "You might find him down at Venice. He likes to play street ball."

"Isn't that a little dangerous for an NBA player?"

"They don't want him to, but he doesn't seem to get hurt."

I stuck that fact in the briefcase of my mind and handed the guy his earbud. It was nice to know Staples Center was in such great hands.

I walked back to my building and got Geraldine and took a spin down to the beach.

VENICE IS A LITTLE CURIO IN LOS ANGELES, SET JUST SOUTH OF Santa Monica. It was built up by a tobacco millionaire in 1904, to resemble its namesake in Italy with canals and gondolas and everything. It drew a nice crowd for awhile, then suffered from urban blight like everything urban eventually does.

In the '50s it became a beatnik burg and it's been pretty artsy ever since. It's been a fashionable place for hipsters to have hangouts. People like Robert Downey, Jr., and Sting and George Carlin.

It's also a place people with muscles can do a little obtrusive flexing. Arnold Schwarzenegger got famous at Gold's Gym here, before he got famous for movies, politics, and domestic intrigue.

And it's a place with a well-known basketball court for those whose hoop dreams stopped short of NBA glory.

Or if you are a seven-foot center for the Clippers, meaning you haven't all that much to lose, you can play here, too.

He was there. The court was surrounded with bathing suited fans, boys and girls, and an old man or two in shorts and black socks. It was a playground game with five on a side and the ratio was nine to one, black to white. The white one was the tallest Italian in the city.

Gamboni looked like he was having the time of his life. He laughed and talked trash. He blocked shots and scored at will. Not just around the basket like a man his size would be expected to do, but from way outside. Downtown, as the bailers like to say.

He was matched up with a guy who was about five inches shorter but a whole lot thicker. He was starting to get a little aggressive with Gamboni, who just laughed all the more as the antics continued.

I watched it all with the slightly bored air of someone who has better things to do than watch strutters strut their hormones all over a blacktop court by the beach.

And then Gamboni got clobbered into one of the basket poles. So hard the basket shook.

The big guy who'd been guarding him stood there with his chin jutting out, looking like he wanted a fight.

Gamboni, meanwhile, crumpled to the ground. His teammates ran at the tough guy and surrounded him and almost started throwing punches.

But then Gamboni sprang—literally, sprang—to his feet.

"No one can hurt the Roof!" he said, and the whole crowd broke into cheers.

The game continued as if nothing untoward had happened. And Gamboni continued to pour in buckets at will.

When the game was over, Gamboni signed autographs for a while. I stood in line. When I got to him, I smiled and reached out like he thought I'd be holding a picture or slip of paper.

Then he recognized me and his face went from smiling Italian to hitman Sicilian.

"You get away from me," he said.

"Relax, Rudy. I'm not going to turn you in. Yet."

"Turn me in? For what?"

"Kidnapping. Maybe murder. You feel like talking now?"

"Not so loud!" He looked around at the dwindling crowd. "We talk on the beach."

So down we went toward the ocean. The ocean I loved as a little girl but could no longer enjoy. Salt. Couldn't get near me.

When we got to where the sand turned wet, Gamboni said, "I heard about you."

"What have you heard?"

"That you are trouble."

"That's why I have a law degree. It's no fun unless you can cause trouble."

"And you eat people. You are the living dead."

"Somebody's been blabbing. Maybe Gus Gilboy." Rudy Gamboni frowned like it was an effort to think. "Here's what I think," I said. "I think Gus is your lawyer, your agent, and he got you the deal of a lifetime. A deal to make you into one of the best players in the league."

When Gamboni didn't answer, I kept heading down that road. "He brokered your soul, which you sold to the devil. In return for giving you a three-point shot and the resilience to come back from injury, you agreed to do a little dirty work. One thing was to get a woman named Gonzalez to come with you. Because her son was basketball crazy and you maybe told her you could get him tickets or something. How'm I doing?"

He actually looked scared then. "How do you know this?"

"Because I have to figure out why people do things all the time. That's my work. That's what I do in court. And with people who are a lot better at hiding their feelings than you."

The waves slapping the beach was the only sound I heard. A couple of kids ran up and asked if Rudy Gamboni was a basketball player. He said no.

"Now look," he said, "I don't know what you think, but I finally got a good thing. I can shoot. I can play. I don't get hurt. I can be the best."

"But at what price, Rudy? Listen, I know something about losing a soul and it's not pretty. It's not something you ever want to experience, believe me. It's a con game." He shook his head but seemed troubled.

"Just tell me what you did with the woman. With Mrs. Gonzalez."

"But if I tell—" He slapped his hands over his mouth.

"Give it to me, Rudy. Give it to me and save yourself."

Slowly he lowered his hand. It almost seemed like a relief to him. "I did not kill her. I did not. They asked me to. I couldn't do it. I didn't do it. I.. ." His eyes started to mist.

"Go on, Rudy, tell me. Is she alive?"

Just then the ocean churned violently, almost as if a storm had hit this one spot of Venice Beach.

And a hand the size of a Dumpster shot out of the water and grabbed Rudy Gamboni.

Rudy screamed. His massive arms and legs flapped around like circus tentpoles in a hurricane.

A massive fluked tail flapped out of the water and slapped back down again.

Then a torso appeared, rising from the surf. This thing had the face of a man, but the skin was scaly. He had a beard that hung down in ringlets. His eyes were aqua colored and gelatinous.

Rudy was screaming still, and he wasn't the only one. People on the beach were fleeing from the waters while desperately grabbing their things.

Then the half man, half fish said, "You will bow down!" His voice boomed like a lifeguard with a bullhorn.

I was used to this. I'd been told to bow down by the best. By Lilith, no less. But I had caught onto something. They couldn't whack me. They couldn't make me. They wanted me to, but when I didn't, all they had was bluster.

And the ability to toss me through the air.

"Put the basketball player down first!" I said.

"Insolent tart!"

Rudy made a pitiful noise, like a harpooned seal.

"What is your name?" I demanded.

"I am Dagon!"

"So?"

"King and ruler!"

"Okay, King and ruler, you want to talk to me? You put Gamboni down here safely and then we'll talk."

"You are to leave him to me!"

"Listen, pal," I said, "I am the Queen of the Clara Shortridge Foltz Criminal Courts Building, and you will treat me as such."

He did not say anything at first. Then a tremendous grunt. "I do not like dealing with women. I never have."

"Welcome to the new world, King. Now let's discuss this like two monarchs, shall we? Put the guy down."

The water roiled under the half-fish, half-man god. But he did as requested. He placed Rudy softly on the sand. The terrified Clipper scampered behind me. Meanwhile, I could hear the distant screams and shouts of the crowd, maybe a hundred yards away. To them it must have seemed like an honest-to-goodness Godzilla movie and they were the terrified hordes.

"What is it you want?" I said.

"You have a boy under your charge," Dagon said. "You alone hold his fate in your hands."

"Okay."

"We want custody of the boy."

"For what purpose?"

"That is our concern."

"What makes you think I would turn over this boy to the likes of you? You're a demon."

"That is the word of an enemy. Why do you believe it? I am a king, and I am benevolent."

"Sez you."

He seemed to sigh. "I do not like women! If this were Philistia, I could have had you thrown in the fire."

"Welcome to L.A."

"This is without point. You are small and undead. Yet you seek to stand in the way of the great rebellion, throwing off the shackles of cosmic oppression! You stand in the way of freedom! Why would you do that?"

"You talking about Lucifer now?"

"The true name that is above all names."

"Urn, I think you have that wrong."

"You will learn."

"I don't have time today. Now why don't you go back—"

"You wish to know who killed you, do you not?"

That brought me up short. I looked into those sea-colored eyes and shivered.

"Ah, your tongue is not so quick now," he said.

"Say what you want and then go."

"It is quite simple. You have something we want. We want the boy. But you have him covered with a protection that cannot be penetrated unless you willingly relinquish him. We have something you want, the information you seek that will lead to reclamation of your soul. We can give you that information, about the man who tried to murder you. And the one who raised you from the dead."

Everything. Everything I'd been searching for without success. Handed to me.

If I could believe him.

But even then, what of it? Give them Jaime?

Wasn't going to happen.

Or was it? For one, brief moment I thought about doing it. Giving up the kid. Why not? What hope did he have in this lousy world? What hope did any of us have? We are all prisoners here, aren't we? We are all stuck inside skins not of our own making. Forces battle around us and use us like playthings.

Maybe it would all be better for death to come quickly and not have to think about it anymore.

But then I knew I couldn't do it. I cursed at myself, silently.

Then I cursed at Dagon, loudly.

His fishy face flushed. He stuck out his chest. "You will be forever sorry for this insult!" he said, then opened his mouth and roared. It was like a hundred Mack trucks blaring their horns at the same time. The force of the sound wave knocked me flat and swirled sand around me.

Then Dagon withdrew into the suds, giving one last smash with his tail, spraying water in the air.

I turned to see how Gamboni was.

But he was long gone.

CHAPTER FIFTY-THREE

I GOT BACK to Geraldine and called Detective Mark Strobert.

"Should I be talking to you?" he said, in a voice that told me he wanted to.

"The trial is over," I said. "We're just waiting for the jury now."

"I need a vacation."

"Not yet. You know about the boy, Jaime Gonzalez, who I've got custody of?"

"Yeah, I know about that. I heard what happened in court. What was that thing?"

"A Rakshasa. Very nasty."

"Okay. And?"

"The boy's mother, his real mother, may be alive."

"You know this how?"

"You follow the Clippers?"

"I try not to."

"You know about Rudy Gamboni?"

"A little."

"Well, he is the one Mrs. Gonzalez was last seen with. It's a long story, but I think you should open up an investigation and lean on him hard. Tell him you know all about his deal with the devil—"

"His what?"

"Just tell him that. He's the only lead and we need a cop to put some fear into him. Would you do that?"

"As a favor to you?"

"No, as the right thing to do. For the boy."

Pause. "I'll look into it."

"Thanks."

I FINISHED THE DAY BACK AT THE CHURCH, HAVING PIZZA IN THE kitchen with Jaime, Nick, and Father Clemente. I picked at my piece, remembering how much I used to love pepperoni.

When we finished, Nick went with Jaime to his little room, to read to him. This gave me an opportunity to tell Father Clemente about my run-in with Gamboni and Dagon.

"Dagon, the god of the Philistines," he said. "This is very big."

"He was very big."

"Mallory, I want you to listen to something. Something I've been thinking about."

He left for a moment and returned with a large Bible. This he set on the kitchen table and opened toward the back.

"Here. Revelation, the eleventh chapter. Listen. 'And I will give power unto my two witnesses, and they shall prophesy a thousand two hundred and threescore days, clothed in sackcloth. These are the two olive trees, and the two candlesticks standing before the God of the earth. And if any man will hurt them, fire proceedeth out of their mouth, and devoureth their enemies: and if any man will hurt them, he must in this manner be killed.' "

Fire, I thought.

He said, "Jaime. What if that is what he meant? That he is one of the witnesses foretold in Scripture."

"A witness to what?"

"To the Light."

"That's a pretty wild theory, isn't it?"

"It's a working theory."

"But it says there's two witnesses."

"Yes! And when they are finally together, you know the end is nigh."

"But what about that a thousand two hundred whatever days?"

"One thousand, two hundred, and three score days, to be precise."

"What's that supposed to mean?"

"According to the lunar calendar John used, that's three and one half years."

"John?"

"The Apostle who was given this Revelation."

"So what's it all mean?"

"John uses the symbolic number three-and-a-half several times in his vision of the future. He speaks of 'a time, times and half a time' and 'three and a half days' and 'forty-two months' and 'one thousand two hundred and sixty days.' These are symbolic numbers referring to the length of time between the giving of the Revelation to John, late in the first century, and the consummation of God's kingdom. There are of course many Christians who insist on fanciful interpretations of all this, with charts and diagrams and timetables. But they are mistaken. We are in the tribulation. The battle is joined."

"I'm getting a headache."

"And there is one more thing," he said, looking at the Bible again. 'And when they shall have finished their testimony, the beast that ascendeth out of the bottomless pit shall make war against them, and shall overcome them, and kill them. And their dead bodies shall lie in the street of the great city, which spiritually is called Sodom and Egypt, where also our Lord was crucified.' "

"Sodom?" I said.

"An obvious reference to present-day Los Angeles."

"Now wait a second—"

"And the two witnesses will be killed, but after three days, it says, they will rise again."

"This is too much."

"God's ways are not our ways."

"You're telling me?"

He read my face. "What are you hiding?"

I shook my head.

"You trust my judgment," Father Clemente said. "Isn't that right?"

"You've got your strong points," I said.

"Then what is it?"

"Let's leave me out of this."

"How can you expect that?" he said. "Your soul is in the balance."

"That's right! What am I supposed to do about that?"

"Turn to God."

"Let him give it back to me and then we'll talk."

"It doesn't work that way."

"In my opinion it doesn't work at all."

Father Clemente trained his eyes on mine. "Ask God to deliver you and empower you."

"For what?"

"For what he has for you to do."

"I don't want power. I just want to be human again!"

CHAPTER FIFTY-FOUR

THREE DAYS later the jury announced it was hopelessly deadlocked.

There is nothing trial judges and prosecutors hate more than a hung jury. It means they've got to do the whole thing again. All that time, all that expense.

Defense lawyers aren't all that thrilled with it, either, but they'll take it because it means their client has not been convicted. Sometimes a prosecutor throws in the towel. But I was sure Aaron wasn't going to do that in this case, a cop killing.

So we gathered back in the courtroom and the judge polled the jury and decided that yes, it was a total deadlock—exactly six to six.

And with that he dismissed the jury.

I told Harry I'd see him a little later to discuss what would happen next. Then the deputies took him back to jail.

Aaron came over to give me a handshake.

"Looks like we tied," he said.

"So we get to dance again," I said.

"Maybe." I finished latching my briefcase. "You saying there's a chance you won't try this case again?"

"I could arrange it so your father walks."

"Why would you do that?"

"You interested?"

"What's the catch?"

"Does there have to be a catch?"

"Yes."

"You always could read me."

"So what is it?"

"Follow your heart. Follow through and marry me."

"That's your catch?"

"That's it."

My heart and mind got into a cage fight and I didn't know who to root for. But something about this didn't sit well with me. I said, "Aaron, you are trading me my father for marriage."

"Now you have absolutely no reason not to marry me."

"This isn't a flea market, Aaron."

"Meet me at City Hall in an hour."

"Aaron—"

"This is going to be the turning point in your life, Mallory. I guarantee it."

FOR THE NEXT HALF HOUR OR SO I WALKED AROUND THE OLD Hall of Justice on Temple Street, thinking things over. The gray brick building that used to be the county jail and main courthouse is boarded up now, almost a ruin. In a way it's a metaphor of the city, the beauty of the architecture still apparent even as time wears it down. Nothing lasts. Not cities or civilizations or zombies. And then I knew I couldn't go through with it. I couldn't lie to Aaron. I couldn't do that to him, even if it meant my father would be retried for murder.

So I started for City Hall. As I approached, it suddenly looked tawdry to me. Because I knew what went on inside. The political dealmaking and breaking. The influence peddling and pandering. Not unlike other towns, I suppose, only more so because it was L.A.

Maybe when Aaron become mayor it would change, but I wondered. The machinery has a way of grinding you down. Aaron was only human. He wanted power and that was going to hurt rather than help.

When I got to the steps, it was starting to cloud up over the city. Looking like rain. Unseasonable, but stranger things have happened, like the Kardashians.

But it was darkness at noon when I finally got to the top of the stairs. There was also an eeriness to the streets, as if people were waiting for something to happen, something bad.

I got that vibe and felt sorry for them. Fear is no way to live. I should know that better than anyone.

"You made it." Aaron was emerging from the large City Hall doors, striding toward me like a guy who already owned the town.

He kissed me, then said, "Are you ready?"

"Aaron—"

"Don't say no. Not now."

"I have to tell you something."

"No, you don't."

"Aaron, please. I have something I have to tell you and it's going to change everything."

"Mallory—"

"Please! Just listen, will you?" A cold wind snapped past us. Aaron said nothing, so I dove right in. There was not going to be any easy way out. "I am undead. I am a zombie. I was shot in a drive-by and they never caught the guy. That much you know. But I died. Then I was reanimated, by someone I considered a friend. Ginny Finn, you may have heard of her."

Aaron said nothing.

"Well, anyway, a cyclops killed her so she wouldn't talk. Something's rotten, and it's not just my flesh. But because she died, I don't think I can ever be normal again. I thought maybe there was a chance, which would mean a chance for us, but now that's gone. And now you know, Aaron."

"But you love me."

"Don't you want to run away now? Don't you want to cut my head off?"

Aaron reached down and took my hand. "I still want you to marry me, Mal. It's very important to me."

"How can you say that? I'm a zombie."

"Nobody's perfect."

"Aaron, I want to eat your head."

"I know it's complicated. But aren't all marriages these days?"

"Not *this* complicated! You realize we can't have children? And forget about a sex life. It just can't work!"

"What if I told you we can see someone. We can bring you back to your normal life?"

"What?"

"Just what I said."

"Aaron, how could you?"

"Will you trust me now?"

"Are you telling me the absolute truth?"

He put his hands on my shoulders. "Absolutely," he said.

Before I could say another word, the world changed behind me. The frigid wind swirled up from the street, blowing trash and dirt around in a mini twister, and it crept up the steps of City Hall.

It grew and blew and thickened and widened, like a curtain of haze dropping on a massive stage.

Then in the middle of the swarm, emerging from the billow, came forms, appearing as if by magic.

Three Rakshasas, taloned and monstrous.

And Gus Gilboy, walking forward like a zombie.

Next to him, Mayor Ronaldo Garza.

And next to the mayor, Charles Beaumont Manyon.

Six across they were, synchronized in their movements forward, like the Rockettes of hell.

And then came a spectral female presence who floated rather than walked. She was naked, with two snakes slithering around her body.

Lilith!

Man, the whole shooting match of the demonic and damned was here and coming up the steps toward me.

For me.

"Aaron," I said, "get out of here. Quick."

He didn't move.

"You can't handle this," I said.

"Don't be afraid," he said.

"*You* should be afraid!"

"I'm not," he said.

The next voice I heard was Manyon's. "It's come to decision time, Ms. Caine. We cannot wait any longer."

Lilith was next. "Join us."

I said, "Why would I join you, snake woman?"

Someone whispered, "To get your soul back, your humanity."

It sounded like it came from inside my head. The voice was so quiet, and even I might say, seductive.

But when I turned and saw Aaron's smiling face, I knew it was his voice this time.

"What have you done, Aaron?"

"Nothing."

"You sold your soul."

"No, I have possession of it. And you can have yours back, too."

"How can you—"

"You simply have to say yes. Say yes to me, yes to our marriage. Come over to my side of the aisle. That's all I've ever wanted you to do."

His eyes were alive now with something so other worldly and seductive that it made every enticing look ever made by Cary Grant seem like ketchup stains by comparison.

And I was filled with a vision of myself, standing on top of these very steps, Aaron by my side, his arm around me. Microphones in front of us. And his announcing that we were going to have a baby.

I was whole.

I was cured.

I was a person again.

And I had power, shared power, as we drew Los Angeles to our bosom, Aaron and me, the first couple of the city.

The vision was as clear as anything I could see with my physical eyes. My whole body vibrated in a way it hadn't done since I'd been with Aaron before I was dead.

My mouth started to open, and I knew I was going to give him that yes, give him whatever he would ask of me—

Until a voice shouted, "No!"

The vision disappeared and I felt the brush of wings.

Max! He hovered in front of me, doing his best hummingbird imitation, which wasn't easy for him. He was puffing. "Don't believe him! The devil is the father of lies! He'll take your—"

Max went stone still, frozen in midair, his beak open, his eyes wide.

I glanced right and saw Aaron pointing at Max, as if a beam of energy came from his finger to my owl guardian. Aaron began to lower his finger, and Max correspondingly went down, down, down to the ground.

And if an owl's face can show pain, Max's did.

"Leave him alone!" I shouted.

Max was unable to breathe or move. He was trembling and mute.

"Stop!" I slapped at Aaron's arm but he pushed me aside and kept the pressure on Max.

Max twitched once, twice. Then his eyes closed. And he moved no more.

"Max!" I dropped to my knees. "Max ..."

His eyes opened, barely. He stuck one wing in the air, almost as if motioning to me.

I put my ear over his beak.

"All things considered," he said, barely audible, "I'd rather be in Philadelphia."

"Don't go, Max."

"Make me proud, *Tchotchke*."

His eyes closed again. He was gone.

I stood, holding him.

"Damn you," I said to Aaron.

"No," he said calmly, "you are the one who is damned. But I can bring you back."

"Are you the devil? Tell me!"

"Almost," he said. "Don't you want the chance to rule?"

"What's that mean, *almost*?"

"I'll tell you everything on our wedding night. No more hesitation, Mal. This is it. Are you in or out? *Out* means certain death and loss of your soul. *In* means power and all your dreams coming true. Home, family. And you can still be a lawyer."

My head was starting to clear of the vision now, and holding Max's body kept me focused. "You've been after me from the start. But I've been protected."

"By what? That dead owl?"

"Maybe."

"You have no idea," Aaron said. "There are things we can do to you that you could not imagine in your worst nightmare."

"I'm already in my worst nightmare."

"Don't you believe it."

I looked into those gemstone eyes again, drawing me in.

And then I looked at Max, cooling in my hands.

"Go to the hell where you belong," I said and started for the steps.

But the crowd of creatures hadn't moved. Garza and Manyon were smiling, the demonic kind.

Was I really convinced I could handle this bunch? Or that someone or something was going to protect me? With Max dead?

"All right," Aaron said to the mob. "Take her."

There was a brief pause, and then, like the start of the L.A. Marathon, they seemed to act as one and rush me.

I held Max close to me, like a teddy bear. Looked like we'd be going out together.

And then a river of fire blasted them back.

There on the steps stood Father Clemente with Nick by his side. And with hands on hips, Jaime Gonzalez.

"In the name of the witness!" Father Clemente thundered, "I say, *Begone!*"

The horde froze, as one.

Until Mayor Ronaldo Garza looked at Aaron and said, "Get rid of them!"

Aaron seemed slightly perplexed at this but made a turn for the priest and the boy.

I kicked his legs out from under him.

Another shot of flame from Jaime—this one as intense as any hillside fire in the history of Los Angeles—almost completely engulfed the hellish company. It stayed and stayed, like a Bunsen burner from Olympus.

And when it finally subsided, the diabolical rabble was dispersed, with Garza and Manyon's backsides scorched as they ran down the hill toward First Street. Nick, Father Clemente, and Jaime gave chase with periodic licks of fire from Jaime as prods.

Aaron clambered to his feet, dusting himself off.

"It was you," I said. "You were the one who had me killed. You were the one who pulled the trigger and took me to Ginny Finn. You wanted to control me, but something went wrong. I wouldn't be controlled."

"You still don't see it," he said.

"All I see is the pathetic excuse for a man I thought I loved."

"Man? You are so naive."

"Then you *are* a demon."

He laughed. "Not even close. But when he comes, it will be all over for you. Once and for all."

"He?"

Aaron said nothing.

"You mean what's-his-name? Lucifer?"

"Don't mock him. It isn't wise."

"And you are in league with him?"

"You could have been part of the family," Aaron said. "You could have been his daughter-in-law."

My head buzzed. "Satan is your *father?*"

"And I can't wait for you to meet him," Aaron said. My head buzzed like a thousand bees doing a Gregorian chant. How much more weirdness could I take?

Aaron Argula was Lucifer, Jr. I've met some pretty low DAs in my time, but none as low as hell itself.

"But Aaron, I would have married you before you killed me. Why didn't you?"

"It was your mind," he said. "I didn't have your *mind.* We knew about you. We knew about your birth and your guardians and that you were supposed to be *something.* But you always were so damned strong willed."

"And you thought if you turned me into a zombie, you could do mind control."

"It was worth a shot," he said.

"So now what, Aaron?"

"Let me put it in movie terms," he said. "This town isn't big enough for the both of us."

"When will you be leaving?" I said.

"Don't think you can resist my father," Aaron said. "Better men and women than you have tried and failed."

"But no better zombies," I said.

I BURIED MAX IN A LITTLE PLOT OF GROUND IN THE HILLS ABOVE the Sunset Strip. There was a view of a comedy club from up there. I thought Max might like that.

I had to wonder what happened to him. He was one of the good spirits, charged with helping those of us on earth. Now where was he? How would I get along without him?

PART FOUR

FALL FASHIONS FOR THE WELL-FED ZOMBIE

CHAPTER FIFTY-FIVE

IT WAS late October and the air had changed in L.A. It was dark early now and it felt like it was overcast all the time.

And it was on just such an evening as I was leaving my office under the watchful eye of LoGo that I had a curious visitation.

Detective Mark Strobert was hanging out in the Smoke 'n Joke, waiting for me.

"Can I walk with you a ways?" he asked.

Not what I needed. Another man to think about. Especially this man. Did he know yet that I was a flesh-eating zombie? Or posed as a hooker named Amanda? Not that he let on.

So why did I go with him? I liked him. Isn't that enough? What was wrong with a little companionship in this nutty world we both lived in?

When we got to Pershing Square he dropped this on me. "You're a darn good lawyer, and I don't say that very often."

"Well, thank you, Detective."

"But there's something about you I just can't put my finger on."

"Best keep your fingers to yourself," I said. And I meant that literally.

"Fair enough," he said. "I wanted to tell you that I may have found Mrs. Gonzalez."

"Where?"

"We don't know if it's her. She's a Jane Doe in a clinic in El Centro."

"Clinic for what?"

"She's a woman without a memory or ID."

"How did you find her?"

"I got enough out of Gamboni to piece together what I think happened. He was supposed to dispose of her, but he couldn't do it. He hit her over the head and left her a few miles from where she is right now. They found this woman wandering in a field and she's been at the clinic ever since. I arrested Gamboni but his lawyer, that slimy one—"

"Gus Gilboy."

"—got him to clam up. Unless we can determine who she is and unless she can remember what happened, we don't have a case."

"I know something we might try," I said.

STROBERT DROVE ME AND JAIME TO THE CLINIC IN THE TOWN OF El Centro. It's a desert city in California's Imperial Valley, way down at the southern tip of the state. Jaime kept close to me all the way, nervous about what he had to do. But he was soldiering up and I was proud of him for that.

The sanitarium was in an adobe-style building, though of modern design. Strobert checked us in and we waited in the lobby for a nurse.

Finally a pretty young Latina came out and said we could see the woman now.

She was in a sitting room with sunlight and plants and a few other patients, some playing board games. She was dressed in a white robe and had on fuzzy white slippers. She wasn't playing anything and seemed to be staring at the far wall.

As soon as Jaime saw her he grabbed my hand. I held it firmly as we approached. The woman, who certainly did look like the Mrs. Gonzalez Rakshasa I'd seen, looked up at us blankly.

And that's how it stayed for a long moment.

A struggle seemed to take place in the woman's head. Behind her eyes were moving parts and the strain of mental gears.

We stood like that for another thirty seconds or so.

And then the woman's face softened and she said, "Jaime."

With that the floodgates opened. Jaime went to her as if he had no doubt. Mrs. Gonzalez hugged him and kissed him and said his name over and over.

And I thought I saw Detective Mark Strobert smile.

On a bright Tuesday morning I ditched the office and went up the hill where I'd buried Max. I sat next to the little mound and said, "Hey Max, I had a Jewish mother on my jury the other day. They had to let her go. She kept insisting *she* was guilty."

A breeze moved the grass.

"Come on, folks, are you an audience or an oil painting?"

In the distance, the whisper of traffic.

"Let's all join hands and try to communicate with the living."

Silence.

"I miss you, Max. I hope wherever you are, there's an audience and they're laughing."

I sat back under the shade of a tree, feeling bone- and soul-tired. Looked down at a large swath of my city. Saw no people but knew they were out there, going to work, looking for work, worrying about their kids, having kids, helping their neighbor fix a faucet, killing their neighbor over a backyard dispute.

And each one of them, potentially, was someone I might eat one day.

I suddenly felt connected to all of them. I don't know what it was except, well, that I cared. I just did. They were part of me and they were in danger. Not just from me, but from the one who wanted to own them all, this Satan, this Lucifer.

What right did he have to any of us? He wasn't a person. He never had been. He'd been this angel from on high. He never got his hands dirty with honest labor. And now he was planning some sort of massive recruitment and then assault on earth and heaven.

I never asked to play a part in this. And I didn't pretend to understand what the big, cosmic game plan was. All I knew at that moment was that I didn't want the devil taking over my city.

I decided then I would stand up against him, and Aaron.

Come what may—come hell itself—I would stand up for L.A.

AUTHOR'S NOTE

When I came up with the idea for a new genre mix—zombie legal thrillers—my agent thought it a good idea to use a pen name, since this series is, shall we say, a bit different from my usual contemporary beat.

That's how the mysterious K. Bennett was born. Now, the mystery is solved. I've reissued the books under my own name.

Please take a moment to:

Leave a review on Amazon

For the other books in this trilogy, please go to the Mallory Caine series page.

I mainly write contemporary suspense, both stand-alone books and series. If you'd like to be on my email list you'll be among the first to know when new books come out. You get a free book, too. I won't share your email address with anyone, nor will I stuff your mailbox with spam. It's just a short, to-the-point email from time to time. For your free book, go HERE. (If this is a print version, go to JamesScottBell.com and navigate to the FREE Book page).

Thanks again!

Jim

MORE THRILLERS BY JAMES SCOTT BELL

The Mike Romeo Thriller Series

"Mike Romeo is a terrific hero. He's smart, tough as nails, and fun to hang out with. James Scott Bell is at the top of his game here. There'll be no sleeping till after the story is over." - **John Gilstrap**, New York Times bestselling author of the Jonathan Grave thriller series

The Ty Buchanan Legal Thriller Series

"Part Michael Connelly and part Raymond Chandler, Bell has an excellent ear for dialogue and makes contemporary L.A. come alive. Deftly plotted, flawlessly executed, and compulsively readable. Bell takes his place among the top authors in the crowded suspense genre." - **Sheldon Siegel**, *New York Times* bestselling author

Stand Alone Thrillers

Your Son Is Alive
Long Lost

No More Lies
Blind Justice
Don't Leave Me
Final Witness
Last Call
Framed

The Trials of Kit Shannon Historical Legal Thrillers

Book 1 - City of Angels
Book 2 - Angels Flight
Book 3 - Angel of Mercy
Book 4 - A Greater Glory
Book 5 - A Higher Justice
Book 6 - A Certain Truth

"With her shoulders squared and faith set high, Kit Shannon arrives in 1903 Los Angeles feeling a special calling to practice law ... Packed full of genuine, deep and real characters ... The tension and suspense are in overdrive ... A series that is timeless!" — **In the Library Review**

ABOUT THE AUTHOR

JAMES SCOTT BELL is a winner of the International Thriller Writers Award and the #1 bestselling author of books on the craft of fiction. He studied writing with Raymond Carver at the University of California, Santa Barbara, and graduated with honors from the University of Southern California Law Center.

A former trial lawyer, Jim writes full time in his home town of Los Angeles.

For More Information
JamesScottBell.com